In Praise of
Everywhere You Want to Be

"Readers will be captivated by this real-life fairy tale, the world of competitive dance, and New York-style pizza."

McCall Hoyle, Award-winning author of *The Thing with Feathers* and *Meet the Sky*

"Christina June weaves a sweet tale of second chances, new beginnings, and finding your own path. We all harbor big dreams and secret wishes, and *Everywhere You Want to Be* will dance into readers' hearts and tug those dreams and wishes out under the lights and onto center stage, where they belong."

Katherine Locke, author of *Second Position* and *The Girl with the Red Balloon*

"Full of heart and humor, *Everywhere You Want to Be* is a nuanced look at what it means to chase a dream. Tilly's delightful narration lets the reader escape into the irresistible energy of a New York City summer."

Lauren Karcz, author of *The Gallery of Unfinished Girls*

"*Everywhere You Want to Be* is a charming story of second chances, facing life's uncertainties, and finding your own way. June's writing captures the heartbeat of NYC, the dance world, and the very essence of a girl on the cusp."

Sara Biren, author of *The Last Thing You Said*

"*Everywhere You Want to Be* is the perfect book for anyone who has ever been stuck at a crossroads at an important point in life. Loosely inspired by Red Riding Hood, it follows Tilly as she fights to choose between a dream that doesn't belong to her and a dream that might not love her back. I absolutely adored it and can't wait for others to read it!"

RACHEL STROLLE, Anderson's Bookshop

Praise for Christina June's
It Started with Goodbye

"Bold, empowering, and all-around fun. A perfect summer story."

ANNA MICHELS, author of *26 Kisses*

"You won't be able to put this book down. This heartfelt read totally sucked m. 'n."

MIRANDA KENNEALLY, bestselling author of *Catching Jordan*

"Honest, fun, and entirely compelling, this is a story about how being in the wrong place at the wrong time can lead to a whole lot of right. Tatum is a character you'll relate to, cheer for, and want to befriend."

LAURIE ELIZABETH FLYNN, author of *Firsts*

EVERYWHERE
You Want to Be

Also by Christina June

It Started With Goodbye

EVERYWHERE

You Want to Be

Christina June

BLINK

For all those who are in my photographs
and
For Tony, who went his own way.

"*One belongs to New York instantly,
one belongs to it as much in five
minutes as in five years.*"
—Tom Wolfe

"*You can't stay in your corner of the
forest waiting for others to come to you.
You have to go to them sometimes.*"
—A.A. Milne

I hated lying to my mother. It always left an unpleasant, metallic taste in my mouth, like I'd accidentally bitten my cheek and it bled a little. But sometimes, I didn't have any other choice.

She'd given me an ultimatum.

"You may accept the spot in New York," she'd said. My heart had inflated like a balloon. "Just as soon as you send in your deposit to Georgetown."

And so began the slow, sad leak. I could almost hear the whistling sound as my heart collapsed in on itself. At least she couldn't hear it. The summer dance program in New York was supposed to be the first step on my journey toward a professional dance career—one that didn't make a pit stop at Georgetown University. College had always been part of my goals, but if anyone knew about plans changing, it was me.

"And check in with your grandmother every once in a while," Mama continued. "She's recovering from her surgery with a friend in New Jersey, so she'll be nearby."

My free-spirited abuela had recently torn her rotator cuff during trapeze lessons. When my mother scolded her for doing something so dangerous "at her age," Abuela just scoffed and said she was fulfilling her dream of being in the circus. Classic Abuela.

In the solitude of my bedroom I pulled out my favorite magenta notebook, the one my stepsister Tatum had given me on my eighteenth birthday, and debated with myself.

Go to College	Dance Professionally
A college degree will help me get a non-dancing job	I love to dance
	I could live in New York or another exciting city
Going to college means being independent	I'll get to perform on some of the greatest stages in the world
I'll meet new people	
Washington, D.C. is familiar	I'll learn more about dance
	I'll have better instructors
I can dance as a hobby	I can make (some) money doing my art, like Tatum does
Mama will be happy	
I might regret it	Having a full-time job means being independent
	I'll meet new people
	Mama might be angry
	I'll be happy

It wasn't even close.

So I'd sent in the deposit holding a spot for me at Georgetown, and then I emailed Sage Oliver, the choreographer, telling her I accepted her offer to dance in a city-wide installation this summer.

What my mother didn't know was that with my deposit submission, I had also deferred my admission for a year. It was a risk—probably the biggest one I'd ever taken—but I *needed* to give dance one last, *real* shot. I'd held my breath as I sent the final email, confirming with the dean that I would not be on campus at the end of August. If I was offered a job with a dance company, then I'd cross that bridge with Mama when I came to it. And if I didn't? Well, as much as I liked things planned and in a neat little row, I'd have to think about that one later.

The icky taste in my mouth lingered the whole train ride to New York no matter how much water I drank or gum I chewed. I read my list probably a hundred times on the trip up, reminding myself I was on the right path. The right path for me. I hoped.

The New York skyline appeared out of the summer haze, like a committee welcoming me to the city. I pressed my face close enough to the train window to see my breath. I drew a heart in the condensation and then quickly wiped it away. I'd only been to New York once, so long ago it felt like nothing more than a faded dream. To prepare myself for the frenzy I knew was about to surround me, I'd spent the past week reading traveler reviews, making a list of all the sights I wanted to see, and memorizing subway maps. But the idea of being in such a big city still made my heart race.

As I stepped through the exit at Penn Station, two things struck me. The first was the smell. It was as if a chemistry experiment gone wrong mingled with burnt sugar and grilled meat. The second was the size of the buildings. Back home in D.C., no building is taller than the Washington Monument. Here, they literally scraped the sky. They made me want to rise up in relevé to try touching them.

Amid the Amazonian structures and semi-noxious odor wafting from who knew where, there were people. Everywhere. All sizes and ages and colors, rushing this way and that. And I was right in the middle of them. Though my heart pounded with sheer terror, I pushed the fear aside. This is where my dream could begin. So I slid on my vintage red sunglasses—a gift from my abuela—and smiled. I'd arrived.

My first decision? Subway or cab. The stairs leading down to the subway platform looked miles long. I took one look, felt phantom pain in the ankle I broke last winter, and turned around. Nope. Not a chance. The broken ankle was the reason I hadn't auditioned for professional dance companies in the spring like everyone else in my dance classes. I wasn't going to injure myself a second time, just to turn around and get back on the train home.

It would have to be a taxi. They whizzed by in a blur of yellow—getting one to see me amidst the bustling tourists looked virtually impossible.

"There's nothing to it, Tilly," I coached myself. "Millions of people visit New York every year and they all manage to get to their hotels just fine. You are intelligent and capable and you want this. You can hail a cab."

I hurried to the corner, my barge-like suitcase dragging behind me, and thrust my hand into the air. Ten seconds later, a little canary-colored hybrid pulled up. My eyes widened—that had been much easier than I thought—and I opened the door as the cab driver opened his.

"Let me put that in the back for you, miss," he said, taking my suitcase.

"Thank you." I slid into the back and across the slick faux-leather seat.

The man returned to the driver's seat. He peered at me through the rearview mirror and then cleared his throat.

"Oh. Right. The Marian Dormitory, please." I rattled off the address on the Upper East Side that I'd had memorized for three days. He pulled into the street.

"First time in New York?"

"Yes, sir. How did you know?" Did I look as clueless as I felt? I hoped not.

"Pretty girl with scared eyes. Big suitcase. Staying in temporary housing." He chuckled again, softer this time.

"Temporary housing?"

"The Marian has a revolving door of interns and apprentices. Temporary New Yorkers. Kids with big dreams."

"None of them stay?" A lump formed at the back of my throat. Would I be temporary too?

"Some stay. Some get crushed and go home right away. Some stick it out the summer and then go back to college or Iowa or wherever they came from. But some stay. Some get the city in their blood."

I blanched. "Like a disease?"

He laughed, loudly this time. "No, like an electrical current. It pulses through you and you feel like all your blood has been replaced with mercury."

15

"You're a writer," I said, with a smile.

"Once upon a time, maybe," he said, a note of sadness behind his words. "I was a teacher in my country. Pakistan. But here, I do this."

My abuelo and abuela had been immigrants as well. But a better job than he'd worked back in Chile had been waiting for Abuelo when they arrived in the U.S. I couldn't begin to imagine not being able to do what you love. And then I realized, sadly, I could. I'd spent the last six months not dancing because of my stupid broken ankle.

We drove in silence for a few minutes before I worked up the courage to ask him, "Do you regret coming here?"

Regret was my biggest fear. I didn't want to find myself wishing I'd chosen to stay home and spend my summer days shopping for dorm accessories with my mother and watching cooking shows with my stepsister. I didn't want to fall flat on my face and regret trying. I didn't want to think about the possibility of my mother being disappointed with me for lying, or maybe worse. Trust was a valued commodity in our house, and though I'd lied in the past, it was never about something this big.

The driver looked at me in the rearview again. "It's hard to be a new person in a new place. But do I regret it? No. Never. Not when I have all this." He gestured to what lay before us. Green trees and rocky hills, dotted with tourists. Carriages drawn by horses with red and purple feathers clomped past. "I hope you don't mind. I took the more scenic route for you."

"I don't mind at all. Thank you. Central Park?" The hair on my arms stood up; it was the same sensation I felt every time the curtains opened seconds before I began to dance. Anticipation was more powerful than guilt. I opened my eyes wider so I wouldn't miss a thing.

"The very one."

I watched the scenery to my left as we continued up town, wondering if I'd have time to explore before rehearsals began tomorrow.

And of course, the thought of rehearsals brought me back to reality. So I picked up my phone to text my mom, the metallic taste creeping back into my mouth.

I made it. I'm in the cab on the way to my dorm.

Two seconds later, my mother responded. **Thank you for letting me know. I'm glad you arrived safely.**

Me too!

Work hard at rehearsal tomorrow. That was her way of saying she loved me.

I always do. My way of saying it back.

Too soon, the driver pulled up in front of a brick structure, not nearly as tall as the buildings near the train station, but still formidable. The double front door was lined with black iron. A gold sign that read "The Marian" glinted in the afternoon sun.

"So, what kind of dreamer are you?"

"Pardon?" I looked at the driver, who was watching me again, amused.

"You come to the big city and you're going to live in this house of dreamers. What kind are you?"

"Oh. I'm a dancer." Pride swelled in my chest. I loved saying that out loud. Being here made it feel real in a way it never had before.

"Ah, wonderful. My daughter is a dancer. It is good for the soul."

"I think so too."

I handed him the fare and a large tip. It seemed like the thing to do for the first person to welcome me to his city. He set my giant bag on the sidewalk in front of the building and made a small, almost imperceptible bow.

"Good luck to you. I hope you find your dream."

"Thank you, sir. I hope so too."

I gripped the handle of the suitcase and stared up. A fluffy white cloud drifted over the top of the building, and a breeze rustled by. This was home for now. And just like the driver predicted, my veins seemed to crackle with electricity.

As he drove away, I wondered how many times he had driven a nervous-looking non-New Yorker to this residence, whose sole purpose was to house kids like me who were here to test out their dreams. I wondered how many excited whispers and heartbroken sobs this building had heard in its lifetime. Where would I fall among them?

In the small lobby, a girl with bright red hair paced, talking sharply to someone on her phone, and a guy holding a motorcycle helmet rushed past me and out the door. When I introduced myself to the woman at the front desk, she handed me a key to room 4F and said my roommate had just checked in a few minutes ago.

"Stairs are around to the left, sweetie." She pointed toward a short hallway.

Stairs. I did my best to ignore my fear of toppling down steps for the second time that day. I inhaled and squared my shoulders. I was a dancer. My legs were strong. My physical therapist said I was as good as new. I hitched my backpack over my shoulders and wheeled my suitcase to the bottom of the stairs. The fourth floor wasn't that high. Not really. Not at all.

Don't look back. Don't look back.

By the time I reached the threshold of the fourth floor, my calves were burning and I might have been panting. Just a little. In my defense, I'd been off my feet for a long time. I slid my bag to a stop in front of the door that read 4F. The F was a little crooked and the paint was peeling in the corners, but never had I been so excited to get somewhere. Or have both feet firmly on flat ground. I was about to put the key into the faded brass lock when the door swung open.

"I heard your suitcase bumping up the stairs. Figured you might need some help, but I guess I was wrong because here you are. Are you Matilda?" Without waiting for me to answer, a girl with long black hair, even darker than mine, and a shock of black fringe over her orange glasses took my backpack off my shoulders and carried it into the room. She plopped it down on the naked bed across from the one that was already made up with sheets and a beige blanket. "I took the bed on the right, I hope you don't mind. I don't like sleeping next to the window—it weirds me out."

The afternoon sunshine filtered in through the window over what was apparently my bed. I didn't think I'd mind being able to wake up looking out at the city every morning. Not one bit. "No problem. And yes," I offered the girl my hand, "I'm Matilda Castillo. Tilly." I hoped my palm wasn't too gross from the alpine climb up to the fourth floor.

She shook it, her long fingers grasping mine firmly. My mother would have approved of her handshake. "Charlotte Tran." Her fire engine red lips parted in a grin.

"It's nice to meet you, Charlotte."

"You too. I've never been to New York. This should be fun, I think." She sat down on her bed and stretched out her long legs, crossing her left ankle over the right and lifting her arms over her head, almost in fifth position. It was as if she was dancing even while sitting down.

"Where are you from?" I asked.

"L.A. The City of Angels." Charlotte laughed at that. Her voice had music in it. "You?"

"A little south of D.C.—Arlington, Virginia. I just got off the train actually. This is my first real trip to New York too." I didn't add that I was more than a little intimidated. If Charlotte was from Los Angeles, she was probably right at home here in this mammoth city.

"Did you brave the subway?" Charlotte drummed her nails, the same red as her mouth, on the bedside table.

I shook my head and pursed my lips. "Not brave enough, I guess. Next time. You?"

"I did," Charlotte smiled broadly, proud of herself. Her lipstick made her teeth look very white. "Nothing to it, actually. You just need to know what direction you're going, that's all."

"That's all," I echoed. Knowing what direction I was going was the whole reason I'd come here. I looked around the room to see if there was another set of sheets somewhere.

"In there," Charlotte said, anticipating what I needed and pointing to the tiny cabinet masquerading as a closet. I opened the door, removed the pile of sheets and blanket, and started making the bed. "That was the first thing I did too," Charlotte said.

"I don't think a room looks right without the bed made, you know?" I scooted around the bed, awkward in the small space, and tugged the fitted sheet down over a corner near the window.

"Agreed. Nice sunglasses, by the way."

I blushed, pleased she'd noticed, and re-centered them on my head. "Thank you. My abuela picked them out." Red wasn't a color I would normally have chosen, but Abuela had ordered them for me and insisted it was the right color. She said red would give me confidence, as if she knew what was in my head and was encouraging my devious plan.

"So, what do you know about Sage Oliver?" Charlotte asked, a sly note in her voice.

"Nothing really. Why? Is there something I should know?" My stomach dropped, just like on a roller coaster, which had never been something I enjoyed.

Charlotte shook her head and her bangs tickled the top of her orange frames. "No, I don't think so. I hope not anyway. I know she's been working overseas for a long time, but that's it. She's a bit of a mystery. But I'm so glad this is strictly contemporary. I love ballet and all, but it brings out the worst in dancers, you know?"

I knew exactly what she meant. The girls in the dance program at my high school had been relentless. If stealing a costume, tripping someone, or starting a ridiculous rumor were guarantees to rattle the competition's nerves, they'd do it. More often than not, though, they tried to sink you with a flash of their eyes, a sneer, a whisper that might have been your name. There was something about tulle and satin that screamed emotional warfare. It was part of what drew me to embrace other styles of dance.

"Yep, me too," I said.

At my intensive with District Ballet Company last summer, I fell head over heels for contemporary dancing. After the introductory lesson, I spent hours playing Alvin Ailey's *Revelations* and Merce Cunningham's *Second Hand* over and over on YouTube as study material. It was the expressiveness that shattered me every time. Ballet dancers are emotional, no doubt, but to me, it always felt contained. You could be happy or sad, but only just so much before it looked sloppy. I realized quickly that the energy in contemporary could be so very raw and explosive. When done well, the walls around you fall down and the whole room is stripped to ribbons and confetti. I've been chasing confetti, while my mother's been rebuilding the walls. New York is confetti. College is the walls.

"So what's your story, Matilda Castillo? Why are you here? Why aren't you getting ready to start in a pre-professional program with a dance company?"

My heart constricted as my ankle ached with pain I

knew was only in my head. I blew out a loud breath. "I broke my ankle last winter. I had to have surgery. There was a cast. Rehab. I wasn't in shape to audition along with everyone else." The volume of my voice decreased with each word until I trailed off completely. I was pretty sure the crack that rang out the day I went down on the icy sidewalk, after slipping on the stairs, was burned into my memory for all of time. That broken ankle changed my life so much in half a second, and hardly any of it for the better.

"Good thing this audition was so late, right?" Charlotte asked, and I nodded.

It *had* been strangely serendipitous timing. Even my teacher remarked as much. The dream of having a chance to dance professionally, to be paid to do the thing I'd been in love with for most of my life, had seemed so far away. Impossible. I'd have to try to remember to thank Sage for giving me a sliver of hope back.

"Yeah, it really was." I smoothed the blanket and folded the flat sheet over it. "What about you?"

"Honestly?" Charlotte cocked her head.

"No, dishonestly," I said and laughed at myself.

"My parents didn't want me to audition. They pretended it was all about performing being a risky career move and not making much money, becoming a professional waitress, and all that, but I knew they really thought I'd just get hurt. Like, emotionally. I tried to tell them I have thick skin, I mean, you kind of have to when you do this, you know?" I nodded. I knew. "They argued, and I screamed and cried a lot, but in the end, I couldn't disrespect them and go against their wishes. So, I didn't go. And after the application for community college began collecting dust on the kitchen counter, my dad finally asked me why I hadn't filled it out. I told him the truth. And, well, long story short, I'm here."

"My mom is protective too," I told her, though *protective* was an understatement.

Charlotte reached across the space between our bed and held her hand up. I high-fived her softly. "So you want to dance professionally, then?" she asked.

"I just want to dance, period."

"Same."

We smiled at each other and then laughed. It felt odd to talk with another dancer without a cloud of tension hovering over us. Storms were always brewing in my program back home, so this was a nice change of pace.

I finished putting my things away while Charlotte messed around on her phone. When my clothes were stashed in the tiny closet and my toiletries were stowed in the bathroom, I perched on the edge of my bed. I stared out the window at the busy street below, taking in my new city. Smiling to myself at the endless possibilities of a summer in New York City, the electricity I'd felt standing outside the building shimmered inside of me.

Chapter 2

*A*ctually *taking* the subway was much less scary than *thinking* about taking the subway. On our way to our very first rehearsal the next day, Charlotte showed me how to get a metro card from the little machine, dipping my credit card and tapping the touch screen. I purchased an unlimited-rides pass for the length of my stay. If everything went according to plan, the card would get a good workout. Maybe better than the one I knew I was in for at rehearsal.

When we got off the train and climbed the steps, we'd been transported from the quiet Upper East Side to the much louder and more chaotic area just below Columbus Circle. We passed men and women walking to the subway and hailing cabs, just as I'd done yesterday, going about their business as if today was just any other day. I couldn't hold in my smile as we turned the corner. Strolling with Charlotte, my dance bag pulled tight across my chest, I felt almost like I was meant to be there. Like this could be my city. This was actually any other day for me now. This was my reality. At least for a little while anyway.

Charlotte stopped in front of a plain gray building and

reached to open the glass door when someone slipped in front of her and blocked her.

"Excuse me," Charlotte muttered, an annoyed edge to her voice.

The girl, who apparently couldn't be bothered to wait for two people to open the door and pass through, turned and gave us a once-over. She was about our age, tall and slender, but I'd been around enough dancers to know that her slight frame was hiding formidable muscles. The definition in her shoulders alone, as she held the door ajar, was like looking at my own shoulders in a mirror.

"Excuse you for what? What did you do?" She raised an eyebrow and whipped her long orange ponytail around, practically snapping Charlotte in the face. There was something familiar about her, but I couldn't put my finger on it. Without waiting for a response to her questions, which were obviously rhetorical, the girl charged into the building and let the door close behind her.

"Excuse me for the things I am thinking about you right now," Charlotte grumbled to the girl's back. She reached for the door again and held it open for me. "After you."

"I hate to say it, but I think she might be in our group," I whispered, remembering where I'd seen that girl before. She'd been in the lobby of the Marian when I arrived, pacing and talking on her phone. "I saw her yesterday. I'm pretty sure she lives in our building too."

"Perfect. Did you notice she reeked of entitlement? My least favorite scent." Charlotte glared at the space the redhead had occupied moments before and then we both cracked up.

We took the dingy stairs to the second floor and found our room at the end of a long hallway that desperately needed a fresh coat of paint. When we entered the rehearsal space, which was nothing more than shock-absorbent Marley flooring surrounded by walls of mirrors, the rude girl was sitting on the floor in a split, stretching nose to knee. Two other girls, seated slightly behind her, were doing their best to follow suit and keep an eye on her at the same time. Charlotte and I dropped our bags in the corner and began our own warming up processes.

After pulling on my socks and making sure my red sunglasses were tucked safely in my bag, I bent at the waist to release the tension in my spine. I let my arms dangle to the ground and peered through my legs, only to see the redhead rise and assume the same position. A second later, so did the other two girls. Odd. I took myself through my normal routine and quickly realized it wasn't a coincidence. Everything I did, they did too. I sighed as the redhead's leg appeared on the bar just feet away from mine, and looked the other way. I'd been pretty good at compartmentalizing when the competition had gotten really intense in high school, so I didn't think this girl was much of a threat to my focus now. But that didn't mean her attempts to get in my head weren't annoying.

Just as I was feeling warm and limber, a woman with a bleached, almost-white, undercut hairstyle and a long, commanding stride came into the studio. She had to be Sage Oliver.

"Are you my troupe?" Her voice was so loud it echoed, even in the tiny space. I was glad to see a grin on her face.

I'd had a teacher years ago whose voice was like a sonic boom every time he spoke. Even when he was just saying hello, it felt like he was screaming.

We were so surprised by her entrance, though, that no one answered. "Can any of you speak? I know you don't have to talk to dance, but I wasn't imagining this being a quiet kind of summer."

Charlotte snorted and raised her hand. The woman nodded at her. "How loud do you want us to be?"

The woman smiled back, one eyebrow up. "As loud as you want to be, sweetheart." A flutter of nervous laughter came from the other girls. "Well, if it wasn't obvious, I'm your choreographer. Fearless leader, if you will." She saluted us. "Sage Oliver. Sage is fine. Please don't call me Mrs. Oliver. That's my mother." Sage poked her thumbs through her black suspenders and stretched them away from her body. Her gray eyes found mine and she winked. "So. Welcome to New York to those of you who made the journey from far flung places. And, to those who live here, welcome home."

I watched Sage's eyes shift to the redheaded dancer. Interesting. So she was from New York City. I wondered why she was living in the dorm with us and not at home.

Sage continued. "I like my dancers to be self-sufficient. I also like hard workers and dancers who take care of each other. I've been around long enough to know what happens if dancers aren't working toward the same goal and I'm telling you right now, I have a zero-tolerance policy when it comes to intimidation tactics."

I resisted looking around the room again. Had Sage

somehow seen the exchange at the door? Had she seen the girl trying to one-up me during stretching?

"I know we don't know each other yet and we're only together for a short time, but this performance is very important to me. It holds a lot of personal significance and I'm counting on your professionalism for the next several weeks. You will work together. You will work as a team. You will watch out for one another. You will help one another."

Those gray eyes met each of ours in turn. I hoped what Sage said would turn out to be true. Either way, I wasn't going to let the possibility of dancer drama ruin my experience. This was my shot to make my dream come true, and I wasn't going to throw it away.

Sage sat down on the floor with us, crossed her legs, and told us to scoot into a circle for introductions. Looking around, I was glad to see girls from so many different backgrounds. Though I had been fortunate to grow up in an area filled with people from all over the globe, the dance world wasn't always so colorful. Last summer, I'd had a run-in with a girl who suggested I was only dancing contemporary because I knew traditional ballet companies wouldn't look twice at "girls like me." I've never stared at someone so hard. She had been careful not to say Latinas or brown girls, so I was careful to say it for her.

"I would recommend reading up on the racial make-up of both ballet and contemporary dance companies," I'd told her. "Brown girls certainly do dance on big stages. I can give you a list of dancers who are black, Latina, Asian, Native, Indian, Arab . . ."

All through high school, I'd reveled in reading about Misty Copeland, Evelyn Cisneros, Michaela DePrince, and Yuan Yuan Tan, among others. They had paved the way to make sure *girls like me* were given a chance.

"I get it." The girl's eyes had almost glowed with anger, but she'd had the grace to blush. She hadn't spoken to me the rest of the summer unless absolutely necessary.

Looking around the circle of girls I sat with now, I had a feeling I wasn't going to run into the same issue here. Sage's choices for the dancers in this performance proved what I already knew—that girl from last summer was dead wrong.

As an ice-breaker, Sage prompted us to give our names, say where we were from, and share one thing about ourselves you couldn't tell by looking at us.

"I'll go first," Sage said. "If any of you decided to internet stalk me before you came here, you probably know I'm originally from outside Chicago, but I've spent the last twenty-ish years working overseas. The last place I lived was Tokyo. And what you can't tell by looking at me is that I have about a million pins and rods in my hip." She knocked a fist on her side. "Part cyborg actually. A long time ago, I sat just where you are right now, bright-eyed and ready to take on the world. But then my partner dropped me and that was the end of my dance training."

I felt the phantom pain in my ankle radiate up my calf. "That's horrible," I whispered without thinking.

Sage nodded. "It was. I thought my life was over. I spent a lot of time being angry—at my partner, at the other able-bodied dancers, at the universe. But it turned out I was good at choreography, which gave me a different but just as satisfying life. I chose not to quit." She nodded her chin at the redhead, seated directly across from her. "Your turn."

The girl sat up straighter and pushed her shoulders back and chest out, as if she were a queen on her throne and we were her subjects. "My name is Sabrina Wolfrik and I live here in Manhattan. I've been dancing since I was two, and last summer I appeared in a national commercial for a theme park. You might recognize me." Sabrina's smile was smug, challenging the rest of us to say something better and more impressive.

"Congratulations," said Sage, not looking all that impressed. I wanted to laugh, but I didn't. I doubted that would fit in with Sage's idea of working as a unit.

The blonde girl to Sabrina's left introduced herself as Ella Cohen. She couldn't have been more than fifteen. Ella told us she was from Connecticut and her dream was to dance in musicals on Broadway. She paused for our reaction, which was polite silence. I smiled, but Ella wasn't looking. Her brown eyes flicked to Sabrina, who pursed her lips into a smirk.

Sitting beside Ella was Arden Davis, with smooth brown skin and bird-like features. She also seemed quite a bit younger than me. Arden came from Atlanta and loved to eat sushi. Sabrina chuckled when Arden said that; Sage glanced at Sabrina and her eyes narrowed, but she didn't say anything.

Charlotte was next in the circle. "Oh, my turn. I'm Charlotte Tran. L.A. native, so I guess I traveled the far-thest. When I'm not dancing, I'm surfing."

I hadn't been expecting that from my roommate, but I wasn't exactly surprised. She seemed like the kind of person who wasn't afraid of anything. As I was thinking about what it might feel like to have the sun beating on my back as my feet gripped the plane of a surfboard riding a salty wave, I realized all eyes were on me. My cheeks flushed.

"Sorry. I'm Matilda Castillo. You can call me Tilly. I live outside Washington, D.C., and . . ."

I didn't know what else to say. Other than dance, my life had been pretty darn boring. I tried to picture myself on a Saturday night at home and realized I was usually studying for something—a test, the SATs, memorizing choreography, or something else equally as nerdy. After my injury, I'd thought the choice to dance had disappeared, so I'd thrown myself into college applications and turned down offers to go to the movies, hockey games, parties, and anything else Tatum could come up with. Without dance, none of it felt worth the effort.

I forced myself to think beyond the past year and come up with something at least partially interesting. ". . . and I like to bake. Usually bread."

Because Tatum was always watching them, I got sucked down the black hole of cooking shows. My favorites were the baking ones—the more hands-on the recipe, the better. One night shortly after my accident, when I'd been feeling particularly angry, I couldn't sleep and took my frustration out on a loaf of honey wheat. My fingers could work even if my ankle couldn't. The ten minutes of kneading did a valiant job of taking away the anger at myself and my shattered ankle. My mother took the sweet-smelling loaf to work to share with her paralegals and I slept well for a few days. Midnight baking became a temporary oasis in the middle of what felt like an endless desert of trying to get my life back to normal.

I looked up. Everyone was still staring at me. I gazed at Sage, silently pleading with her to move on. Thankfully, she got the message.

"Right, well, I'm super excited to have all of you with me this summer. As you know, we're going to perform as part of an installation project sponsored by the Collective Arts Foundation. Other companies and independent teams will be putting on short productions all over New York, some in unexpected places. There will be many support-ers of the arts in the audiences and, as you already know, scouts from dance companies may attend. So, those of you still looking for a home with a company may find yourself with a job offer by the time this is all over. I'll warn you, though, there may be only a handful of spaces open, from what I've been told. It's late in the year, so they'll only be able to hire the crème de la crème."

So few spots? That meant that most of the dancers performing in the installation could be left without jobs. It meant that every turn, every point of my toes, every lift of my arms, every jeté, every facial expression, every line, would count a million times more for me.

Sage went on, a cat-like grin spreading across her face. "And, you're the first to know that I am using this oppor-tunity to—fingers crossed—move toward the launch of my new company."

"Right on," Charlotte said, giving Sage two thumbs up.

I tried to fix a congratulatory smile on my face, but I could feel my shoulders sinking toward the floor. If Sage was starting a brand-new company, she would most likely be on the hunt for patrons to fund her efforts. Patrons who could be in the audience for our performance. I knew a little bit about this after watching my teachers in high school hustle for donors. Even though I'd attended a public performing arts magnet school, they were forever trying to raise money for better costumes, guest choreographers, and workshop opportunities. I put enough stress on myself having the prospect of a job at the end of the summer dangled like a carrot, forcing me to keep going. And now knowing my performance could contribute to Sage's success? That was a lot to carry. I hoped I—and my ankle—could hold it up.

I looked over at Charlotte, who didn't seem nearly as burdened as I felt, but she wasn't smiling quite as easily as she had been moments before. The other girls, even Sabrina, seemed subdued and thoughtful, maybe even a little scared as well. It was obvious they had jumped to the same conclusion I had.

Breaking the sudden tension, Sage hopped to her feet in one swift movement, still displaying the grace of a dancer, and motioned for us to join her.

"Besides the rule about working as a team, I have one more request." Her gaze circled the room and found each of us. "I just ask that you work hard. You're only as good as the effort you give. Whether your goal is to get a job, make connections, or just dance the heck out of what I promise will be an amazing piece, you have the power to make it happen. I don't want anyone to leave with regrets."

My heart grew three sizes when she said the magic words. *No regrets.* Even though my senior year hadn't gone exactly as I'd planned, this was my second chance, and I was going to make the most of it.

Chapter 3

When Sage said she wanted us to work hard, she hadn't been kidding. By the time our first rehearsal let out, my skin was slick with sweat, and my socks, black tank, and shorts were suctioned to my body, completely soaked through. My muscles were screaming with fatigue, but I had loved every single minute. From the looks on their faces, my new teammates were just as wiped out and just as amazed at what they'd accomplished.

There had been days in the past when I'd come home from a particularly long class—physically long or emotionally—and told myself that I was done. That the toll the work was taking on my body and mind wasn't worth it. But I would inevitably remember the sheer joy I felt when my body did things I had only imagined. Even in the painful moments when I wanted to walk away, there was something to celebrate.

I never gave up because I knew the next day could be the best day I would ever have.

This was that best day. The day I felt fully alive. And I knew, deep down in my dead-tired bones, that it wouldn't be the last.

Charlotte and I walked slowly back to our room from the subway, the late afternoon sun doing its part to dry our damp clothes. "So, that was pretty wild, huh?" Charlotte asked. "I have to give Sage props for thinking outside the box for the theme. Slaying dragons and battling inner demons? Bold. It's got purpose," she said.

I nodded fervently. "I love it. I think Sage is a genius."

At the end of rehearsal, Sage had explained the theme of our piece for the installation project.

She had crouched down in front of us, like she was about to share a secret, and whispered, "We're going to explore the idea of defeating the demons that keep us from living life to the fullest. As you could probably deduce from what I told you about myself earlier, this is something I hold near and dear to my heart."

I'd thought about what Sage had shared about finding a new path in life. I knew I'd been lucky to have recovered from my injury, even if it still made me a little wary of stairs, but I wasn't sure what I would have done or felt if I'd been told that the moment of disaster had been my last.

"And each of you is going to do a little self-reflection while you're here." A collective groan echoed softly through the room. Sage chuckled. "Nothing you can't handle. The theme I want you all to remember while you're dancing is 'slaying the dragon.' That could mean an actual dragon, like in a fairy tale. It could mean defeating an enemy in a war, like Joan of Arc. It could mean something within yourself. But you need to do some thinking on what, or who, inspires you to keep going. Get a book. Watch a movie. Observe the people in your life." Sage's voice grew quieter. "Some of my favorites are the ones who battled and lost. For example, I've often used the music of Amy Winehouse and Janis Joplin in my pieces because you can hear them wrestling with their emotions when they sing."

Sabrina had wrinkled her nose when she'd heard the musicians' names, and Sage had raised one eyebrow and stared her down until she'd turned beet red. "Sorry, but why would someone dance to sad, screechy music by people who looked like they hadn't taken a shower in decades? It's just gross."

"Sometimes the most beautiful lessons we can learn are from the people who lived with the biggest demons," Sage explained. "Are these artists the ones I want you all to choose for personal role models? Maybe. Maybe not. But if we only live our lives paying attention to unicorns and rainbows, we miss out on all the stuff that makes us human. We read history books so we know which choices were successful and which ones crashed and burned, right? And I also think there is something to be said for being able to recognize the demons in ourselves and knowing we have the power to fight them."

Sabrina muttered something unintelligible and looked away. Ella and Arden stared at their feet. Charlotte smiled politely, as if she approved but wasn't sure what to say. From the look on Sage's face, I knew she'd been expecting quite a different reaction.

"I like it," I said quietly.

Sage had winked at me as she stood up. "So, that's settled then."

To wrap up our practice, Sage went around the room and told each of us how we'd done. Charlotte, Arden, and Ella were each given one note of praise and one "action item," as Sage called it, to work on the next day. Then she looked Sabrina up and down, as if she wanted to say something and then thought better of it, simply telling her to watch her posture. When it was my turn, Sage smiled broadly and told me to keep doing everything exactly the same.

"Superb, Tilly. Looking forward to more." And she winked.

I thanked her quietly, feeling four pairs of eyes swing in my direction. Charlotte looked happy for me, but I could feel Arden and Ella side-eying me. Even though the two younger girls weren't competing for a job at the end of the summer, dancers were programmed to size each other up. When I caught Sabrina's eye, I flinched. Whether or not Sage had meant to, she'd just painted a bright red bulls-eye on my back and Sabrina was ready to take aim. For a fleeting moment, it seemed as if Sabrina even bared her teeth at me, like she was about to growl. I was grateful when Charlotte threaded her arm through mine and pulled me out of the studio after we'd packed up.

Standing outside the Marian half an hour later, Charlotte and I both paused at the gate.

"Do you want to walk around the city?" I asked at the same time she said, "I'm exhausted but I'm not ready to go home." We giggled together.

"Why don't we shower, because we might scare some tourists, and then go for a stroll?" Charlotte didn't wait for me to agree before jogging into the building, apparently getting her second wind.

I followed quickly behind her, excited to start exploring my new city.

"Let's play a game," Charlotte said as we stepped back out of the building and into the early evening air.

The day was still warm, but the promise of the sun setting slowly made the heat more bearable. I'd put on a new outfit, a skirt that twirled when I spun, fixed my red sunglasses on my head, and borrowed Charlotte's *Pink Pout* lipstick. She said it would make my skin glow golden, so I'd trusted her. I wasn't sure I was exactly glowing, but it made me feel pretty, like I was dressing up for something special, which my first evening exploring New York definitely was.

"What kind of game?" I asked as we started down the block.

"One photo, one story. We played it at the program I did last summer. Kind of a getting to know you game. I choose one photo on your phone and you tell me the story behind it."

"They might be boring stories," I warned her.

"You let me be the judge of that."

"Fine. But you go first."

Charlotte handed over her phone and I scrolled through her photographs, stopping at one that jumped out at me. A girl who looked just enough like Charlotte to make me think they were related was fitting her hands into the prints left on the sidewalk outside Grauman's Chinese Theater, which I knew from TV. I handed over the phone. "This one."

"Ah, yes. This was from last spring break. That's my older sister, Sophia, and she is as close as she'll ever get to her idol, Julie Andrews."

"The actress from *The Princess Diaries*?"

Charlotte snorted. "That, and classics like *The Sound of Music* and *Mary Poppins*. Soph is obsessed. She's in film school and is doing her thesis project about movie musicals. She was a big choir geek in high school, so this was the likely next step. Mom and Dad hate it."

"Because the film industry is grueling? Superficial?"

Charlotte shook her head as we paused at Lexington Avenue to wait for the traffic to stop. "No, they just don't like musicals. The whole breaking into song in the middle of a scene baffles them." She put her hand out. "My turn."

I gave her my phone. Charlotte scrolled for what felt like forever and I tried to think about what she might be looking at. I didn't take many photographs, so I was curious what she might land on. Most of them were of *things* . . . things like a pink sunrise on the way to school, the flowers in our yard, or something pretty I noticed during a performance or rehearsal—sometimes the trim on a costume or the line of a dancer's shoulder.

"There are no people in these," Charlotte commented.

"Sorry," I said, and we crossed the street. "I told you they'd be boring." I made a mental note to take more pictures this summer. Pictures with people. Preferably of Charlotte and me in front of all the landmarks I'd written on my New York bucket list.

"Oh, jackpot. Here we go." She held it out to me.
"What is happening here?"

I almost groaned. I should have known she'd pick that
one. Charlotte had chosen a picture from last summer. The
Christmas lights strung across the homemade stage twinkled
in the darkness as The Frisson, the band playing on the stage,
mesmerized the crowd. I'd been in the audience that night—
somewhat reluctantly at first—and listened intently, totally
under their spell. Tatum had dragged me to the concert, my
first, and it only took me a matter of minutes to recognize
in their songs the same emotion I felt when I danced. There
was something about experiencing music live and in person
that could never be communicated in a recording or a video.

"That is The Frisson. That's my stepsister's boyfriend
on the piano there. Seamus. And her friend Abby's boyfriend, Hunter, is the lead singer. Tatum and I went to hear
them play. They were amazing. I can play you some of their
music later if you want." I didn't add that I had all of The
Frisson's songs on my phone, like any good fangirl would.
But I hadn't let myself listen to them in a very long time.

"I want. And who is this fine specimen playing the
drums?"

"That is Paolo Sansone." I bit my tongue. I didn't
want to talk about Paolo. My day was going entirely too
well to mess it up by rehashing old mistakes.

"Hello, Paolo," said Charlotte. She blew a kiss at the
screen and then handed the phone back to me. I hoped
she didn't notice how red my cheeks were. "So this looked
like it was a lot of fun. I love concerts. Maybe we should
look for some live music while we're in the city."

"Sure, I'd like that." A concert would be great, as long a certain band wasn't playing—and there was zero chance of that happening here in New York.

With my next photo pick, Charlotte told me the story of the day she and her younger brother, Henry, tried to teach their dog to surf. The picture was of a smiling golden retriever perched on a red board, seemingly riding a wave into shore. "Except two seconds later, poor Bandit wiped out. He wouldn't go near the board after that, which broke Henry's heart, but what can you do?"

When she'd finished her story, I realized we'd wandered into Central Park. The city had fallen away and was replaced by a lush, green fantasy world. While Charlotte scrolled through my phone trying to find something worthy of a story, I led us across the twisting paths that took us through literary-themed statues and past parents trying to hold their kids back from jumping into fountains. We both stopped talking, letting the beauty soak in, and just walked. My veins sparked with excitement, just being here, right in the middle of it.

"This is magic," I whispered to Charlotte as we passed what I knew was the Bethesda Fountain, thanks to the map my stepfather Ken had highlighted for me before I left.

"I don't even feel like we're in the city anymore," Charlotte replied. "Let's come here every day. Or at least find some place kind of like this. I'm sure there are more, and probably hidden, spots."

"Deal." That was one proposition I didn't hesitate to agree to.

We heard the drumming before we saw the drummers, and Charlotte practically leapt in the air.

"Oh, music! Just like we were hoping for. Let's go. I might even have some change in my purse." She handed my phone back and tugged me along the path until we could see a small crowd gathered.

Charlotte apologized to the people she jostled as she squeezed into the middle of the audience, taking me with her. Five musicians were beating on overturned ten-gallon buckets. Their heads dipped low over their drums, knees bent as they sat on plastic crates. A symphony of rhythm embraced us. Every time they struck their makeshift drums, the sound echoed pleasantly in my chest. My legs felt itchy to move, my toes wanting to be pointed and flexed in time with the vibrations.

"You want to dance, don't you?" Charlotte whispered in my ear.

"Of course." My need to move had increased a million percent, both from hearing the rhythm and from standing in the middle of this beautiful park.

"I wonder if they would want us distracting them though."

"Probably not."

We stood still, eyes glued to the ten drumsticks that flew through the air like birds flitting from one space to another, until all five of them raised their arms in the air in five V's, heads still down, like they were bowing for us. The crowd, which had doubled as we stood and watched, erupted into applause. I clapped until the palms of my hands were sore. They were fantastic. This was exactly the kind of New York moment I had dreamed of. Stumbling across a world-class musical performance just walking down the street was an everyday occurrence here.

Just a regular day, I told myself with a smile. I quickly snapped a photograph, capturing my first magical New York memory.

The audience members approached the drummers to toss coins and bills into the red velvet-lined guitar case lying on the ground. I dug a few quarters and nickels out of the bottom of my purse and approached. I tossed the change into the case, admiring how much money they'd earned in such a short time, and wondered if Charlotte and I should think about coming up with a little something to perform somewhere.

"Grazi," said a low, gravelly voice. I started—I recognized that voice. I lifted my eyes to the drummer closest to me.

"You're wel—" I began, but couldn't finish. My eyes met a pair of amber-brown ones I'd know anywhere. They bored into me, straight through to my core, and my stomach clenched. I silently willed the protein bar I'd eaten on the walk over to stay down. Throwing up on his feet would just be the cherry on top of this humiliating moment.

I blinked to make sure he wasn't just a figment of my imagination. How was *Paolo* here in New York? Was Central Park actually magic and making him appear just as I was passing by? His eyes, so warm and friendly when we'd first met, were now void of all emotion, and his lips were pressed into a firm line. I opened my mouth to say something—what, I had no idea—and closed it again. I knew he didn't want to hear anything I had to say, and I couldn't blame him. If I were him, I'd hate me too. I half-nodded and backed away. This time, I grabbed Charlotte's arm and pulled her along with me, trying to get us away as fast as possible despite her confused protests.

But of course, fifteen paces away, I couldn't resist looking over my shoulder to see if he was watching me leave. He wasn't. He wasn't even looking in my general direction. Even worse, he had his arm wrapped around the shoulders of the drummer next to him—a pretty girl with hair the color of the ocean. They were both laughing, and it felt strangely intimate, like I was interrupting something by watching them. My heart squeezed. I turned away and marched myself, and Charlotte, away from the wreckage of our almost-relationship.

Chapter 4

*W*hat's the rush?" Charlotte asked. "I thought you were into it."

"That was Paolo." The arches of my feet protested as I half-walked, half-ran across the park.

"Paolo from the picture you just showed me?" Charlotte hurried, two steps behind me. "How is that even possible?"

"I don't know. I thought it *wasn't* possible." I picked up the pace and didn't stop until I reached the opening in the gate that led to 72nd Street. I put a hand on the low stone wall and panted a little, trying to catch my breath. Five seconds later, Charlotte did the same.

"Why did we run away from the cute drummer who appeared out of thin air? That's the kind of thing we run *toward*, Tilly."

I inhaled slowly and let out the breath, forcing my heart to stop pounding. "Normally, I would agree with you, but that particular cute drummer wants nothing to do with me. Hence the running away."

Charlotte's red mouth popped open. "But you're so nice."

"I try to be. But I screwed up. Big time. He has every right to hate me."

We started walking slowly downtown. "So what did you do to him?" Charlotte asked curiously.

I sighed. "I pushed him away."

"And why did you do that?"

"Because apparently I make really, really bad decisions when I'm stressed."

There was a reason—plenty of reasons actually—why I hadn't wanted to have regrets that summer. Because I'd had months and months of them. My injury was just the beginning.

I patted my purse, digging for my cell. "I need to call my stepsister." Tatum was the only one who knew about the mess between Paolo and me, making her the only one who would understand why I was freaking out about seeing him. Had she known Paolo would be in New York? If she had, I was totally going to kill her.

Tatum picked up right away. "Please tell me you're eating something delicious. Your mother made kale salad for dinner and I am wondering how I'm going to make it through the rest of the summer if she keeps this up. I'm going to need you to send me pictures of all the bagels and all the cheesecake. Yes? Yes. Glad we agree on that."

If I hadn't been so all over the place, I would've laughed. "Hello to you too."

"Hi." I knew without even seeing her that she was smiling. "How's it going? Is it fabulous? I can't even tell you how jealous I am right now."

I wasn't up for small talk, so I dove right in. "So something kind of weird just happened."

"Yeah?"

"Yeah. My roommate and I were walking through Central Park and I ran into someone." I paused to see if she'd volunteer his name, but there was just silence on the other end. "Paolo." Tatum kept up the silence and my heart raced. Was she in the same state of shock I was or was she quiet because she felt guilty? "Tatum? Are you still there?"

She exhaled loudly, making the receiver crackle. "I'm here. I was hoping the city was so big you'd never cross paths. But, of course, you'd see him right away. Of course," she said in a low, defeated voice.

I sucked in a sharp breath. "You knew he was here?"

"I did."

"And you didn't tell me?" I must have gotten louder because the people sitting on the bench nearby turned to stare at me, puzzled expressions on their faces. I walked faster. "How could you withhold that kind of information?" I whispered into the phone. "You knew things were awkward between me and Paolo. Why wouldn't you at least give me a heads-up?"

It had been a long time since I'd been snippy with Tatum. We'd spent our first decade together fighting or ignoring each other before realizing we could actually be friends. Now we got along great, but I definitely didn't appreciate her keeping this from me.

A long pause. "I thought you'd be upset if you knew," Tatum finally said, with a sniff.

I sighed, but resisted raising my voice again. "But I'm upset now. He was playing the drums in the middle of the park. Before I realized who he was, I gave him money like he was any old street performer. Do you know how mortifying that was?"

"I can guess," she said in a small voice. "I'm sorry. I really didn't think there was any chance of you guys running into each other. I assumed if you knew he was there, you'd be anxious and it would stress you out and you would have a terrible summer with that hanging over your head."

I closed my eyes. It wasn't hard to see how she could think she was protecting me. "I get it. I just wish you'd told me because then I could have prepared for it. I wish you'd thought about it from my perspective."

The second I said it, I regretted it. I love Tatum. She was the closest thing I had to a best friend. We might've disagreed on delivery, but I didn't want to make her feel bad for her good intentions.

"I'm sorry," Tatum said again. "I don't know what else to say, Tilly. I didn't mean to hurt you. I thought I was doing the right thing."

I stopped walking and Charlotte paused next to me, cabs and buses honking in the wide street ahead of us. "I know you did. And I understand, I do."

"Do you want me to call him? Have Seamus call him? What can I do to make it better?"

I shook my head and then realized she couldn't see me. "No, thank you though. I think the only one who can make this better is me." A lump formed in the back of my throat as soon as I said it. "I still have his number. I guess I'll reach out and see what happens."

There were a million things I'd rather do than humiliate myself more, but seeing Paolo in the park was probably a sign that I needed to stop hiding. This summer was all about being brave and leaping into the unknown. Deep down I knew I wanted some closure with the only boy I'd really ever had feelings for.

"Well, just remember how awesome you are, and if he can't get over himself, then he's not worth it." Gone was Tatum's small, apologetic voice and back was the brash, confident stepsister who had worked since the winter to bring me out of my funk.

"Thank you for that."

"I love you. You're the best."

"I love you too."

Tatum raised her voice, probably for my mother's benefit. "And send me pictures of pizza!"

"Will do."

I disconnected, a reluctant smile on my face.

"Everything okay?" Charlotte seemed torn between concern for me and fear that I might start speed-walking again.

"No, not really," I said with a laugh. I bent at the waist and buried my face in my hands. I didn't want to talk to Paolo. But I did. Rather, I wanted everything to be fine, as if we'd never met. That way, I would have been saved from death-by-embarrassment.

"Wanna talk about it?"

I lifted my head to look at Charlotte. "Not yet. But I will. I promise." I needed to work things out in my head first.

Charlotte nodded. "Okay. How about we keep walking?"

"In the opposite direction?"

"And slowly."

We grinned at each other and started down 5th Avenue. In the dwindling evening light, the city was a different shade of exciting. I concentrated on breathing in and out, in and out. We walked for ages, watching businesspeople and shop owners head home for the day, while tourists swam upstream, in search of dinner or happy hour. We stopped to admire the jewelry in the windows of Tiffany's and Cartier, and Charlotte lingered in front of the inventive displays at Louis Vuitton and the Gap.

We wove in and out of the long city blocks, Charlotte pointing out interesting buildings or restaurants, while I tapped out quick notes into my phone about the things I wanted to save for later. I mentally recorded the hours of the Museum of Modern Art and told Charlotte we'd have to come back one Friday night when admission was free. We passed Rockefeller Center and took a quick photo of ourselves with the 30 Rock address sign. As we neared Times Square, which was growing brighter with neon as the sun set, my stomach growled.

"Want to grab a bite?"

Charlotte rubbed her belly. "Yes, please. How about pizza? There isn't much that's more New York than that."

"Really?" Pizza was definitely not on the approved list of food for dancers, even though Tatum always encouraged me to break the rules.

"Sure, why not? I like to live on the edge." I shrugged. "Well, we probably earned a slice, with all the calories we burned today." My feet ached, as if they agreed with me. "Plus, I promised my stepsister I'd send her a picture of New York pizza."

"That's the spirit," Charlotte said, and we ducked into the nearest pizza shop.

After pizza, we'd wandered around until dark before heading back to the Marian. Charlotte, to her credit, didn't push me for details on Paolo again, and distracted me for the rest of the evening with a movie instead. But despite her efforts and my own exhaustion, I couldn't stop thinking about whether or not I should reach out to Paolo like I'd told Tatum I would. If I did, what would I say? Would he even reply? There wasn't a pro and con list long enough for this.

Charlotte conked out in a matter of minutes once we turned off the lights for bed. I, however, stared at the ceiling for what felt like hours, kicking the blanket off, then covering my feet, and kicking it off again, over and over. Suddenly, my phone lit up the room. I grabbed it, grateful for the distraction, and checked to see what the notification said.

Check out my new machine!

It was a text from Abuela. I mentally kicked myself for not going to visit her tonight. That might've taken my mind off the Paolo disaster more than pizza, even though it had been very delicious. The photo she sent with her text was a selfie. She was smiling broadly, as she always did, and there was a blue wrap, connected to some kind of tubing, around her injured shoulder.

Hola! What is it? I texted back.

It pumps cold water to my shoulder, so poor Ginger isn't constantly changing my ice. Neat, yes?

Abuela was staying with her old pal Ginger in her apartment in New Jersey, as it was close to "the best surgeon my insurance can buy" as well as "a crackerjack team of rehab specialists." Nothing less than the best for Abuela, even if it meant she had to sleep in an unfamiliar bed for several weeks. I would've preferred recuperating at home, if it had been me, but she was used to couch surfing. She spent more time staying with friends than in her own apartment, so I shouldn't have been surprised she would travel for doctors as well.

Instead of texting back, I quietly crawled out of bed, went out into the dim hallway, and pressed the video chat button for Abuela. She picked up right away. Despite being in recovery, her short silver hair was perfectly styled and her ever-present red lipstick lined her bright smile. She was a comforting sight.

"Isn't technology wonderful, mija? I may have sweet-talked my physical therapist into letting me borrow it the whole time I'm here." Like Tatum, Abuela launched into conversation without even saying hello.

I grinned at her, sliding down to the floor and propping myself up against the wall. "It looks very efficient. How is the recovery going?"

"As well as can be expected. I'm not sure I'll be back on the trapeze anytime soon, but my therapist believes I am making progress."

"That's great, I'm glad to hear it. My therapists were

miracle workers. I don't think I would be here in New York without them." That was certainly the truth. They had shown me that my body was capable of much more than I thought, which was saying a lot given my lifetime of dancing.

Abuela waved her hand dismissively. "We are all a little bit broken. But that doesn't mean we aren't still strong. I never had any doubt you would be back on a stage."

"Well, I'm glad you didn't, because I had plenty of doubts." I smiled and shook my head.

"But you are in New York now. And I am sure you are having much more fun than an old lady stuck on the couch." Abuela turned her phone and gave me a tour of Ginger's small living room, complete with floral sofa that didn't look nearly comfortable enough for a woman in a sling with a torn rotator cuff.

I sighed. Did I tell her about Paolo? Did I tell her about Sabrina? Did I tell her Tatum kept her mouth shut when she should've told me an important piece of information? No. My abuela deserved a stress-free recovery, so I stuck to the positives.

"Things are great. I really like my roommate, Charlotte, and our choreographer is great too. The theme of the show is slaying dragons, which is great, really inspiring. Charlotte and I took a great stroll through the city earlier tonight too."

Abuela paused and pursed her lips before speaking. "And you're feeling great?"

I nodded emphatically. "Yep, super great." Inside, I cringed, knowing she'd caught me. I'd never used the word "great" so many times in my life.

To her credit, Abuela knew when to push harder and when to leave well enough alone. She nodded, her eyes crinkling in the corners, probably amused at my attempt to cover up the truth. "Well, once I'm a little more mobile, you can bet I'll be coming into the city to see how great everything really is."

I laughed softly. "Is that a threat?"

Abuela smiled. "Just a promise."

"I would be happy to show you around. And I'll come out to Ginger's apartment to visit you as well. Can I bring you anything? Ice cream? Cupcakes?" It was the least I could do for her.

She waved me away again. "Just your smile."

Instinctively, the corners of my mouth turned up. "Definitely."

Abuela's face turned serious and she waggled a finger at me. "Shouldn't you be in bed, mija? Dancers need to rest."

"Yes, I was just going to say good night. I'll talk to you soon, okay?"

Abuela waved good-bye with her free, non-sling-bound hand. "Good night. I hope you have sweet dreams."

"Good night, Abuela." I waved back and then her face disappeared from view as we disconnected.

Chapter 5

*S*o, how are you feeling?" Charlotte asked the next morning, stuffing extra practice clothes into her dance bag.

I yawned and stretched my arms up over my head. "How am I feeling about what? The part where I ran into the boy I burned but still have feelings for, or the part where my stepsister left out the part where she knew he was spending his summer in New York?" I stood up, went to the tiny almost-closet, and plucked out a fresh tank and dance shorts.

Charlotte shrugged cheerfully. "Either one."

I flopped back on the bed, buried my face in my pillow, and groaned.

"Are you ready to talk about it? I mean, you don't have to, obviously, but I'm a good listener."

And she had been, about everything so far. There was just something about Charlotte that put me at ease. I sighed and recounted my tale of bad decisions as I got back up to dress and pack my bag.

"Everything started last summer at the concert I was telling you about. The one in the photo. I noticed Paolo on stage immediately. You know that expression 'golden

boy' and how it normally describes a nice, accomplished
guy who everyone loves? That was the first thing that
popped into my head when I saw him, except I was
thinking *actual gold*. You saw the picture. His hair, his
eyes, his skin. Everything about him just radiated light
and energy. Tatum introduced us after the show and we
exchanged numbers. We started texting right away, and I
was hooked. He was so easy to open up to."

I remembered feeling that, even though we'd only
known each other a short time, there was the possibility of
more. And I wanted that more. I wanted him to be more
to me. I'd never felt that way about anyone before.

Once both of us were fully dressed, I gestured to
Charlotte to go ahead of me as we breezed through our
doorway and into the hall.

"A couple weeks later, Tatum invited me to go to the
movies with her and Seamus. When we got there, Paolo
was waiting for us in the lobby. I sat through the whole
movie, stiff as a board, side-eyeing him to see if he was
side-eyeing me, which he was. We would both look away
and grin. I was such a mess."

I smiled and blushed, remembering. I could still feel
the two inches of space between my leg and his as we sat
there in the dark, both pretending to watch the movie
and trying hard to look like we didn't care about what the
other was thinking.

"We went to dinner afterward and I couldn't eat a
thing. I pushed my rice around on my plate, making little
piles. I didn't even realize what I was doing until Paolo
leaned over and asked me if I had aspirations of being an

architect." I had chuckled, caught. When I looked down at my plate, the rice looked like a badly formed sand castle.

Charlotte and I stopped at a silver food cart a block from the subway. Charlotte ordered an everything bagel; mine was plain with veggie cream cheese.

Her bagel hovered near her mouth as I dove into mine. "Not seeing anything to run away from yet. Also, not seeing bad behavior on your part. Sounds like you really liked each other." Charlotte hip checked me.

I chewed and swallowed as we descended the subway stairs. "I was totally smitten. He was funny and nice and so talented. He and Seamus are musical geniuses. When we were sitting there at dinner, they mimed this whole piece for us. Paolo with his fork and knife as his drum sticks and Seamus playing an invisible piano. They wanted me and Tatum to sing, but we couldn't stop laughing." I suddenly stopped talking because I couldn't remember the last time I'd laughed like that. Which was more than a little distressing. And totally part of my problem.

"These sound like my kind of people," Charlotte said, taking a huge bite of her bagel. We stepped into the waiting train and sat down in two miraculously empty seats.

I smiled sadly. They were my kind of people too. "So we texted a lot after that. And there were some long, late night phone calls."

"The kind where you stay up until the sun's about to rise and you're totally exhausted but it was completely worth it because of the adrenaline rush you got from the conversation?"

"Exactly."

"Been there."

We smiled at each other with mouths full of bagel. "We went out once more with Tatum and Seamus, but then things at school got hectic. I was in the dance program—you know how that goes—and he was practicing with the band and playing gigs on a lot of weekends, so it was hard to find a time when we were both free. Which, I didn't like, obviously, but I knew he got it. If anyone understood what it was like to be committed to something you love, Paolo did."

At our stop, we exited the train, pushed through the turnstiles, and ascended once again to the bustling streets and morning sunshine.

"I wasn't really close with any of the dancers at school, so it was nice talking to someone who was just as passionate about his art as I was." It was one of the things I liked best about Paolo, really. When we compared schedules, he wasn't jealous, or upset, or put out that we had to wait several weeks until we both had a free evening.

"His high school was having their homecoming football game on one of the only free Friday nights we had, so I went with him. We ate hot dogs, drank cocoa, and cheered for his team, even though they lost. I met some of his friends from school and they were all super nice. It felt like I was a normal girl who went to their normal school. Just for a night." I'd loved it. For that night. And the next day I went back to sweating and stretching and working hard to become the best dancer and student I could.

"Sounds awesome. I'm still hearing zero reasons why you would push him away." Charlotte held the door to the building housing the rehearsal space. Thankfully, there was no Sabrina in sight.

I sighed loudly as we approached the stairs, still angry at myself for what came next. "We kept talking and texting, but it was coming up on holiday performances and we were both swamped. Plus, we were working on college essays and there was the SAT and my grandmother visited and then his did and . . ."

My heartbeat picked up in anticipation of what I was about to say. Reliving the nightmare was never an easy thing. My body still reacted over and over again. ". . . and then there was a freak cold streak in December, and the stairs out front of school hadn't been salted yet. I slipped."

Chapter 6

I had been at the top of the stairs when I felt my feet leave the ground. My arms went wide, hands splayed to catch myself, but my ankle took the brunt of the fall. There was a deafening crack when I finally crashed to the ground. Agony shot through every limb, every nerve in my body. It wasn't until I cried out from the pain that I looked at my legs and saw my ankle twisted in an unnatural way. And possibly worse than that, a crowd began to form the minute I landed on the sidewalk, at the bottom of the stairs. My fellow dancers stood there, gaping, no doubt thankful that it was me and not them. An injury can be a like a death sentence for a dancer. Like it was for Sage.

"I was in a cast, then therapy, for months," I told Charlotte. "I was in so much pain, not just physical, that I shut everyone out. I was so angry and humiliated. I felt this wash of rage all the time, dripping over me. I was mad at myself for not being more careful, for not wearing shoes with better traction, for not thinking ahead and realizing the stairs could be icy. The accident was completely my fault, and I hated knowing that."

I pinched the bridge of my nose. The next part was the worst.

"After surgery, I laid there in my hospital bed, a ball of rage and tears, thinking my dancing career—my *life*—was over. Tatum called Paolo to tell him what had happened, so of course being the nice guy he is, he came to visit. He even brought a gorgeous bouquet of lilacs. Who knows where he found them in the winter." Shame flooded my insides. I could barely say it out loud. "I refused to let him in. I was so humiliated and mad. Like if I saw him, I would explode. Maybe scream. It was like the best thing in my life couldn't share space with the worst thing that had ever happened to me. My stepfather sent Paolo away and promised he'd have me call him when I got home. But I never did. I couldn't do it. A week or so later, he sent a text to ask me if I was feeling okay. It was really sweet. There were even heart emojis. And instead of thanking him, like a rational person, I texted him back and said to leave me alone. That I couldn't deal with us—with him—right then."

My face burned with the memory. In hindsight, I knew it had been a coward's move, and one that earned me his silence. Paolo had every right to never want to see me again.

"My mother suggested I try to find a way to channel my anger, so I spent weeks and weeks in my room, finishing college and scholarship apps, making sure my homework was perfect, memorizing the choreography I couldn't perform. Tatum was amazing, even though I was horrible. She kept inviting me to things and I always turned her down, unless it was a movie on the couch at home." I smirked at the ground. "One time, she made this website to cheer me up. She does graphic design, even has her own business actually. So she did a fake personal website for me and gave me all of these fake talents. Tatum said I was an award-winning poet and novelist, a radio DJ, a Supreme Court justice, all kinds of stuff."

"They're all things you can do sitting down." Charlotte's face lifted and she smiled at me.

I nodded. "Or on crutches, which I was at the time. It was really sweet. But it also reminded me of the one thing I couldn't do—dance."

We climbed the stairs slowly. Even talking about my ankle made it ache, just a little, with each step up. "And you never once talked to Paolo through all this?" Charlotte asked.

"No," I said quietly. "I was so embarrassed. And angry. Always angry. I didn't want him to see what a mess I was. And I somehow got it into my head that if I couldn't dance, I had to have a backup plan. I mean, before the injury, I'd always planned to go to college and dance on the side, maybe with the university. Georgetown has a few options on campus. But when I wiped out— boom. Dancing was suddenly the only thing I wanted to do, and it wasn't possible."

"You always want the thing you can't have," Charlotte said sadly.

We entered the rehearsal space—the first ones to arrive—and dropped our bags in the corner before sitting down on the floor to stretch.

"Bingo. I was a girl on a mission. College acceptance

needed to happen and tuition needed to be paid for. There was clearly no chance of a dance scholarship anymore, so I filled out so many applications, wrote so many stupid essays." I half-snorted. "Injuries make for very compelling essay topics. By graduation, I had enough to pay sticker price for my whole first year and then some." Because of my brilliant—or delusional—leap of faith, I knew I'd have to return the money. It would be worth the sacrifice, though, and someone else could benefit from my change of heart.

Charlotte switched to the other side as I worked into a splits position. "And you made it happen. But something changed, obviously, because you're here."

"Exactly. I got into college, but I don't want it. I know that is the height of privilege for me to say, but I just want to dance."

"And you will. Think about all that anger—that's got to be great material to draw from when you're dancing, you know? You're trying to slay your dragon right now."

I nodded slowly. I appreciated Charlotte's optimism. "The only problem is, I promised my mom I'd go to college. The deposit has been sent. They're probably assigning me to a dorm as we speak. Georgetown, here I come."

As soon as I said it, the tin-can sensation flooded my mouth. I swallowed hard but it lingered, reminding me of the promise I'd already broken.

"Maybe, maybe not," Charlotte said, her nose touching her knee as she lifted her arm overhead.

I inhaled sharply. "Actually, can you keep a secret?" I looked around the room to check for intruders, even though I knew we were still the only people there.

Charlotte's eyes widened. "Of course I can."

I leaned closer to her and whispered, "Here's the truth. I'm not going to Georgetown. I deferred and told them I'm taking a gap year. Good-bye back-up plan." Saying the words out loud for the first time both thrilled and terrified me. There was so much riding on this performance. Everything, actually.

"Get out." Charlotte slapped the floor with both hands. "Seriously?"

"Seriously. You're the only one who knows, so shhh." I put a finger to my lips.

Charlotte shook her head in disbelief, which made me a little bit proud, crossed an invisible X over her heart, and like any good conspirator, changed the subject.

"So why didn't you call Paolo while you were recovering? Other than the rage blackouts and all." She said the last bit with a cheeky smile. "You could've fixed it. He sounds like a good dude. I bet he would've forgiven you, given the circumstances."

I sighed. Past-Tilly's actions made zero sense to me now. "Even though I kept thinking about him, I'd convinced myself that he was a distraction. An obstacle to my goal. It sounds ridiculous, I know, but that's what I thought. I was laser-focused on making my new future happen. Plus, after I told him to leave me alone, he did. No more texts or calls. I never gave him a reason, even though I bet Tatum explained some of it. The punch line is I screwed up big time, and now he hates me."

"He definitely doesn't hate you." She raised an eyebrow. "You feel bad about the way you treated him. Maybe this is the universe telling you that you're supposed to make it up to him. I mean, he's here in New York. Drumming in Central Park. What are the chances? This is like something out of a movie or Jane Austen novel. Maybe you and Paolo are meant to be together, and this is your second chance."

"You're a hopeless romantic." I shook my head. "Which I like and thank you for trying, but you didn't see the way he looked at me. If he could've reduced me to dust with his eyes, he probably would have done it."

Charlotte shrugged. "Fine. Maybe he's feeling anti-social where you're concerned. But that doesn't mean you can't try."

"True, but I think the fact that he had his arm around a girl ten seconds after he saw me is a good reason why I shouldn't." I wish it hadn't hurt so much to see him embrace her. He wasn't mine anymore—not that he'd really ever been mine to begin with. I hadn't let it get that far.

"That's fair, I guess. But what if she wasn't his girlfriend?"

I raised one eyebrow back at Charlotte. Even if the blue-haired girl wasn't his girlfriend, it certainly looked like he wanted her to be. But I couldn't help thinking that Charlotte had a point. Maybe this was my second chance, even if it was only a chance at friendship. At the very least, if I worked up the nerve, I could explain . . . if he was willing to listen. Girlfriend or no girlfriend, I'd regret not saying I was sorry.

Charlotte flexed and pointed her feet. "If you guys were really into each other, I bet he'd be down for at least talking. It would give you a chance to apologize. You know, if you want to."

The door swung open and Sabrina sauntered in. "What did you do, Tilly? Why do you need to apologize?" Ella and Arden skittered in behind her, and I wondered how much they'd heard.

"Don't worry about it," I muttered. I may not have known Sabrina well, but I was certain she was the *last* person I'd want to spill my deep dark secrets to.

Sage burst through the door as we were all getting warmed up. "Who's ready to work?"

For the first half of the rehearsal, Sage took us through a series of movements that reminded me of toy soldiers I'd seen in a Christmas movie years ago. If one of the six of us bent our knees slightly or our toes weren't perfectly flexed, Sage made us all do it again. And again. And again.

"I wasn't just telling you that you would learn to work as a group because I like to hear myself talk. I *do* like to hear myself talk," Sage said with a low chuckle. "But I meant what I said. Part of the beauty of contemporary dance is the precision involved. Remember that guy in high school with the perfect hair?"

Crickets. We didn't know what she was talking about.

"Come on! You know the one." Sage finger combed her upper cut until it started to stand up a little, defying gravity. "This guy exists in every school. His hair is messy, but artfully so. He looks like he walked through a car wash or a windstorm and his hair just happened to blow into the most interesting arrangement and you can't take your eyes off it." Sage tapped her chin. "Think of Eddie Redmayne. Or all the guys in One Direction."

Ella giggled and covered her mouth. "That guy is my

brother. He spends longer on his hair than my mother and me combined."

Sage touched her nose with one index finger and pointed at Ella with the other. "Exactly. It looks like a mess but a lot of thought and planning and details goes into it, right?"

Five heads, including my own, nodded.

Sage pointed to her own hair. "I might be guilty of this myself." All of us laughed, even Sabrina. "I've heard audience members say that contemporary dancing looks like everyone is jerking around on stage. A woman I met in London compared the dancers' bones to rubber bands. One critical man I came across in Brazil said it looks like the dancers are just winging it. They've used the words flopping and flailing and ugly, but you know what? I say bravo. Because I know how much hard work goes into these performances and how much care and attention to detail."

Sage started pacing around us. "And you know what else those audience members said? They all said how *moved* they were. That's why I'm working you so hard. So what you do looks effortless and so it causes an emotional reaction. Be the guy with the hair. Can you do it?"

"We can do it!" I called, as Charlotte, Ella, and Arden burst out with the same. We looked at each other and laughed, while Sabrina just rolled her eyes and pressed her lips into a thin line.

As we went through a new combination, I concentrated even harder on making sure my steps were perfectly precise. There were moments where my ankle cried out and sweat dripped down my back and arms, but I willed myself to stay focused. I thought about what Charlotte had said to me earlier, about using all my months of anger in my dancing. Against my better judgment, I brought up a hazy vision of Paolo's face in Central Park, his eyes narrowed and his mouth clamped shut because he was appalled to see me. Emotion—*power*—exploded through my limbs, forcing me through the motions until time and music and movement began to blur into pure freedom.

We ended the combination on the floor. Five mouths panted as five pairs of lungs filled with much needed oxygen. I bent over my knees, eyes wide in disbelief. I'd never danced like that before. In all my years in ballet, I'd been trained to make tiny adjustments and be elegant and long. When I first started with contemporary, it was new and unfamiliar, and while I loved it, I'd had no real life experience to draw from. When my teacher told me to look angry, I'd thought about the times I'd done poorly on tests or when I was fighting with Tatum. It felt completely different to use those months of frustration and disappointment and turn them into movement. If there was the smallest silver lining to my disastrous senior year, this was it.

Sage clapped twice. "Well. That was fine, team. Let's not forget the theme of the performance, yeah? Fight the thing that is fighting you." Sage looked pointedly at me. "There's a difference between being mad and pouting and being mad about something and deciding to change that something. Think about that tonight. That's what I want you to marinate on. Come back tomorrow so we can start cooking with gas, all right? And don't forget, we're having fun!"

We broke up and headed for our gear. I wiped my

slick arms with a towel and slipped on my flip-flops as the adrenaline rush of using my anger flickered and sputtered within me. I was mad at myself for being horrible to Paolo, and it was up to me to make it right.

I threw the rest of my stuff into my bag. As I did, my hand brushed against the handful of change leftover from my bagel purchase this morning. I pulled out a penny and without even thinking, tossed it up in the air.

"Call Paolo, heads. Don't call, tails," I whispered to myself. I didn't even try to catch it.

The penny clattered to the floor. Charlotte, startled, looked over at me as if I'd set off an alarm.

"Sorry." I bent over to inspect the coin. Heads. The burn in my cheeks spread down my neck and to my ears in seconds. Call Paolo. I gulped in a breath, stood, and squared my shoulders. I could do this. He was just a boy, and I owed him an apology. We'd never have to talk again after that, unless he wanted to, and my conscience would be clear.

On the way home, a text buzzed on my phone. I entered my passcode to find a picture of my abuela on the couch, but turned around backward with the TV screen behind her.

When I get out of this place, I'm going to hunt down where the NJ housewives get their hair done!

I laughed out loud and passed the phone to Charlotte to show her. She laughed and shook her head.

"My abuela just had surgery. She's probably seen a little too much TV at this point," I explained.

"If she found the salon, do you think she'd go in?" Charlotte asked.

I smirked. "I wouldn't put it past her."

I texted back. **Is this you checking up on me? I thought I was the one who was supposed to do that.**

I'm just fine. What's happening with you? Everything still great? She sent a winking face emoji.

Just rehearsing. Nothing scandalous like your housewives.

GREAT.

I took a quick picture of me and Charlotte on the subway, colorful map behind our heads, and sent it off. I wasn't interested in scandals this summer. I'd settle for calm and smooth sailing and leave the waves, even if they were just on TV, to Abuela.

Chapter 7

*D*espite the courage-inducing coin flip, it still took me a whole day before I got up the nerve to send Paolo a text. After rehearsal, I searched for the number saved under Paolo Sansone. It had been months since I'd used it. I'd saved it with a close-up of the picture Charlotte had been looking at from The Frisson concert. His longish golden brown hair waved over his brow; he grinned, lopsided and rakish. The muscles in his arms were well-defined as they contracted to grip the drumsticks. He looked like he was having the time of his life, and I hated knowing my text would probably give him the opposite expression.

> **Hi, Paolo. This is Tilly. I'm sure I'm the last person you want to hear from, but I wanted to apologize for disappearing on you. I'd like to explain, if you'll let me. Please.**

Before I could talk myself out of it, I pressed send. I hoped he'd write back, but I wouldn't blame him if he didn't. He'd probably deleted my number a long time ago or even blocked it.

Hastily I added, **If you don't want to, I'll understand. But if you have even ten minutes . . .**

He didn't respond in the time it took to pack up my bag, or the time it took me and Charlotte to ride the subway home, or the time it took us to shower and decide which neighborhood we wanted to wander through that evening. Charlotte and I were settling on Chelsea and maybe the Meatpacking District if we weren't too tired, when my phone *finally* buzzed.

I jumped.

"Is that him?" Charlotte asked anxiously, trying to grab the phone out of my hand.

"I don't know. I can't look." I handed it to her.

"Yes!" she screeched, waving the phone around.

"What does it say?" I'd never been so nervous to read something in my whole life. Well, maybe Sage's email telling me if I'd gotten a spot in her performance was slightly more nerve-fraying, but it was a close second.

Charlotte read aloud, "'I'm in class until seven and then I have a thing, but if you can meet me at nine, I'll come.'" She looked up, her brown eyes glittering. "This is your shot, Till."

"What do I say back?"

"You ask him where, obviously."

"You type—I can't do it." My hands were shaking, and I couldn't chance autocorrect sending something that made no sense, or worse, dug me deeper into the shame hole.

Charlotte tapped out a message. "How's this? 'Nine works for me. Where should I meet you?'"

"That's fine." No autocorrect errors. Phew.

My phone buzzed again.

"He sent an address," Charlotte reported. She clicked on it, and the map that came up on the screen showed a blue dot not far from where we planned to explore. "I think this is a sign. We're going to be near here tonight. The universe is pushing you together, I'm sure of it."

I cracked a nervous smile. "You and your theories of the universe."

I took the phone from Charlotte.

See you there, I typed, and sent it before I could change my mind.

He didn't write back.

On our trip downtown, my phone rang in my pocket, and I yelped when I saw the name on the screen.

"Scare much?" Charlotte teased.

I thought it was an appropriate reaction, given the caller was my mother. "Hi, Mama."

"Hello, Matilda." Her voice was crisp and business-like as usual. "I haven't heard from you in a few days and wanted to see how things are going with the installation."

This was no surprise. She didn't need to know how I was enjoying the city or how I was getting along with my roommate or even if I was missing home. The most important thing to my mother was whether to not I was doing a good job and working hard. I knew better than to take it personally or read too much into it. Keeping people on task was her love language, just like pro and con lists were mine.

"It's been really great, Mama. Sage is very dedicated to her art. I've never worked this hard before, but I'm really enjoying it."

"Hard work is good for you. It makes the finished product even more worthwhile." This was something she'd said enough times throughout my childhood that it ought to have been embroidered on a pillow in my bedroom.

"How is everyone at home?" I'd texted with Tatum, of course, but she never mentioned what else was going on in my absence.

"We are all fine." She cleared her throat, and sounded almost excited—or maybe it was nervous—when she spoke again. "Your stepsister and I started a photography class at the community center last night."

"Really?" I couldn't contain the shock in my voice. My mother and Tatum had never gotten along. It wasn't until fairly recently that they had come to a sort of mutual agreement that Tatum wouldn't try to rock the boat so much and my mother wouldn't get all bent out of shape if Tatum wanted to do something Mama didn't approve of. It was their way of being more open-minded about each other, I thought. But taking a class and spending actual leisure time together seemed a little extreme.

"Yes, really."

"Wow. That's great, Mama. Will you send me some of your pictures?"

"They won't be very good, but I will send them to you."

There was vulnerability laced through her words.

I was the one who was used to being in the spotlight, not her. Mama definitely preferred to kept things running smoothly behind the scenes, so I was actually kind of proud she'd taken a step outside her comfort zone. I imagined it was scary for her.

"And will you send me a video of you dancing?" The statement lying quietly under her request was that she missed having me around.

The distance between us suddenly felt strange and prickly. Mama missed me, and I was lying to her. World's. Worst. Daughter.

"I'll ask Sage if she minds," I mumbled.

"Thank you." She sounded pleased. "Well, I will let you go. I'm sure you are exhausted and need your rest. Make sure you're drinking enough water and eating protein, please."

"I will, Mama."

"Speak to you soon."

"Bye."

I put the phone back in my pocket and hitched my purse back up on my shoulder.

"Everything okay?" Charlotte asked.

"Yeah, everything is fine. My mother was just checking in."

Charlotte nodded. "Mine is texting me constantly. She's thinks I'm going to get mugged or kidnapped or something. Big cities scare her."

"You live in a big city." I'd never been to Los Angeles but I couldn't imagine it being terribly different from New York in terms of potential dangers.

"We don't live in L.A. proper," Charlotte clarified.

"We're out closer to the beach, so it's just easier to say we live in the city. But my mom texts me like this when I'm at home too. I shouldn't be surprised." Charlotte gave me a wry smile.

We rode the subway to the 14th Street subway stop. Navigating the city had gotten easier over the last day or two; I was starting to feel a little like a New Yorker. I smiled as we stepped off the train and pushed our way through the turnstiles, just like everyone else. I smiled as we trudged up the steep steps and back onto the street. I smiled as we made our way to the enormous brick building that I knew, from reading my guidebooks, housed one of the most impressive collection of shops and eateries anywhere. I kept on smiling as Charlotte and I spent an inordinate amount of time strolling through Chelsea Market.

But despite my smile, my insides were trembling. Fear. Anticipation. Relief. I did my best to keep it together, but I was sure Charlotte, and anyone else even glancing my way, knew I was a mess.

At 8:45, after we'd eaten salads at a gluten-free, dairy-free counter in the market, just because we could, Charlotte looked at me and gave me a small salute. "Well, my friend, this is it. You think you can make it to the address on your own?"

The place I was supposed to meet Paolo was only a few blocks away. "I'm sure I can manage."

I didn't doubt my ability to follow a set of directions from my phone. I was a little fuzzier, though, on my ability to apologize tactfully and without running away.

Charlotte placed both hands on my shoulders in a

decidedly parental fashion. "Look. You've got this. If the only thing you say to him is 'I'm sorry,' then you did what you needed to do and you can sleep tonight, okay?"

"Okay. You're right." I inhaled loudly and blew it out, sending the hair that had fallen out of my braid flying. "Thank you."

"You're welcome. And if he doesn't see how genuine you are, then he's not worth your time."

"Right." I hoped that if Paolo *did* blow me off, I could have a little bit of Charlotte's confidence and just let it go.

"I'll see you back at the dorm. You got this." She squeezed my shoulders, winked, and walked away.

Chapter 8

After heading a few blocks south, I began walking west, toward the river, when my phone buzzed in my pocket. My nerves got the best of me, and I nearly dropped it facedown on the sidewalk before I saw Paolo's message.

Take the stairs up. I'm at the top.

He was early. And what stairs was he talking about? I made my way to the cross streets he'd sent in his original text and found, oddly, a giant metal staircase. Awesome— more stairs. A placard with a maple leaf and the words "The Highline" was affixed on a pillar at the base of the stairs, next to a map. I held the railing, white knuckling it all the way to the top. At the pinnacle, the stairs opened up to a wide wooden plaza, dotted with tourists strolling past a breathtaking view of the Hudson River.

I spotted Paolo immediately. His back was to me, but there was no mistaking his hair, poking out from beneath a gray beanie. The hat was completely unnecessary in summer, but it looked good on him. An equally unnecessary plaid flannel shirt was tied around his waist. Paolo's arms rested on a wooden railing. He was looking out at the last few rays of sun as it slid into the harbor. I noticed a scroll of black text peeking from beneath his sleeve. He hadn't had a tattoo . . . before. I would've remembered that.

For a moment, I just watched him. Not in a creepy way, but in that way where everything is still possible, that moment before words are spoken and decisions are made. Everything I needed to say was still perfect in my head. His answers were figments of my imagination.

In profile, Paolo was just as striking as he had been the first time I'd seen him on stage. He played his role of laid-back, fun-loving drummer well, but I knew from our private conversations that he was also thoughtful, intelligent, and driven. Those were the same things I liked most about myself. I watched him, without breaking the spell, so all of those things kept still for a moment longer.

Finally I blinked and sucked in a grounding breath. I approached him with as much confidence as I could muster.

"Hi," I said.

Paolo didn't turn his head, but kept on staring at the last golden-red bit of sun about to disappear. "Hey," he said in his gruff, gravelly voice. There was a reason he wasn't the lead singer, but I liked his voice just the same.

"How are you?" My question was automatic.

"Tired," he replied.

I imagined he was. If he was practicing for hours a day, just like I was, and then doing "a thing"—whatever that meant—after, and going on dates with the girl with the blue hair, then of course he'd be exhausted.

"I won't keep you," I said carefully. "Thank you for meeting me. I'm sure I'm the last person on the planet you want to see and I get it. I wouldn't want to see me either after . . . the last few months."

Paolo slowly fixed his golden gaze on me, making my stomach drop. I shifted from one foot to the other and inhaled, hoping to steady myself. I wasn't the type to get nervous at auditions or before shows, probably because of the way my mother raised me to believe you work hard and everything will come together. Even if you fall apart, you know you put in the effort and that counts for a lot. Except, I knew in my heart of hearts, that I hadn't put in my best effort with Paolo. Or any effort at all, really. I quit him. Without a word. And that's why I was in pieces.

"I'm listening," he said, turning back to the harbor.

I could see New Jersey across the water. Lights atop hotels and office buildings twinkled in the distance. I stepped forward and leaned my elbows on the wooden railing, just like he was, and we both looked out over the rippling water. Maybe this would be easier if we weren't looking at each other.

I inhaled, counted in my head to three, and began. "After I fell, I was in the worst place I'd ever been. Humiliated that I couldn't save myself. Horrified that my dancing days were probably over. I didn't want to talk about my injury, not even with Tatum. I was so touched that you came to the hospital, but I couldn't face you. Not then. I told myself I'd text you soon, let you know I hadn't disappeared. But I was angry and I literally had no outlet for all the rage I was feeling. I was ready to peel off my skin. So I didn't text because I didn't want to say anything I'd regret." I closed my eyes before saying the worst part. "And when I did finally write you back? I regretted it immediately. I didn't actually want you to leave me alone. I just didn't know how to be me with you anymore."

Paolo had turned his head slightly toward me. I guess that was progress. "I convinced myself I was never going to dance again, so I threw all that negative energy into college applications. I labored over every word, every sentence, until they were perfect."

Paolo cleared his throat. "Is there a point in there somewhere? I mean, I'm sorry you got hurt. I really am. And I'm not trying to be rude, but like I said. I'm exhausted."

I flushed, glad it was dark and he couldn't see. "Yes. There's a point. I promise. I just need to get this out. I didn't think I'd ever have the chance to say it, so just bear with me. Please."

He nodded, the hard lines of his jaw softening slightly. Maybe it was the *please*.

"I had it so stuck in my head that anything that wasn't essay-writing or application-perfecting would be a distraction. Including you. Tatum came up with all kinds of ideas for ways to get me out of the house and I turned her down every time."

"You were supposed to come to one of our shows," Paolo said flatly.

"Yeah," I replied sadly. "Long story short, I caused an avalanche, so to speak, and I've been trying to claw my way out ever since. I got into Georgetown, but I don't want to go. I'm so thankful for the opportunity, but it's not the right path. Being down for so long made me realize that I love dancing enough to want to make it my career. So, I'm here for the summer because it's my last chance to try to get a job as a professional dancer."

I paused, waiting for Paolo to respond. He didn't, so I went on. "When I got hurt, I saw myself as a destroyed china plate—shards and fractures all over the place. My whole life broken, I guess. I'm trying to put them back together. Dancing is a big piece, obviously, and I'm doing my best to glue that one in."

At this, Paolo nodded a bit, and I knew he at least understood that.

"I think . . ." I started and then stopped. I curled my fingers around the edge of the railing and dug my nails into the soft wood, willing myself to keep talking. "I think when I saw you in the park, even though you were obviously angry with me, and rightfully so, I realized that you're an important piece that needs to be repaired. I mean, I knew it before that—I've known it for months—but I wasn't in a good place to apologize. Now I am, and I'm sorry. I need you to know that I didn't mean to hurt you, but I know that I did. I was in pain and not myself. But I'm trying now."

I couldn't look at him when I finished my speech. All the ticking and whirring of my body stopped for a moment as I waited for his reaction. Paolo still didn't say anything, like he was purposely torturing me into rambling. My lungs filled back up and my brain switched back on, turning somersaults of panic. Had I said the wrong thing? Was it too much? Not enough?

Hastily, in case I hadn't been clear, I said, "And I hope you can forgive me. But, if you can't, I get it. Disappearing after two great dates is kind of unforgivable." And for good measure, I added, "*Really* great dates."

Finally, after I shifted to the other foot after realizing pins and needles were dancing up my calf, Paolo said, "Did you know this is where the *Titanic* was supposed to dock?" He pointed into the darkness. "Right there. If it had made it, that is."

"I didn't know that." It was, obviously, a total change of subject, and not even close to a metaphor for forgiveness. But I wasn't going to stop him from talking to me.

"And just a few blocks from here is the Jane Hotel, where the surviving crew members stayed after the *Carpathia* rescued them. It's still a hotel today, and the staff tell stories about how they hear wailing at night."

I wasn't sure why he was telling me this. "That's, um, interesting."

Paolo pushed off from the railing and jerked his head slightly, as if asking me to follow him. I did. He went north on the strange wooden walkway. It was half-park, half-boardwalk in the middle of the city. I wondered how long it went and how far we would go. I figured if he was talking, I'd keep following.

He stopped at the next clearing. "This used to be railroad tracks." Paolo pointed to our right and I could make out metal tracks between tufty grass and flowers. "The city elevated the trains because people kept getting killed on the tracks. They even hired these guys on horseback to warn them away, but it didn't really work. When they no longer needed trains transporting goods into the city, they eventually turned it into this park."

Okay, first the *Titanic*, and now death trains. What was happening? "It's nice," I said, fumbling for a response. "A good way to repurpose something they didn't think they needed anymore."

We kept walking and every once in a while, Paolo would offer a historical fact or story to go along with something we saw. For someone claiming to be tired, he didn't show any signs of stopping, which was fine with me. Eventually he paused at an overpass. We looked out onto the wide, lit up street, watching cabs drive along and people making their way home along the still-busy sidewalks.

As much as I was enjoying being there with him, because there was no way to deny that, the frenzy of my attraction to him and my need for him to shout "yes, I forgive you," was building. All at once, the anticipation of whatever he was going to say became too much. I looked at my watch and decided to take a risk.

I wrapped my arms around myself, maybe for protection, and said, "Not that I'm not enjoying the history lesson, because I am, but you said you were tired. I don't want you to think you can't leave on my account. You know, if you need to go back to . . ." I trailed off. Where was he staying? A dorm like me? An apartment?

"I want to keep talking to you, Tilly. I like talking to you. I always have." Well, that was something. "And I do want to talk about what you said earlier. Eventually. But like I said, I'm tired, and this is what I have to give right now. This is what I can say."

My cheeks burned again, this time all the way up to my

ears and down my neck. "I understand. Um. Whatever you need. It's fine."

If telling me the entire history of New York City, spanning hundreds of years, would ultimately put him in a place to forgive me, I'd listen to every word.

Paolo nodded and sat down on a low concrete wall. I sat next to him, not too close but close enough that it didn't look like I was avoiding being near him, and let my legs dangle.

I changed the subject, but kept it neutral, in an effort to keep him talking. "So you're here for the summer in drumming classes?"

"Yeah. You know that movie *Whiplash*?"

"I do." One night Tatum and I had streamed the movie about a young drummer studying under an abusive professor. Neither one of us could tear our eyes from the screen. It had been physically painful to watch. "Please tell me that's not what it's like for you here."

"Nah," he said with a low chuckle. "But it is intense. Hence the tired."

I chuckled too. "Same. I've never worked this hard in my whole life."

"It's like when you come into the city, the expectations automatically rise."

"And the stakes do too."

Paolo glanced over at me with what I hoped was a sympathetic smile. "I'm sorry you got hurt."

"Me too," I said, with a small sigh. "But I'm healed now."

"So this is really your last shot at a job?"

I assumed his interest was a good sign. "Yeah. I missed

the window to audition with everyone else, but this came up and here I am." I described the installation and Sage's vision for our performance. Paolo nodded, as if he approved.

"College will always be an option," he reasoned, with a shrug.

I hoped my mother would agree. "So what about you?" I ventured. "College? Not college?"

"College."

"Nice. Percussion?"

"Yeah, double degree actually. Percussion performance and history. Oberlin."

I laughed. "I probably should've guessed the history part. Your recall is impressive."

Paolo smirked and sat up a little straighter. "I'm a nerd, what can I say?"

We smiled at each other, our expressions laced with that mutual respect that comes with understanding exactly what it means to be in someone else's shoes. Even though our chosen crafts were completely different, we got each other.

"I'm happy for you," I said, looking away. "And I'm happy you met me here. I'd been wanting to say that for a long time, but I didn't know how."

Paolo pressed his mouth into a line and then spoke again. "I forgive you, Tilly. Thank you for the apology and the explanation."

I looked up at him and offered a closed-mouth smile. Inside, though, I was bursting. If no one else was around, I might have hopped off the wall and started turning cartwheels.

"But," he continued. Oh. There was a *but*. My inner

cartwheels screeched to a halt. "I guess I need to share some context too. I was pretty confused when you blew me off. I tried to think of what I could've done wrong and kept coming up with nothing."

"You didn't do anything wrong," I whispered.

"I know that now. But it's kind of a blow to the ego when the girl you really like tells you to get out of her life and just drops off the face of the earth."

"I'm so sorry," I whispered, tears pricking in the corners of my eyes.

"I know you are. I'm sorry it went down like that too. At any rate, it's going to take me a minute to get there, Tilly." Despite his now somewhat-sharper tone, I wanted him to say my name again. And again. "How do I know you won't bail on me or run away again?"

"I won't," I said quickly. "I promise."

"My head knows that, but here," Paolo said, patting his chest where his heart was. "I'm willing. But it's going to take a minute."

"I get it," I replied, echoing his sentiment from earlier. "I'm willing too." I squinted at him in the fluorescent streetlight. "Friends?"

I didn't think it was the right time to come out and say I wanted to pick up exactly where I'd dropped us months ago, when we were decidedly more than friends. Not when he clearly felt like he couldn't trust me. Plus, there was that tiny detail of the girl drummer.

"Friends," he said, with his trademark lopsided grin. My insides went liquid again. Paolo stretched his arms above his head and yawned. The black script on his arm became visible once more. I'd ask him about it next time, if there was a next time.

He hopped down off the ledge. "I really should get going, but I'm glad you texted me."

"Me too."

Paolo hesitated. "I'm gonna catch a cab. Are you going downtown too?"

I wished. "Uptown. I think I'm going to walk for a bit and catch the subway when I get tired."

Paolo looked skeptical. "Are you sure? By yourself?"

It was cute that he was worried about me. "Yeah. I'm almost a real New Yorker now."

Paolo slid the gray hat back on his head and lifted his chin in my direction. "Well, good night then."

I wanted to close the distance between us, only about two feet, and walk into his arms for a hug. But I wasn't sure he would allow that. I lifted a hand instead. "Good night. Thanks again."

"You're welcome." Paolo flashed his sideways grin at me and ducked away into the darkness.

I continued my walk on the Highline alone, past sculptures and murals. It seemed such a contrary place—a green respite hovering above a still-busy city. But I was discovering there were oases everywhere here, if you looked hard enough. At 30th Street, I took the stairs down to street level, turned left onto 7th Avenue, and walked toward the neon lights ahead.

Chapter 9

*I*n the morning, Charlotte pounced, quite literally, on me.

"Wake up, wake up. How was it? I am dying to know if cute drummer boy forgave you. I was dying last night, but I was good and didn't text you just in case you would be compelled to look at your phone during that super important conversation."

I opened one eye. Charlotte knelt in the six inches of space between my leg and the edge of the bed, an arm on either side of my head as she hovered over me.

"Good morning?" I said groggily.

"Good morning. It's time to get up. It's also time for you to tell Charlotte how it went."

"You're referring to yourself in the third person now?"

"Will you quit stalling?"

"Yes, ma'am. As soon as you get out of my personal bubble." I gave her a light shove off the bed.

Charlotte pouted, but retreated to her own bed, sitting cross-legged and revealing her socks, which were printed with tacos. "So?"

"So, it was good."

"Just good?"

"I wasn't expecting perfect. But yes, he forgave me."

"Was there kissing?"

I made a face. "No. I'm still pretty sure he has a girl-friend." Even though he hadn't mentioned the girl with the aqua-blue hair, I wasn't going to assume she was just a friend and be humiliatingly wrong. "But we're friends again. Or almost friends. Quasi-friends."

Charlotte stuck her tongue out at me. "Well, that's boring."

"Would you prefer me to be crying my eyes out because he wouldn't listen?"

"Of course not. I was kind of hoping for a grand gesture. Something out of a movie. All good romance movies set in New York have them. Too bad he didn't ask you to meet him on top of the Empire State Building."

"One, this isn't a movie. And two, I'm kind of hoping this isn't the end. A second beginning maybe?"

Charlotte grinned. "Okay. Yes. A second beginning. Don't screw it up this time."

As if I hadn't had enough excitement in the past twelve hours, Sage decided to ramp things up at rehearsal.

"Team, now sounds like as good a time as any to let you know I'm ready to start assigning roles for the perfor-mance," she said. "I think I've got a good handle on each of your strengths and I've started to visualize where I need each of you on stage." Sage grinned at us as we sat in a semi-circle around her after warm-up.

Sabrina sat up a little straighter and jutted her chin out, batting her eyelashes. She looked just like a preening parrot.

"Before you all start dissecting the number of minutes you're on stage and comparing your minutes to someone else's, know that I've very deliberately given you all equal amounts of stage time." Sage's tone was amused, but it was also a warning.

I flicked my gaze to see Sabrina's reaction. She was frowning, while Ella next to her at least had the grace to blush because she'd been caught thinking about her time in the spotlight.

"I know I'm a broken record, but we're a unit," Sage went on. "No one will be the star. This team is going to blow everyone away with your ability to work together, not apart."

The passion in Sage's voice, coupled with the fact that she was literally pounding this idea of teamwork into our heads, made me wonder what other details from her past influenced her. Was there possibly more to her own story than just an unfortunate injury? I could blame my accident only on myself, but her partner dropped her. What if it hadn't been an accident? The idea of someone possibly going to such horrible lengths to get ahead made me shudder.

As we stood up to begin work, I saw Sabrina leaning over to Ella, looking like a hurricane about to make land-fall. Ella shook her head, her face just as stormy.

Abruptly, Sabrina raised her hand, but didn't bother waiting for Sage to acknowledge her. "Um, Sage? I get the whole togetherness thing you're going for here and obviously, that's awesome and everything, but how will we get noticed by the scouts?"

I hated to admit it, but that was a valid question. The dancers who were featured most prominently got the most attention. If none of us was the star, how would we stand out?

Sage had just taken a sip from her coffee mug and looked as if she was trying not to spit it out all over the floor. She kept her voice quiet and even. "A strong dancer will be noticed, regardless of how much time she's on stage. Scouts will be impressed by our unity. Provided we achieve it."

There was a challenge in those words, not just to Sabrina but to all of us. To rise above our competitiveness and pettiness to achieve something bigger than ourselves.

And I never walked away from a challenge.

The opening song for the show was both modern and vintage at the same time, sassy and serious, and as Sage said, the perfect way to set the tone of the show. I would be in the piece, mostly in the background, but got a small solo combination near the end. Sage blocked most of the choreography and began to break it down into small segments to practice. As expected, she worked us to the point of perfection. And just like each day before, instead of being ready to flop down on the bed, as my body wanted, my mind was racing a million miles an hour with excitement. I danced better than ever, in part from Sage's motivation but mostly because I'd let go of the Paolo guilt I'd been dragging around for months. I felt stronger and lighter than I had in ages.

At the end of rehearsal, Sage said, "Great job, friends."

EVERYWHERE YOU WANT TO BE

She clapped her hands slowly and complimented each of us in turn. When she got to me, she said, "You nailed it today, Tilly. I was impressed. Whatever you were channeling, keep doing it."

I blushed furiously, the heat spreading up my neck and the back of my head. "Thank you, Sage."

I'd been thinking about Paolo and how, even if we didn't actually end up being true friends again, I'd said what I needed to say and he'd heard me. I'd been thinking about how much I was enjoying the hard work and the delicious ache of my muscles that woke me up each morning, reminding me of what I'd accomplished the day before. I'd been remembering my stroll back to the Marian last night, through Times Square in all its glory like a midway at the state fair. The frenetic energy was both thrilling and nauseating. I loved it. As I danced, I realized I was finally ready to pick up my life from where I'd left it last December.

"Oh, and team?" Sage said with a grin. "Remember what I said on the first day about looking for inspiration? Now is the time for research if you haven't started thinking about this. Find someone—real or fictional—who faced a battle. They didn't have to win. But they had to fight."

That sounded like homework, and the nerd in me rejoiced.

"I think we're going to take a field trip today," I whispered to Charlotte, who nodded and started for her bag in the corner of the room.

Sabrina, antenna always up for any compliments that weren't for her, sneered at me when Sage stepped out of the room. "Keep doing it," she mocked, in a frosty whisper. I stared at her, my brown eyes locking with her green ones. I should've been paying closer attention to the rest of her, though, because two seconds later, instead of walking over to my bag, her foot shot out and I hit the ground with a thud.

"Tilly!" Charlotte cried out. She rushed over, Arden and Ella right behind her, hovering over me. "Are you okay?"

I nodded and rubbed my tailbone. "Yeah, I think I'm fine."

"What happened?" Arden asked, her voice filled with concern.

"Do you need an ice pack or something?" Ella blinked her doll eyes, waiting for my answer.

I looked over at Sabrina, now sitting down cross-legged, her face completely calm as she packed her socks away into her bag. No one else had seen her trip me, but I wasn't about to play into whatever trap she thought she was setting. I could rise above her pettiness and mind games. "I stumbled over my feet. No big deal."

"Is your ankle hurt?" Charlotte knelt down next to me.

I stretched out my leg and rolled my ankle, just to be sure. "No damage done. Thankfully," I said loudly, for Sabrina's benefit.

"Glad you're all right," Ella said, and Arden nodded. I smiled at them, pleased and a little surprised by their concern. So far, the two younger girls had mostly stuck together, and I hadn't had a chance to get a good read on them. They both waved before heading out the door, which cemented my opinion that if nothing else, they definitely weren't clones of Sabrina. I let out a sigh of relief.

Charlotte stood up, extended a hand, and pulled me up from the floor. "Sure you're okay?"

I nodded. She picked up my bag for me and we quickly packed up and left. I didn't want to share space with Sabrina any longer than I had to.

Instead of doing more damage to our sore legs—and my sore tailbone—by crisscrossing the city, I dragged Charlotte to one of New York's most famous bookstores, The Strand, to find some reading material based on Sage's assignment. When people described The Strand as eighteen miles of books, they weren't kidding. If our task was to find inspiration, we'd certainly come to the right starting point.

I sifted through the aisles of bookshelves twice my height for almost an hour, coming away with an anthology of classic fairy tales and a volume of translated poems by Chilean poet Gabriela Mistral. I recognized her name from my abuela's bookshelf; she told me Abuelo had carried several of Mistral's collections with him when they came to America. I figured if it was so important to them, there had to be something for me inside as well. I paid for my treasures and met Charlotte at the entrance.

"What did you get?"

She pulled three books from the canvas bag with The Strand's logo printed on it. "A variety of butt-kickers." She held them up so I could read the titles.

"*Sheila Rae's Peppermint Stick*? A picture book? Really?"

"You can read it and then you'll know. It was my

favorite book as a kid because the little sister wins."
Charlotte grinned.

"Can't wait." I looked at the other books. "*When I was Puerto Rican* and *The Hours After: Letters of Love and Longing in War's Aftermath*," I read.

"One's about the struggles of being an immigrant and the other is about a Holocaust survivor. I think I've covered all kinds of fighters, yes?"

"For sure. You'll have to let me borrow those when you're done."

"Definitely."

We left the store, stopped at the farmers' market a block away at Union Square to buy a bag of hard pretzels and two fresh-pressed lemonades, and continued on until we found an empty bench at the edge of the park. It was the perfect spot to people-watch and skim our books.

Charlotte and I planted ourselves and I dug into the fairy tales first. I turned my nose up at *Sleeping Beauty*— the prince was the one who slayed her dragon, but I did appreciate her fairy guardians. I considered *Cinderella* and how, though she didn't exactly battle her stepmother, she took advantage of an opportunity that presented itself, via the fairy godmother, and ran with it. I paged through *The Ugly Duckling, Beauty and the Beast,* and *Rapunzel* and filed away lines and lessons to draw from later. At *Little Red Riding Hood*, I lingered longer.

A mother who wanted her daughter to stay on the path. A girl who didn't and ended up a wolf's dinner. Even though the story turned out okay in the end, I felt a stab of guilt for continuing to keep my future plans from Mama.

"I think I identify with Little Red Riding Hood a little too much," I mused.

Charlotte looked up from her novel. "Does your grandmother have really big eyes?"

I laughed. "No, not especially big."

"The better to see you with, my dear," Charlotte said in a high, screechy voice, and made a clawing motion with her fingers. "But hey, speaking of big bad wolves, isn't that Sabrina?"

She pointed across the street to where a familiar looking redhead was ducking out of a storefront.

"Maybe?" I stood up, shielding my eyes from the sun, and squinted. The figure was walking in our direction, which was also the way to the subway entrance. "Yes, I think so. She's got her dance bag with her. And she looks a hot mess. What was she doing?"

Charlotte and I looked at each other, clearly having the same thought. "Let's check it out," Charlotte said with a troublemaking grin.

We gathered our belongings and quickly walked toward Sabrina, narrowly missing her as she ducked into the subway. Peeking over our shoulders to make sure she wasn't following, we headed toward the building Sabrina had just left. We cupped our faces and peered through the glass door.

"This looks just like the entrance to our rehearsal room," Charlotte said, voicing the same thing that had just flashed through my mind. Definitely some kind of performance space.

"What is she doing? Dancing? more? Why would she do that?"

Every dance teacher I'd ever had drilled into our heads to rest our bodies and not to push too hard for fear of shin splints, broken toes, or worse. Had Sabrina's teachers not done the same?

Charlotte put a hand on her hip and shrugged. "Maybe she hired a private dance teacher to make her stand out more since Sage isn't buying her 'but I need to be in the front' nonsense. It's probably nothing. And besides, you know as well as I do that if Sabrina is putting in extra time, she's going to be exhausted."

"And that's just counterproductive," I said, finishing her thought.

"Exactly. She's shooting herself in the foot."

Last year, when the seniors in the dance program at my high school were getting ready to audition, our teachers showed several examples of contracts for apprentice, trainee, and corps positions. All of them had clauses about the number of hours a day dancers could be active. The clauses included required rest. Dancing was serious business when it came to the toll it took on the body.

"I guess it's none of our business, right? She's a big girl. She can make her own decisions."

"You said it." Charlotte slurped the dregs of her lemonade from her plastic cup. "And now that we put that mystery to bed, what next?"

"Are you sufficiently inspired for today?"

"I am. And now I'm hungry."

"You just ate a bunch of pretzels."

"And we also burned a million calories today."

"Point."

We walked back uptown past the amazing triangular Flatiron building and ran into an orange and black tiger-striped food truck selling Korean tacos. We ate as we walked back to the Marian, but even though Charlotte claimed we'd solved the Sabrina mystery, something felt off to me. Surely Sabrina would know extra practice could cause injuries or strains that would affect her performance. Sage pushed us to the limit already, and heaping on additional training was definitely testing fate.

If Sabrina and I had gotten off to a better start, I might have thought about stopping by her room, which was only down the hall from ours, and asking her if she needed to talk. But, Sabrina had so obviously made me her number one enemy, I doubted she'd want to unload whatever she was dealing with on the girl she liked sneering at in class.

"Maybe she has a less meticulous twin," I murmured to myself once we were back in our room.

"Who has a twin?" Charlotte called from her bed, nose in one of her new books, highlighter at the ready.

"No one," I sighed. I stood and unhooked my robe from the inside of the wardrobe. "I'm going to shower."

"Good, you stink," Charlotte said, without looking up.

I giggled, grateful for the thousandth time since we'd arrived that the roommate fairies had paired me with her and not someone else. I gathered up my shampoo and soap, ready for the hot water to melt away some of the tension in my shoulders, when my phone rang. Knowing my hands were full, Charlotte answered.

"Castillo Funeral Home, you kill 'em, we chill 'em."

I nearly dropped my soap. "You can't answer my phone like that! What if that's my mother?" I hissed.

Charlotte winked at me behind her orange frames. "Mmmm-hmmm. Yes. Yes, she is working very hard. Sure, I'll put her on right now. Mmmm-hmmm. Can't wait to meet you as well."

I practically threw my bathroom gear across the room and grabbed the phone out of her hand. "Hello?"

"Your roommate is a riot. She is definitely invited to hang out when Seamus and I come up."

I exhaled loudly with relief. If my mother had been calling . . . well, at least I didn't have to think of a good reason as to why my roommate was masquerading as a mortician.

"Tatum. I'm so glad it's you."

"And not your mom? Cosigned. How's it going in the Big Apple?"

I stepped into the bathroom and closed the door behind me, taking a seat on the toilet, with the lid down, of course. "Really good, actually. Sage is a genius."

"Groovy. Can't wait to see the show." There was a pause. "And what about Paolo? Have you seen him again?" she asked, a note of hesitation in her voice.

At least I had something better to report than last time she and I talked. "Yes. I met up with him the other night and I apologized."

I gave my stepsister the abbreviated version of my meeting with Paolo, but couldn't keep the smile out of my voice. She knew it too and even called us star-crossed lovers until I pointed out that our families weren't feuding and I didn't think he and I were going to swallow poison.

"But there's hope. I think. For friendship again, at the very least."

"Or *more*. You totally want to kiss him, right?"

Even though no one could see me, I blushed redder than my sunglasses. "I don't think that's going to happen. But yes." I was only a good liar about some things, it seemed.

Tatum sounded awfully pleased about my change in circumstance. "Maybe you're being rewarded after having endured such a craptastic year."

I laughed. "That's pretty much the same thing Charlotte said."

"Glad to know there's someone with my good judgment looking out for you. I have to run, but I'll call later in the week and we can plan my big visit to the city, okay?"

I laughed. "Sounds good. I'll talk to you soon."

I hung up and headed for the shower. The steam filled the tiny bathroom and I inhaled deeply. Maybe Tatum and Charlotte were right. Maybe this exact moment in time was the exact place and the exact situation I was supposed to be in. Maybe I had proven I could make it through a stressful situation—an obstacle, as the college essay prompts called it—and now I was being rewarded. *Good job, Tilly*, I imagined the universe whispering.

I sighed and pulled back the shower curtain to step in. If this was my reward, though, then why did Paolo have his arm around another girl? Why was Sabrina trying to pick fights and sneaking off to extra practices that could compromise our group? And why had I still not gotten up the courage to come clean with my mother?

Chapter 10

I couldn't do anything about my feelings for Paolo, and I definitely wasn't ready to talk about the college situation with my mom. But I figured I could at least get the Sabrina thing off my mind, which was why I found myself on the same bench in the same park across from where I'd seen her yesterday, hoping she'd walk by again.

I brought my book of Gabriela Mistral's poetry to pass the time, and quickly found myself entranced. Mistral's words in my head were the literary equivalent of dancing. There was passion in her lines, whether she was writing about pine trees or grief. She had even written a poem about the different ways you can dance—with your feet, with your heart, on the wind. I smiled to myself and sent Abuela a text with a picture of the poem.

She wrote back immediately. **One of your abuelo's favorites. My heart is full.**

I texted her back a row of fat red hearts.

Thirty poems later, my favorite lines written in my notebook for safekeeping, I stretched my arms above my head, stiff from the hard bench. Realizing I'd lost track of time during my stakeout, I looked up to see Sabrina across the street. She was exiting the same door we'd seen her at yesterday, her hair mussed and her face even paler than usual. Sabrina's shoulders slumped as she hurried, almost staggering, toward the subway, her dance bag sliding off her shoulder into the crook of her elbow.

"What were you doing?" I murmured to myself. I grabbed my own bag, stuffed the book back in, and marched toward the rehearsal space.

I hesitated outside. Should I go in? It felt like I was crossing a line if I did. Was I betraying Sabrina's trust? There was nothing to betray. Sage's trust maybe? Was it team-friendly behavior if I snuck around after one of my teammates? I blinked at my reflection in the glass door. It wasn't very team-friendly behavior to tire yourself out when you've been explicitly told to take care of your body. Which was the bigger sin?

Before I could answer myself, the door swung open and a tall girl with curly blond hair spilling out of a bun on top of her head stepped out.

"Oh, excuse me. I'm so sorry, did the door hit you?" She smiled her apology.

"No, I'm fine, I shouldn't have been standing in front of it anyway." I stepped aside to let her, and my dignity, pass.

"No worries. Were you thinking about going in? You're a dancer, right?"

In? Dancer? "I was thinking about it. And yes."

"I thought so," she said with a nod. "We can recognize each other from a block away, right?"

"Uh-huh, right," I said, clumsily.

"Well, I can vouch that En Avant is the best. The class

schedule is behind the desk, just down the hall and to the left. Maybe I'll see you?" The blonde looped her bag over her head and across her chest.

"Maybe. Thank you." Charlotte and I had been right. Sabrina was doing double duty, which broke so many unwritten rules.

"No problem." The girl flashed a million-watt smile at me and headed down the block.

I peered through the door again. I didn't dare go in, lest someone somehow connect me to Sabrina and tell her I was creeping. But I committed the name En Avant, to memory, rolling my eyes as I did. It meant "in the front." Exactly the thing Sabrina hoped to be.

Charlotte was out treating herself to a massage when I got home, so I flopped down on my bed, almost hitting my head on the window, and reached for my laptop.

"En Avant," I murmured to myself as I typed the words into my search bar. After several French to English trans-lation links and a site for ballet terms, En Avant School of Dance popped up. "Bingo."

I scrolled past photographs of smiling dancers of all ages in frilly costumes and stage make-up. I clicked on the class schedule, not sure what I was looking for. Sabrina's photo-graph would have been evidence . . . of what? I sighed, but kept clicking. In the gallery section, my finger cramped from scrolling, but one picture made me stop. There, serenely surveying a class of tap dancers, was a woman who looked exactly like Sabrina, plus thirty years or so. Her red hair was graying at the temples, and she had smile lines around her eyes and mouth. But there was no mistaking the expression. Peaceful as it may have been, there was a familiar steel in her green eyes. She wanted those girls, in their shiny patent leather tap shoes, to be the best. Just like Sabrina.

I shuddered a little. Perhaps this was what seeing a ghost was like. "The ghost of Sabrina's future," I muttered. My eyes flicked to the caption under the photo. "Donna Wolfrik, senior teacher," I read aloud. "Like there was any question."

I immediately reached for my phone. Tatum picked up halfway through the first ring.

"Quick, your mom and I are about to leave for photography class."

"I have a problem."

"You have sixty seconds."

I sucked in a breath. "There's this girl in my dance troupe and she's kind of mean, especially to me, and I caught her twice coming out of a different studio looking like she had definitely been rehearsing overtime which is a big no-no because she's wearing herself out, and when I looked up the name of the studio I saw her mom teaches there and it all seems kind of fishy and I don't know what to do."

Tatum laughed. "Stream of consciousness much?"

"You said your time was limited."

"Have you talked to this mean girl about what you saw?"

I paused. "No. She's not exactly the easiest person to talk to."

"Well. That could present a problem. But let me remind you, dear sister, that sometimes people have secrets for reasons." Tatum hesitated pointedly. "Maybe her mother has something to do with it. Do you think that might be possible?"

She dragged out the word "mother" so there was no question she was actually talking about herself. And me. Last summer, Tatum managed to keep an entire business secret from my mother, and I'd kept my love for contemporary dance quiet. We both told the truth in the end, but we thought we were doing the right thing at the time.

"Point taken." I knew I'd have to give this some more thought, though. Engaging with Sabrina felt like approaching a cobra about to strike. "Thanks. Enjoy your class."

"No charge. Enjoy your talk."

Tatum hung up and I groaned out loud. I didn't want to talk to Sabrina. I wasn't sure that she was worth my time, actually. If she wanted to ruin her own career by exhausting her body, getting stress fractures or worse, she could be my guest. But—and unfortunately this was a big but—I needed her. If she wore herself out, her performance would suffer. The company owners and artistic directors would see just her sloppiness and dismiss all of us. Including me. It sounded so incredibly selfish in my head, but it was true. This was what I wanted. Could I take a chance that Sabrina's intentions were on the up and up?

I leaned across the bed toward my bag and pulled out my magenta notebook. I cracked the spine, opened to a fresh page and ran a hand over the smooth paper. I slid the matching pen from the holster on the side of the notebook and started a new list.

If I Talk to Sabrina	If I Don't Talk to Sabrina
It'll clear up why she's been going to En Avant	She might get even meaner
Perhaps I'll convince her to stop going	It's none of my business
It'll remind her of what's at stake for all the dancers	I won't be a tattletale
Getting a job becomes more secure if she cooperates	We could end up embarrassing Sage
Getting a job becomes less secure if she doesn't	I risk losing my job
She might get target me even more	She could get hurt

When I finished writing, I examined my list, nervously tapping the end of the pen on the paper. Even though there were more points on the "don't talk" side, the weight of the "talk" column was much heavier. Was I risking it more by saying something or keeping my mouth shut? I had no idea.

Like the perfect distraction she was, Charlotte sauntered into the room and collapsed on her bed.

"Do I look like rubber? Because I feel like rubber. That was amazing. Like, otherworldly. I wish I had the cash to get a massage every day after rehearsal."

I laughed. "That good, huh?"

Charlotte reached both hands overhead and stretched. "Yep. Maybe when I'm an internationally famous dancer, I'll be able to afford a massage every day. Or even a personal masseuse. That's definitely the way to go. And this performance is just the steppingstone. World domination, followed by relaxation, here I come."

She laughed at her own joke, stood up, and grabbed her towel. "And now I will further relax by letting the hot water turn my bones from rubber to Jell-O." She went into the bathroom and shut the door.

Charlotte's little fantasy was a good reminder that I wasn't the only one who needed a job at the end of this summer. I looked at the list again. When I added a line about Charlotte's future employment, it was clear I couldn't keep silent. As soon as the water turned on, I stood up, opened the door to our room, and peeked down the hall.

Sabrina's single room was three doors down on the other side of the hall. If I leaned just far enough over, I was reasonably sure that I could see if her door was open or not. I planted my feet and leaned. Couldn't tell. I lifted up on one foot to lean further, as if en pointe, extended my arm for balance, and shifted my weight as far down the hall as I could. And still, I couldn't tell.

"Get it together," I told myself. "She's just another dancer. Same as you. You are perfectly capable of having a civil conversation with her. No big deal."

I shook my head at myself and strode down the hall like I did it every day. Two steps before the door, I inhaled slowly. Then I stepped up and knocked. "Sabrina?"

"Come in," a voice called. I highly doubted she realized it was me.

The door was unlocked. I stepped into the empty room, which was set up exactly like mine except everything was reversed. A lacy white bedspread covered my bed's mirror image, and the soft floral scent of what had to be Sabrina's shampoo wafted from the bathroom. She must have just showered.

"Um, hi," I started. "It's Tilly. I was hoping to talk for a few minutes. Is now a good time?"

Sabrina's head poked out of the open bathroom door, her red hair dark and dripping in long strands against her pale green bathrobe. She held a wide-toothed comb in her hand as if she were brandishing a knife. "Why do you need to talk to me?" Her eyes flashed a warning. Like if I came too close, she'd comb me to death.

"Well. I saw you," I said. "Today. And the other day."

"Obviously. We've seen each other every day since we started with Sage. This is not news." Sabrina raised one eyebrow as if to suggest I was being ridiculous.

"No." I locked eyes with her. "I. Saw. You."

Sabrina's pale face went bubblegum pink, and I knew she knew what, and where, I meant. "I have no idea what you're talking about." She grabbed a towel and distracted herself by drying the ends of her mane, turning away from me.

"Fine. I'll spell it out for you," I said, not meaning to be too snarky but it just came out that way. I'd never had patience for game-playing. "Two days in the last week, when I was reading near Union Square Green Market, I've watched you come out of the En Avant Dance School. You appeared to be leaving a rehearsal, given you were still dressed for dancing and you carried your dance bag. And when I did a search on the school, I saw that a woman who I'm pretty sure is your mother works there.

So I'm hoping I'm wrong about this, but it seems like you are either taking extra classes or you're in two shows. Whatever you're doing, it's not a good idea."

Sabrina scoffed and turned back to me, eyebrow still in the air. "And how would you know what's a good idea for me?"

I'd expected her to be defensive, so I was glad I'd written down my pro and con list to make sure I hit all the important points during our little chat. "Well, for one, I don't think Sage would like it."

"Sage isn't the boss of me."

Was she five years old? That was something Tatum would have said to me when we were younger. "I understand that," I said, doing my best to remain calm. "But if you've been rehearsing for hours, to the point of muscle failure, with Sage, just like we all have, there is no way doing it all over again every day is good for your body."

"My body is none of your business. Thanks for the concern and all, but it's not necessary. I can take care of myself." Sabrina put the comb down on the sink with a surprisingly loud crack and stood with her hands on her hips, as if to tower over me, even though we were virtually the same height.

I kept going. "All right, then point number two: if you exhaust yourself, all of us look bad. Your dancing becomes sloppy and the whole team gets thrown off."

"I'm not here to make friends," Sabrina spat.

I should have seen that one coming. "I didn't say anything about friendship. Trust me, I don't want to be friends any more than you do. Think about yourself. You want a job, too, don't you? I know it probably seems like the right thing to do—to practice and practice until you can't feel your limbs anymore—but you could get a stress fracture or severe dehydration or something even worse. Do you think any company worth its salt is going to want someone who doesn't take care of herself? I mean, have you ever seen a professional contract? You could lose your job over something like this. Your mom should know better too, if she's the one making you do this. You're going to get hurt." I hoped that turning the consequences of her actions back on herself would help. I didn't hold my breath though.

Sabrina narrowed her eyes at me, one hand still on her hip and the other raised in the air, one pink-polished finger pointed at my face. She stopped with about six inches between us. We were so close I could practically feel her breath on my face and the scent of her shampoo became stronger, making my stomach curdle. Everything in me wanted to pivot and get away from her, but I stood my ground.

Sabrina shocked me by curling her lips into a sickening smile. "Speaking of mothers, do you think *yours* might be interested in knowing that you're planning to take a job at the end of the summer, if you're offered one? I'm guessing Mommy Dearest has already purchased her Georgetown Mom sweatshirt and a Georgetown flag for the front of your house. She'd probably be disappointed to know that her dream for her perfect little girl is just a joke to you." She grinned wider, victorious, her teeth looking sharp and white.

My jaw dropped. "How do you know about that?" I whispered.

"You didn't invent internet snooping," Sabrina said with a sneer. "Your college plans were right on the front of your high school newspaper's website. One of the first links that comes up when you search Matilda Castillo. They're so proud of their seniors." She raised an eyebrow at me. "And you might think about paying attention to open doors when you're having 'private'"—she made air quotes—"conversations. You told Charlotte you lied to your mother and you actually can't go to college if you don't get a job because you deferred."

"What—how did—" I stammered. "You were listening to that?" I'd been *sure* no one was in the room.

"Seems like your mom would be pretty upset if she found out about that, huh?" Sabrina went on, almost gleeful. "Like she might even make you come home from New York."

Sabrina's words were a punch to the gut. She was probably right—if my mom knew what I was planning, I'd be back in Arlington before I danced another step.

"I don't appreciate being threatened," I said coldly, trying to keep my fear from showing. "Especially when I came here out of concern for you and your health."

Sabrina rolled her eyes. "That's rich. You came here out of concern for yourself. You think that if I screw up the routine, you won't get a job."

My cheeks colored. She wasn't wrong, but I'd convinced myself I was there for altruistic reasons first.

"Or, maybe," Sabrina wagged her finger close enough to my face that I could see a small chip in her polish. "Maybe you're intimidated. By me. Maybe you know I'm a stronger dancer and you want to sabotage my efforts."

"I never said you weren't good," I said through gritted teeth. I wasn't sure how I'd lost the upper hand in this conversation, but if the sweat forming on my palms and along my hairline was any indication, I was in well over my head.

"I know I am. But thanks so much for noticing." She winked at me and flashed a brilliant smile, as if we'd just had a moment of bonding. "If you want me to keep your little secret, keep your mouth shut. Now, you have a good night."

Sabrina stepped closer to me and I backed up. She didn't stop until I was out the door, which she promptly slammed in my face. The sound of the lock sliding into place shattered the silence of the hall.

Chapter 11

Charlotte was flipping through a celebrity gossip magazine when I walked back into the dorm room. Tatum had had a subscription to the same magazine for as long as I could remember and the sight of the familiar yellow font of the title tugged on my heart. I wished Tatum was here. Though I liked Charlotte a lot, we were still getting to know each other and really, there was no substitute for my stepsister.

Like she knew I needed it, Charlotte greeted me with a wide smile. "Where did you disappear to? I was just getting ready to pick out a show. I was thinking we totally have time to binge on something while we're still here. What about *Friends?* My parents used to watch it a million years ago, and it's set in New York. What do you think?"

I shook my head, maybe in an effort to mix up the conflicting thoughts racing around in there after the conversation with Sabrina. "Not right now, but maybe later, okay?" Charlotte nodded, and I was glad she didn't ask questions. I did remember to smile back, though, as I slid onto my own bed. The smooth fabric of the comforter was cool under my warm skin, and I reached under the bed for my laptop.

If Sabrina could get her blackmail from the internet, then so could I.

"I need more evidence," I whispered to myself. I glanced over at Charlotte, who had put on her neon green headphones and was covering her mouth to stifle a laugh. She caught me looking at her, pointed to the screen emphatically, and gave me a double thumbs-up.

I gave her one in return, turned back to my own laptop, and opened a browser. Last time I'd searched, the most interesting information about Sabrina had been on the En Avant website, so that's where I started. En Avant's list of classes and teachers didn't yield anything new, but then I noticed a link I hadn't seen before. I hovered over the word "blog" and clicked. A string of short posts about summer classes and birthday parties for tiny dancers told me nothing. They'd all been posted since we joined Sage's troupe, so I knew I'd have to go back further. I flicked to June, scrolling down the screen until I found exactly what I'd been looking for.

"Jackpot," I said quietly.

There, at the very bottom of a flurry of recital pictures of little girls in pink leather ballet shoes and a mess of tulle, was the photo of the studio's recent graduates. In bold letters, I read the words "Departing Seniors," above two rows of smiling students, all standing at attention. I enlarged the picture and found Sabrina immediately. She was on the far right, in the back row, the only one with red hair. The defined muscles in her shoulders were obvious even in the small photograph and she held her head high. But, unlike the others, Sabrina wasn't smiling.

In fact, she wasn't even looking at the camera. Her gaze was fixed on some point off to the side; her pale eyebrows furrowed ever so slightly. It wasn't that different from the expression she wore most of the time during rehearsal—a mix of anger and disappointment, somehow.

I scanned the text under the picture. It read:

> En Avant is so proud of our graduating seniors! All the years of hard work, dedication, blood, sweat, and tears have paid off. Though not everyone is choosing to pursue dance as a career, we know they will all set the world on fire. We have loved working with these young people so much and we can't wait to see them on a stage—whether they're performing or earning a degree. Congratulations, seniors!

It went on to list the senior's destinations; my school put out something very similar. Of the fifteen or so dancers, four were off to ballet companies with names I recognized as being in New York, several were planning to dance in California and Chicago, one was starting at a military academy, a handful had earned scholarships to dance programs at various colleges, and one was dancing for a cruise line. I could see why the school was proud of their students.

I looked over the names again and noticed Sabrina's was missing. I checked a third time to make sure I hadn't overlooked her, but there was nothing.

Sabrina Wolfrik was the only one of her graduating class from En Avant Dance Studio with no place to go.

This was a game changer. What if Sabrina had auditioned and been rejected? What if she'd applied to college and hadn't gotten any acceptance letters? What if Sabrina had put all her eggs in one basket and found them all smashed and dripping on her feet?

I sighed. It seemed par for the course that now I would feel bad for her . . . empathize with the girl who was basically my nemesis. It was hard to dislike someone you knew was having a bit of a moment.

It occurred to me that Sabrina's mother was somehow wrapped up in this mystery too. She knew Sabrina was working with Sage, but she still allowed her daughter to pull double-duty practices. I knew a thing or two about intense mothers—mine was in the top ten in Virginia, maybe even the country. But I also knew she loved and supported me unconditionally, and that she'd *never* let me risk my health and wellbeing. I wasn't sure I could say the same for Sabrina's mother.

I typed "Donna Wolfrik" into the search bar, and of course, En Avant's website came up first and then various articles. I scrolled through the first two pages of links and randomly clicked on an interview Mrs. Wolfrik had done for a dance magazine. It was a few years old, but she hadn't aged a bit. Her hair was cut in a bob and pushed back behind one ear in the photograph included with the article. The interviewer started at the beginning of her career and asked about her influences and turning points. As I read, a familiar name leapt off the page and practically pirouetted in front of my face.

> One of the most terrible times in my dancing career was when my dear friend, Sage Oliver, was injured. We were both dancing for the Elisabeth Ballet, a tiny

company that went under right after this tragedy because they'd lost their brightest star. I remember it like it was yesterday. You don't forget something like that, let me tell you. Her partner was learning the one-handed presage lift, which is very difficult and requires a lot of strength. Well, he didn't have it, obviously. One second Sage was rising into the air like a dove taking flight, and the next, she was lying broken on the stage.

I winced and looked away from the words. I could feel Sage's crash in my own ankle.

I screamed. We all did. And then we cried. For days, we cried. When Sage left, we were incredibly sad but we understood. Who would stick around after that? I feel like that was a turning point for me personally and made me realize my real gift was teaching. To make sure that young dancers have excellent technique as well as the self-awareness to know when something is going wrong. To know their bodies.

I frowned and shook my head. This woman talked a good game, but she was not practicing what she preached—at least not with her daughter. Had she convinced Sage to take Sabrina on this summer as some kind of favor?

"Poor Sabrina," I whispered. Not words I ever thought I'd say out loud, or think at all—but it was the truth. If Sabrina had no job, no college, no alternative plan, and her mother was willing to put aside her personal beliefs to change that, there was no other way to view her. A victim of her own circumstances.

I flicked my gaze to Charlotte, who was still

engrossed in her show, blissfully unaware of everything I'd just discovered. I squeezed my eyes shut and felt the pressure of trying to find a solution settle on my shoulders.

At least now I understood Sabrina's attitude toward me. It was easy to recognize an emotion I knew really, really well—desperation. What if, just like me, Sabrina saw this performance as her last shot? What if she felt the pressure from her mother, and herself, to be perfect enough that some prestigious company would offer her one of the very last available positions? I tried to swallow but it stuck in my throat, like sandpaper. I knew exactly why she hated me so much. I was her direct competition, and I didn't doubt Sabrina would do everything in her power to make sure I stayed out of her way. And I had just gone into her room and poked the bear. In retrospect, not my brightest idea, but I hadn't known then what I knew now.

I sighed again, this time so loudly that Charlotte looked at me and cocked her head to the side as if to ask "everything okay?" I flashed her a weak smile.

If Sabrina was desperate, how far would she go? One time, sophomore year, there was a senior who locked another senior in the bathroom right before a show. It turned out that girl had been spending hours and hours learning the other girl's part and was planning to dance both parts in the show, since they weren't on stage together at all. Luckily, someone noticed there was a dancer missing, checked the bathroom, and the whole ridiculous plan unraveled. I wondered if Sabrina was that desperate. What if she tried to lock me in a bathroom and

I missed my last chance? Or worse . . . told my mom the truth? I'd get a one-way train ticket back home, for sure.

I closed the laptop, my hands beginning to shake. I sat on them and stared straight ahead, suddenly seething. Who was Sabrina to try to take away my chance? I didn't know her endgame, but I knew for certain that even if all she was doing was spending extra time practicing, she was hurting herself and that would hurt all of us. I sucked in a sharp breath through my nose and blew it out slowly through my mouth. There was no easy solution. I could picture myself somehow getting hurt, no matter what I did or didn't do.

I had to be smart with Sabrina going forward. I had to be careful. So the question now was, *what was my next move?*

Chapter 12

*O*ver the next few days, I didn't get more than four or five hours of sleep a night, wondering if Sabrina would spill my secret to my mom and ruin everything before it began. Every time I closed my eyes, my heart raced like I'd just downed a venti coffee with an extra shot, while scenes from my potential near-future played on a loop in my mind like a horror movie. In addition to the locked bathroom, where I could almost feel the walls closing in on me, I imagined more broken limbs, cruel rumors whispered behind my back, and worst of all, my mother coming to New York to take me home.

It felt like an elephant had decided my chest looked like a good place to take a rest, my lungs folding inward on themselves, and my ribs screaming out and threatening to crack. My skin was a rubber suit, suffocating me, blocking all the oxygen from flowing. I felt like I was withering, staring at nothing, with sleep never coming, until it was morning.

After the fourth day of this, I packed my bag as usual. Socks, water bottle, protein bars, extra hairbands, ankle brace—just in case—and an extra set of clothing in the event of total body soakage. When Charlotte and I arrived at our space, I dropped the bag and went to the restroom. As I was washing my hands, I looked into the mirror and almost scared myself. The bags under my eyes were almost as dark as they'd been just after my accident. My normally bronzed skin was pale and sickly looking. *Get it together, Tilly. She's not worth it.* I splashed cold water on my face, squared my shoulders, and marched down the hall, determined that today would be a better day.

Everyone was warming up when I returned to the room. I unzipped my bag and felt around for my socks; I came up empty handed. Had they fallen out? I looked around the room to see if an extra pair was lying around, but there was nothing. My heart began to race. Had I forgotten them? I knew I was tired, but could I have hallucinated packing them just an hour ago? Intellectually, I knew I could dance without the socks. They were merely a personal preference. But I also knew making that tiny adjustment to bare feet could have an impact on my performance, especially in my current state.

"Does anyone have an extra pair of socks?" I called out.

Arden shook her head and made a sad face.

"Sorry, roomie, wish I did," Charlotte called back.

Ella didn't even look up.

Just as Sage opened the door and strolled in, Sabrina said loudly, "That's a real shame you forgot your socks, Tilly."

The moment Sabrina opened her mouth I realized I hadn't forgotten anything. There was no doubt in my mind that if I opened her bag, I'd find my "missing" socks.

As if she knew exactly what I was thinking, Charlotte

shot me a sympathetic look as we were called to the center of the room to get started. Sage's gaze on me felt cold. Was our leader judging me for not coming prepared? I hoped not. The floor felt almost sticky under my bare feet, but I willed myself to ignore it. It was harder to ignore the angry thoughts that invaded my brain space. Why was *I* the target? What had I done to offend Sabrina, other than breathe? I didn't get it at all. And, maybe the most puzzling of all, why was she so bitter that she felt the need to sabotage a fellow teammate?

An hour into rehearsal, Sage pulled me aside. We'd been working on a combination where all five of us were circling the stage, rallying each other to fight something invisible that was between us, keeping us apart. She'd asked us to crouch and leap, then roll. Crouch and leap, then roll. My thighs were burning with pain, but I kept going, hoping, perhaps foolishly, that adrenaline would save me.

"Tilly, come here, please," Sage said with a crook of her finger. "Team, take a break. Get a drink." The other girls eyed me curiously and dispersed, but I knew they'd be straining to listen to whatever Sage had to say to me.

I crossed the room to where Sage stood, waiting for me. "Hi," I said cautiously.

"Are you feeling okay today, Tilly?"

My cheeks warmed. "I'm okay."

Sage pursed her lips and her face took on the same concerned look my mother wore when I had a fever or stayed up too late studying. "You look tired. Are you getting enough sleep?" At least she didn't mention the socks.

I nodded at the floor and hoped she couldn't tell I

was lying. "I am. Everything's great," I said with a weak laugh. I looked up at Sage through my lashes. I couldn't tell if she was convinced or not.

She ran her fingers through her hair and it stood up an inch higher than usual. "Maybe you're just having an off day then. I know you're working hard. That natural spring in your step just isn't there today."

I realized it probably wasn't my bare feet tripping me up, but instead, *thinking* about having bare feet. That was probably exactly what Sabrina was hoping for. "I'll do better," I promised, hoping I could make it true.

The last thing in the world I wanted to do was disappoint Sage, and my fellow dancers, because then I wouldn't be any better than someone who was exhausting themselves with extra practice. I would be just like Sabrina. Who was currently watching me with a satisfied smirk on her face. *Poor baby*, she mouthed with exaggerated fake sympathy. I resisted the urge to stick my tongue out at her.

You've got to get her out of your head, I told myself. And I knew just how to do that.

On the walk home, I stopped at the market that was a few blocks from the dorm. I methodically went up and down the unfamiliar aisles looking for the ingredients to make my favorite crusty Italian bread. I put the flour, eggs, yeast, brown sugar, and a handful of other items into the blue plastic basket I'd grabbed at the door. I picked up a disposable metal tray, just in case the dorm kitchen didn't have a pan.

I lugged my treasures back home, my anxiety already beginning to be replaced, ever so slowly, with anticipation. Baking was luxurious and comforting at the same time—it was magical in a way. What other activity could relieve my stress, let me use the skills I'd picked up in chemistry class, allow me to be a perfectionist, *and* produce something amazingly delicious when I was finished? When I thought about it that way, I wondered why baking therapy wasn't a thing.

In the dorm kitchen, I located a bowl and a dishtowel I'd use for proofing, or letting the dough rise, and then I set to work. The second the silky flour sifted through my fingers, I felt like I could breathe again.

"Why didn't I do this earlier?" I scolded myself aloud.

When the dough was ready to proof, I covered the bowl and left it on the counter, lights off, hoping no one would disturb it. I washed my hands again and went back to my room. Charlotte left a note tacked to the door saying she was going to shop for her siblings, so I had the room to myself.

When I pushed open the door, I saw, with equal parts surprise and rage, my lost socks sitting on my bed, as if I'd just left them there that morning. *What if I did forget them?* No. Not possible. I sighed loudly and sat down, tossing the socks from one hand to the other like a juggler. Sabrina was really messing with me now.

The bread-making had cleared the cobwebs from my mind, and I was ready, I hoped, to make a move of my own. Confronting Sabrina wasn't an option—clearly I'd screwed that one up the first time—which meant my options were to stay quiet or talk to Sage.

Tell Sage	Don't Tell Sage
Sabrina could be removed from the show	Everything will proceed as normal
Without Sabrina we have to re-choreograph = more work for everyone	Keep group unity
	Don't make enemies
Sabrina might ruin her relationship with her mother	Sabrina gets hurt
	Sabrina sabotages me
I could prevent more sabotage	Sabrina sabotages the show
Sage thinks I'm a tattletale	

I was up a creek no matter what I did. My head hurt thinking about it. There literally was no way everyone got out of this unscathed.

Ugh. Pro and con lists definitely weren't helping. I went back to the kitchen and found my dough had doubled in size exactly as it should. I kneaded it again and let it rise once more.

"Why can't everything be like a recipe? You follow the directions perfectly and you end up with something good at the end," I said to myself as I slid the dough into the oven. Knowing my fate was in someone else's hands was maybe the scariest thing possible to me. My mother's "work hard" mantra had gotten me through for so long, but now, working hard didn't seem to be enough.

I clicked on the oven light to make sure the bread was positioned well inside, clicked it off again, and went back to my room. My notebook was lying open on my bed and I read over my list once more. I knew what the right answer was. I knew what the rule-follower part of me should do—talk to Sage. But the other, more self-centered part? She said to keep quiet and let Sabrina sink her own ship.

I picked up my phone to tell Tatum I was baking again—a warning sign and hopefully a conversation starter—when I found a text waiting on the lock screen.

I have a performance tomorrow night. Feel like coming?

Paolo. I gripped the phone, completely unsure of how to respond. Did I want to go see him perform? Of course I did. Did I really think he wanted me there? I wasn't sure. Maybe this was a test to see if I was serious about not bailing again.

But I didn't think Paolo was the kind of guy who would test me.

I'd love to come. Send me the details?

He texted back that the performance was on the NYU campus, sent the time, the address, and how to find the space in the building.

Looking forward to it, I wrote back.

The space in my chest that had opened up when the elephant vacated his spot, after I kneaded the stress away, began to flutter and ripple. Was this a date? No. It couldn't be. Could it? No. This was just a friend inviting another friend to listen to some music because they happened to be spending the summer in the same city.

I typed a new text to Tatum.

Paolo just invited me to see him perform tomorrow.

SUCCESS! He's totally still into you. Seamus and I were right.

You guys talk about us?

Of course we do. They're bandmates, we're sisters. How is this even a question?

You're so weird.

You love me.

I do.

What are you going to wear?

Did friends dress up for performances of other friends? I didn't want to seem like I was trying too hard. I went to the minuscule closet and flicked through the outfits I'd brought.

Probably a skirt and a shirt.

Does the skirt twirl?

Of course it does.

Then I approve.

Day made.

XOXOXO

I sent Tatum a wink emoji and put the phone down. I picked up Charlotte's celebrity magazine and flipped through the pages until the timer for my bread went off.

The hallway smelled like heaven, or what I imagined heaven would smell like. I took the perfectly round loaf from the oven with a pair of worn, yellow oven mitts and left it, with a knife, stack of paper plates, and a stick of butter, on the counter. After stealing a piece, I scribbled a note on the top paper plate that said "Please, eat and enjoy!" I knew that a warm loaf of homemade bread was hard to resist—Mama always told me exactly how fast my treats had been consumed when she took them to her office—and I wouldn't have been surprised if it disappeared within an hour or two.

Pleased with myself that one, I had banished the anxiety at least for the moment and two, that I'd made something with my hands that might make someone else happy, I left the kitchen and went back to my room to figure out dinner. For the first time that day, a little bit of the hope I'd felt when I first set foot in this building dared to return.

"What are going to wear on your date?" Charlotte asked with a gigantic grin on her face as we walked to the subway after rehearsal.

Of course she'd ask the same question Tatum did. "My swirly skirt and my red top. The red matches my sunglasses."

Charlotte nodded her approval. "And then you can wear them on top of your head, all casual-like, even after dark because obviously, you have better things to do than worry about having your fabulous sunglasses still on. I like it. It fits with the image you're going for with Paolo."

I'd just been thinking that red and red go together,

and that the sunglasses made me feel confident and I knew I could use every ounce of confidence I could get. "What image am I going for exactly?"

"Friend. Trustworthy. Loyal. Flawed, but able to apologize. Interesting. Perhaps also a good kisser, if you manage to convey all of the rest."

"That sounds like a lot of conveying. And perhaps a lot of pressure. Thanks for that." I hip-checked Charlotte to let her know I was kidding. She put a hand up to dismiss me, but giggled at the same time.

I showered and dressed, tucking the loose red tank into the wide waistband of my black skirt. I towel-dried my hair and let it fall in damp waves down my back. I knew when it dried completely the waves would tighten a bit. I checked myself out in the bathroom mirror and couldn't help but feel pretty. I tried not to wonder if Paolo would notice, but it was a losing battle. I wanted him to notice.

"You're perfect," Charlotte declared.

"I'm not perfect." I knew Charlotte meant it as a compliment, but I was starting to embrace my flaws.

"You're right." Charlotte reached into her purse and pulled out a tube of lipstick. She slashed my mouth with a red that was both dark and bright at the same time. "Now you are. That color is fantastic on you. You look effortless."

"I'm anything but effortless."

"Okay, fine, you're hopeless. Better?"

I giggled. "No, not better. I'm just me. Take it or leave it."

Charlotte winked. "Let's hope he takes it."

I hoped so too.

Chapter 13

I was comfortable enough with the New York transit system that my heart didn't even pick up its pace in the slightest when I descended into the station, swiped my card, and got on a train to a part of the city I hadn't been yet. Paolo's recital was going to be held in a theater, at the Steinhardt Department of Music and Performing Arts Professions, which was used for chamber orchestra performances, recitals, and other small shows. Or so Google told me.

I got off the train at the West 4th Street station, intending to walk along the edge of Washington Square Park on my way to the theater. The sun was setting behind the mammoth buildings surrounding me and the huge marble arch looming over the park. I walked slowly, watching the people sitting on benches and reading paperback books, nannies pushing expensive-looking strollers, cyclists and skaters, and shoppers with full bags. It was a different crowd than the one I walked through to get to my own rehearsals every day, but it was lively and energetic, just like the city surrounding us.

For a moment, I tried to imagine what it would be like to be a student here at NYU. I pretended my purse

was a large messenger bag full of textbooks and maybe a
laptop. Imaginary me was headed for a chemistry class,
to fulfill a science requirement perhaps, and I'd probably
meet with a lab partner to work on analyzing our data.
And maybe after, as I was passing the massive library with
its glass front, on the other side of the park, I'd study at a
long table, stack of books next to me, laptop open, maybe
even chatting with Tatum back home and venting about
challenging professors. In my mind, my dorm looked just
like the one I shared with Charlotte, and I walked back
there after class, through crunchy autumn leaves and crisp,
city-scented air.

It was easy to see it in my mind. And if I stretched
even a little more, I could transfer those ideas to a different setting—Georgetown University. My mom's dream
wasn't a bad one. In fact, it was a great one. But it wasn't
mine anymore.

I arrived at the hall with ten minutes to spare. I sat
down in the fifth row, on an aisle, just in case I needed to
make a quick exit. Just in case I looked up on stage and
saw Paolo scowling at me, realizing he'd made a huge
mistake by inviting me. Just in case, after the show, I
happened to see the girl with the turquoise hair with her
arms around Paolo.

I took a picture of the empty stage and texted it to
Tatum, then scrolled through the other photos I'd taken
in the last week. I hadn't forgotten my vow to add more
people to my collection, so there were a few of Charlotte
warming up before rehearsal, one of Sage instructing
Arden on the correct placement of her left leg, and a selfie

of me and Charlotte just hanging out in our room. I felt like, through the pictures, I was proving to myself that I was actually part of something. Back in high school, I'd stuck to the prescribed schedule and followed all the rules. And somehow I'd missed the rule that things are better when you don't go it alone.

A few minutes later, the house lights darkened and the stage lights turned on. This was one of my favorite moments as a dancer, when the stage is still empty and the orchestra gives the audience a pause of anticipation before the music begins and then we're off. In the beginning, there are no mistakes, only possibilities. It's only as we go that we misstep, but most of the time the audience never knows. This was probably true in other areas of life, I reasoned.

The musicians filed on stage. Paolo was fourth in the line, walking out as if he were strolling down the street, without a care in the world. His black T-shirt was snug in all the right places and his tattoo was visible on his bicep. Paolo's drumsticks were conveniently stuck in the back pocket of his dark jeans and even on stage, he had on his gray knit cap. The ends of his hair stuck out from the edges like little tufts of grass. He sat down behind a drum kit.

The other musicians, ranging in age from high school through early twenties, carried instruments and took their places, standing behind music stands. There were ten of them total. A tall, thin man with a goatee and thick glasses was the last to come out. He took his place at center stage and picked the microphone up out of its holster.

"Ladies and gents, thanks for giving your time tonight to support the Summer Musicians Symposium. This is

a pre-recital for our jazz track students, and as I'm sure
you're aware, musicians enjoy playing for an audience.
So even if all you hear is cacophony, clap loud, okay?"
He gave a little sheepish shrug as the musicians on stage
booed at him good-naturedly. "Away we go," the conductor said, more to the people on stage than anyone else.

Paolo, sticks at the ready, tapped out three counts
and the music flooded out from the instruments, loud
and clear. It was a jubilant, bouncy song, one I didn't
recognize. My toe began to tap along with Paolo's beat,
my legs wishing they could dance. Some people say they
feel music or they experience emotion, an actual physical
reaction, when they hear music. Me? I choreograph in
my head. I can feel my arms moving, sweeping across my
body, a leg lifting slightly behind and then in front. I can
feel the whole dance in the song.

Once when we were much younger and definitely
not friends, Tatum took dance lessons with me. Not *with*
me exactly, but our classes met at the same time, so my
mother drove us together. After a really fun class for me,
I left the studio with a big smile on my face and a sticker
on my hand, while Tatum looked utterly miserable. I hid
my smile from her and in the car on the way home, she
asked me why I liked dancing. "It's sweaty and itchy and
weird," she declared. I wanted to tell her even then that it
was beautiful and fun and I was good at it.

I'd never lost that feeling. Judging by the look on
Paolo's face, he would have understood everything I
couldn't say to Tatum. As the piece went on, all I could
do was watch his movements and the sheer, unbridled joy

on his face. I felt like we were closer than we'd ever been, even though we were an auditorium apart.

After the happy number, the jazz ensemble switched out a few musicians, including Paolo, who left in favor of the girl with the ocean-blue hair. Paolo tapped his drumsticks against hers as they passed each other on stage, a sort of drummer high five. My heart gave an unexpected twist. If anyone looked effortless tonight, it was him.

Under the bright stage lights, and sitting in the audience with literally nowhere else to look, I watched the girl. It was such a masochistic thing to do, but I couldn't look away. The first thing I watched was her hands, sticks in a gentle grip, never missing a beat. She was good. She didn't have the same magnetic flair that Paolo did, but she definitely knew was she was doing. Her hair, shiny and so very blue, was braided and hung over one shoulder. She was undeniably pretty. I sighed.

I shook my head and focused on the guy playing the clarinet instead. I shouldn't compare myself with her. This wasn't a competition. If she was with him, good for her, and I would be nothing more than a friend.

I closed my eyes and just let the sounds fill my head, replacing the catty thoughts and doubts. When I opened them again, I was impressed with the unity of the musicians on stage, which changed with each song. This was what Sage wanted us dancers to achieve. I'd have to remember what this music sounded like when I was dancing.

During the performance, I took a handful of videos. I wanted to make sure, no matter what happened next, I would have these memories and could recapture the feelings if I wanted to.

When the show was over, the musicians took a bow in a long line stretching from one end of the stage to the other. Paolo was standing next to the girl with the blue hair, and as they bowed, they held hands. To be fair, all the musicians were holding hands, but still. In that moment, as if I hadn't known it before, I wanted to be with him. I wanted a second chance. I felt so foolish for pushing him away last winter. I regretted it. If she was his girlfriend, I had no one to blame but myself.

As the audience began to disperse, I stood, wondering what to do next. Did I go up on stage, shake Paolo's hand, tell him that he had done a great job, and say good night? Did I hug him? Did I introduce myself to the girl drummer and wish her and Paolo a lifetime of happiness?

I watched Paolo shake the hand of the conductor and then get brought in for a warm hug. There was a mutual respect between them and I smiled. Paolo waved goodbye or called out his thanks to the other musicians and then, to my surprise, he made a beeline down the stage stairs right to me.

"Thanks for coming," he said in the gravelly voice I enjoyed so much, hands stuffed in his front pockets. No hug for me then, but I did get a small smile.

"Thanks for inviting me," I said to his feet, clad in black Converse. My heart pounded and I hated myself for it. Why was I getting all bent out of shape over a guy? He was just a guy. Just a guy I liked. A drum-playing, history nerd guy I liked.

"What did you think?" Paolo asked. He sounded nervous. Like my opinion mattered to him.

"Is she your girlfriend?" I blurted out, and slapped my hands over my mouth, horrified. I'd meant to tell him I liked the show.

I slowly lifted my eyes to meet his, afraid he'd be mad or embarrassed or beaming with love for the blue-haired drummer. I didn't expect him to be amused.

"You mean Zelda?" Paolo pointed to the stage, where the girl, Zelda apparently, was chatting up the conductor.

"Her name is Zelda?"

"No, it's actually Zoe but she thinks Zelda is a more memorable stage name."

"Oh, well, that's interest—"

"No," he said, stopping me midsentence.

"No?"

"No, Zelda's not my girlfriend. We're just friends. She's got someone back home actually, in San Francisco. But even if she didn't—just friends." Paolo smiled shyly.

I smiled back and then before I could think about what I was doing, I hugged him. I launched myself forward and wrapped him up in a big bear hug and squeezed. I inhaled against his shoulder and breathed in his clean, cotton scent. And then I held my breath. What if he hated it? What if this was all wrong? I let out the breath when, thankfully, his arms wrapped around me in return.

We stood there in the middle of the auditorium, in each other's arms, for what was becoming an awkward amount of time, no matter how great it was. Did I pull away first? Did he? There wasn't a pro and con list for this kind of thing.

Gently, Paolo softened his arms and we stepped away from each other at the same time.

"Sorry. I, um, just wanted to check," I said, tugging on a lock of hair.

"Don't be sorry," he said, his amber eyes intense on mine. "I'm the one who should be apologizing."

I frowned. "Why? You didn't do anything wrong."

"I'm sorry for how I reacted in Central Park. And for being standoffish last time. On the Highline. I was just reacting, that's all."

I shook my head. "Please, don't apologize for being genuine. You had every right to be mad. *I* was mad at me. So mad," I trailed off.

"Are you still mad at yourself?" Paolo gestured for me to follow him down the aisle.

We passed dozens of empty red seats and he led me out of the auditorium and backstage. "No, not anymore." I offered him a small smile. "It took me a while, but I think I've forgiven myself." Paolo nodded approvingly.

We stepped out into the dark, balmy night. I looked up at the inky black sky. "You know, the one thing I don't like about New York is that you can't see the stars. If I could see the stars, it would be perfect."

"Are you going back to the subway?" Paolo asked. I nodded. "I'll walk you."

"Thank you." Now that I knew Paolo and Zelda were just friends, which filled me with a lot of relief and little hope, this seemed more and more like a date.

We took off down the sidewalk. "So, there are actually a few places you can see the stars in the city."

"Yeah?"

"One is actually the Highline. Ironically."

"Ironically," I echoed.

"Next time," he said with a grin and my breath caught. *Next time* was like a promise, right? At this stage of a fragile non-relationship, it meant he wanted more. It meant he *wanted* to see me again. Flawed, tunnel-visioned, sometimes angry me.

I inhaled slowly and deeply. "Thank you."

"For what?"

"For giving me a second chance to show you I'm not a terrible human being."

"You're not terrible. You acted on instinct."

"Bad instinct."

"Self-preservation."

"Fine. But thank you for not writing me off."

"You're welcome."

And as if he wanted to seal a pact between us, Paolo took my hand.

In science class a long time ago, we built electrical circuits. I remember when the final piece was joined and the tiny light bulbs at the other end glowed red and green. The second Paolo's skin connected with mine, it was like a whole string of twinkle lights—like the ones on the stage the night we met—glowed within me.

"I want you to make me a deal," he said.

"Okay?"

"No more talk about what didn't happen between us this last year, okay?"

"Okay," I agreed. This was a pact I could definitely get

behind. "By the way, sorry I didn't say it earlier, but I really loved your show. I don't listen to a lot of jazz music, actually. It was nice. And you all were really in sync up there."

"Thanks. John, our professor, says we have to all be on the same wavelength. We have to reach out psychically to one another and make sure we're all feeling the same thing at the same time in order to perform as one. Music is all about emotion, right? We cry at sad movies because of the emotion on screen, we laugh at comedians' jokes. This is kind of the same, if you really think about it."

I loved how earnest he was. How he truly believed in what his group could do together.

"Oh, I totally get it. And you can tell it's working from the way you play. My choreographer, Sage Oliver, says something similar. She's spent the whole summer so far basically hitting us over the head with team and unity and working for the good of the group."

"And how is that going?"

I shrugged. "Um, it's going. I try. My roommate, Charlotte, who is a fantastic dancer and really fun, tries. But not everyone is into the whole teamwork thing."

"What does that mean?"

I sucked in a breath. Here we go. "There's this other girl, Sabrina—she's kind of a piece of work." I spilled the whole story. The snarky comments, tripping me in class, finding out about Sabrina and En Avant, my completely unproductive conversation with her in her dorm room. "Sabrina threatened to tell my mom I'm lying about going to college, which would be bad for me at this point, obviously. But ultimately, I'm afraid she'll take away my chance for a job."

Paolo clung to my hand even tighter as I spoke. "Man. What are you doing to do?"

"Still not sure. I've made a pro and con list for telling our choreographer and I can't come up with a solution that doesn't come with a boatload of consequences."

Paolo looked at me with a smirk. "You made a pro and con list?"

I hip-checked him. "They help me make decisions. Organize my thoughts."

"Did you make a pro and con list about me?"

"No, but I might have to now."

He grinned. "Ouch." Then his voice went serious again. "I'm sorry you're dealing with that. Seriously. It sucks big time. But you're a good person, Tilly. You'll figure it out."

I squeezed his hand. "Thanks."

At the mouth of the subway station, we paused. It was like that moment in movies and TV shows when the couple, just finishing their date, had a choice to make. To kiss or not to kiss. I definitely wanted to kiss Paolo. I had for months and months. But I didn't want our first kiss, if I was so lucky to get one, to be colored by dance drama. So, I made the move.

I faced Paolo, smiled at him, and gave him a hug. His bare arms were warm as they encircled me, and goosebumps tickled up and down my skin. We stood there for a moment, the city still busy around us, people passing by, laughing and chatting, a street performer playing a saxophone in the distance. And we were still.

It felt like the first moment of real peace since I got to

New York. I loved the pace and the energy of the city, I loved the hustle and the movement of being a dancer and using my body to make art, and on some level, I enjoyed the intellectual challenge of solving the problem of Sabrina. But sometimes it was nice to be still and quiet. It was even nicer to be still and quiet with someone else.

"I'm glad I came tonight," I said into his shoulder.

"I'm glad you did too," he said into mine.

I unwound my arms from around him and stepped back. "Have you talked to Seamus lately?"

Paolo cocked his head slightly to the side. "We text every few days. Why?"

"He and Tatum are coming up this weekend. Did he tell you? We're supposed to go sightseeing. Do you want to join us?"

"That's this weekend? Man. It's easy to forget what day it is around here, you know?"

"I know," I agreed. Did that mean he was busy?

"Shay mentioned something about visiting a while back, but I forgot the date. Thanks for the reminder, by the way, because he's supposed to stay with me." Paolo grinned sheepishly at me. "But yeah, I'm in. I haven't had much time to hang out. Most of the time, when I'm not rehearsing, I'm helping at my aunt and uncle's store."

I bit my lip, trying to be cool and calm. "That's great. I'll text you the details when we figure out a plan. What kind of a store does your family have?"

"They own a flower shop in Little Italy. My great-grandparents opened it when they came to the U.S."

The thought of Paolo surrounded by flowers was almost

too much. "That's really cool," I said. "I'm sure it's nice to have relatives close by when you're far from home."

"For sure. We should swing by on our touristing. Say hello."

"Sounds perfect." I smiled broadly at him. If he wanted me to meet his family, I must be doing something right. "I should probably get going. Busy day tomorrow. I'm sure it is for you too."

"Back to the grind," he said, matching my smile. He hugged me again briefly. "I'll see you soon."

"See you soon."

I started for the stairs and then turned back, remembering something. As I did, I caught the intensity of his gaze. It was completely magnetic and I felt it in my knees. "One more question." Paolo raised an eyebrow, amused. "What does your tattoo say?"

He grinned and shook his head, as if it was the most predictable question on earth. "Tamburo. It's drum in Italian." He held his arm out for me to see up close.

I laughed. "Of course."

He winked. Knees still wobbly, I waved and quickly ducked down the stairs into the subway, not looking back. I thought if I did, I might run back up and hug him again.

When I made it back to the Marian, I sent a text, smiling as I typed.

Made it back. Thanks again. I'm glad tonight happened.

Two seconds later, he replied.

I'm glad too.

Chapter 14

Unfortunately, even Paolo couldn't keep away the Sabrina dreams that night. After waking up from a nightmare that she'd gone for my knee, Tonya Harding style, I was back in the kitchen surrounded by the items needed for banana bread and trying to keep my anxiety at bay. There was something about whipping the ingredients into shape with a wooden spoon that was almost as satisfying and happy-making as kneading dough.

When I'd left the Italian bread out on the counter, it hadn't lasted long. I knew our floor had more than dancers on it—there were some summer interns who wore company polos when we passed them on the stairs in the mornings, and some guys who were probably musicians or actors judging by the hours they kept. I didn't know who had chowed down on my gift, but I assumed they'd enjoyed it based on how fast it disappeared.

I left the banana bread out as well, with another *Alice in Wonderland*-style "eat me" note. When I was finishing wrapping my hair up in a bun on top of my head before leaving for rehearsal, Charlotte, who I assumed had gone out to get a coffee, came sauntering back in the room with her mouth full like a chipmunk.

"Good breakfast?" I asked, as she swallowed.

"Yes, the carb fairy left something delicious for us. Banana bread. It just appeared in the kitchen, like magic. This is the second time, actually," she said, her mouth still stuffed. "There's a little bit left, but you should probably run if you want some. Arden came in after me and she was definitely headed for the knives."

I laughed. "So do you think I should get a pair of wings to wear when I bake then? Maybe a crown of fresh flowers?"

Charlotte's eyes doubled in size and her mouth dropped open. I was glad she'd finished her bite. "You're the carb fairy?"

"If you mean the girl who stress bakes, then yes. I was thinking about sourdough or honey oatmeal next. Do you have a preference?"

Charlotte smacked herself on the forehead. "You told us you bake on the first day of rehearsal. I should've put two and two together. And did you say stress bake? Are you okay? How are you stressed after you had such a great night?"

When I'd gotten home last night, I'd dished to Charlotte, no doubt with actual stars in my eyes, about how well things had gone with Paolo. Remembering how freeing it had felt to tell him about Sabrina, I decided to go all in and tell Charlotte too. "So you know how Sabrina is kind of mean?"

"Kind of? She's a lot of other four letter words, my friend. Mean is tame."

"I'm trying to be diplomatic."

"Fine. Continue."

I told her everything, starting with the day I'd gone to Union Square by myself and seen Sabrina a second time and leading up through my online discoveries. And then I told her about Sabrina's blackmail, how she tripped me the day I fell after rehearsal, and what I suspected about my socks.

"Shut the front door. This is not what I signed up for this summer," Charlotte said, her hands balled in fists at her sides, the effects of the magical banana bread having clearly worn off. "Who does she think she is?" Her face was pink with anger.

"Well, I don't know for sure that she's actually going to do anything . . . else." I felt that lack of evidence was important to point out and somewhere deep inside, I wanted to believe that Sabrina wouldn't really hurt us. "But it would be hard to say I don't think it's a possibility."

"So, let me just make sure I have it straight." Charlotte held up a finger. "Sabrina has been observed at a dance studio twice after regular rehearsal." She held up another finger. "Sabrina was the only one from said studio's seniors to not get a job. Sabrina's mother is her teacher and Sabrina's mother and Sage used to be in the same company." Four fingers were in the air. Then she lifted a fifth. "And, Sabrina's been a major jerk to you, specifically, which I will draw my own conclusion about and say that she's jealous of Sage's attention."

"I wouldn't call that a fact, exactly," I said, and this time my face was the one that turned pink.

"Well, I would. It's so obvious. Just watch today. You'll see."

I smirked. "I try to avoid watching Sabrina, but I'll pay closer attention."

Sage had taught us roughly three quarters of the show and we ran through the whole thing, as far as we'd gotten, a few times, so she could determine if it all flowed together the way she envisioned.

As Sage's favorite rock, dance, and hip hop songs filled the room, I took Charlotte's advice and started observing more closely. Not just Sabrina, but the other girls as well. Ella's bright blonde hair was a beacon in the center of the floor. She was tiny and quick, with sharp, angular movements. Sage always complimented her on the flexing of her toes. Arden was tall and slight, yet surprisingly muscular. She was particularly good at leaping and jumping; she exuded power and strength. Unsurprisingly, Charlotte was larger than life on stage. She was the visual representation of bold in everything she did. I was a little jealous of how she commanded the stage—there was no way an artistic director wouldn't notice her during our performance.

And, if I squinted my eyes, I could pretend the graceful girl to my left wasn't Sabrina. She was solid. I wasn't petty enough to convince myself she wasn't. The thing she lacked, I realized, was confidence. The way she carried herself and second guessed the motions she was making, as if she didn't trust her body to do as she willed, made me sad. I wondered how much of that was natural and how much of it was the result of not getting a job last spring. How much of it was pressure from her mother? How much was pressure she put on herself? I knew it was good to have a goal. I also knew, from personal experience, how becoming obsessed with the goal can make you miss out on some really great experiences.

The other thing I noticed was that Sabrina looked tired, which wasn't a surprise. It was as if she could barely lift her arms above her head. She nailed the looks of angst and longing Sage wanted, but everything else was fuzzy around the edges.

As we ran through a section that involved all five of us, Sabrina wasn't the only who started fading. My muscles burned and I knew I was nearing the point of failure, but I pressed on.

"Stop, everyone," Sage shouted, interrupting my concentration. We froze in place. "Tilly, step forward please."

A lump formed in the back of my throat as I advanced toward Sage. I didn't dare steal a glance at the other girls, but kept my eyes on our director as she sifted her fingers through her hair, lifting it higher. There was a look of concern and maybe a little bit of annoyance on her thin face. I gulped as I stood before her, my body automatically settling into first position.

"Everyone watch, please." Sage swiped her arm in a flourish, from right in front of my face to the far corner. "Leap, please, Tilly. Like we've been doing."

I leapt.

"Again."

I leapt again, this time back in the opposite direction. Without looking at them, I could feel the four pairs of eyes shifting from me to Sage and back again, wondering what she was getting at. I'd been corrected in class many times over the years. It was a part of dance life. But no matter how many times it happened, I never got used to being the example for what *not* to do.

"Tilly, can you tell me what you're doing wrong here?" Sage's tone was firm, but not mean.

I ran through my body position, the line of my neck and my arms, the height I'd gotten, and tried to come up with what Sage might have caught that needed fixing.

"My ankle on the landing?" It was a safe bet.

Sage tilted her head slightly and watched me before turning to the rest of the girls. "Team? Is she right?"

Sabrina's hand shot up in the air like the space shuttle launching into orbit. She didn't wait to be called on. "She's looking at the ground." Next to her, Ella nodded.

"Correct. Looking down while leaping is a common mistake, usually tied to an unrealistic fear of falling," Sage said matter-of-factly.

My cheeks burned. Maybe it was an unrealistic fear for everyone else, but not for me. It made complete sense that I would be nervous on my landings. I hadn't realized that my fear was showing in my dancing though.

Sage moved directly in front of me and put her hands on the sides of my face. "Let's take a look at the floor, shall we?" Her hands guided my face downward.

It was the same gray Marley floor I'd seen every rehearsal since we started, and just like every other dance room floor I'd seen in my career. After a moment, Sage lifted my face gently back to center.

"Not so interesting, is it?"

I resisted a nervous giggle. "No, not really."

Sage's eyes connected with mine and crinkled in the

corners, amused. "Let's look up from now on, okay? The audience needs to see your face. And you need to trust yourself. You're not going to shatter, Tilly." I nodded. I knew she was right. To the entire group, she said, "That goes for everyone. I know you're working hard, but these small tweaks are really going to make a difference. For you and for the people watching." The unspoken message was that we needed to get everything perfect if we wanted to be noticed by the people who mattered.

We ran through everything once more and I kept my eyes up. When we finished, Sage asked us to sit down in a circle. "All right, we're so close to having the whole thing out in the open. Ready for the world, right?" We nodded. "One more segment and then we will work on perfecting. You're doing a really nice job so far, but we want to punch it up. If you need to refocus, pull out whatever you used for inspiration those first few days."

Arden raised her hand. "Will we get to practice at the Whitney before the day of the show?"

"Good question. Yes, we will. The day before, so not so far off, actually." The performance was only about two weeks away. "Anything else?" The room was silent. "Fine, make sure you drink your water and go out and enjoy this marvelous city. More tomorrow." Sage patted the wooden floor with both hands and leapt up. I was amazed at how fluid she still was, despite her robot parts. We all stood up.

Sage chucked me on the shoulder. "Good correction. And, I see you have the spring back in your step. Get to sleep a little earlier?"

I smiled shyly. I couldn't help it. I didn't want Sage

to think I was one of those girls whose life was complete because of a boy. I did want her to know I was the kind of girl who tried to make difficult things better, though. "I resolved an issue with a friend."

Sage nodded. "Forgiveness can be transformative. Invite this friend to the show. Maybe you'll leap even higher."

"Maybe." I laughed and headed for my bag.

Arden was already packed up and had darted out the door. Charlotte zipped her bag and said she'd wait for me outside; she wanted to return a call she'd missed from her sister. When I finished stripping off my wet socks and slid on my sandals, I glanced over at Sabrina and Ella, who were standing entirely too close together to not have been whispering about something. Sabrina was staring at me with such intensity that I nearly took a step backward. Tatum told me once that she thought my mother was capable of shooting lasers out of her eyes when she was upset. I'd never experienced that myself, but now I thought I might know what that felt like.

I cleared my throat, hoping she'd take the hint and say whatever it was she was insinuating with her glare.

"It must be terrifying to dance after such a tragic injury. Sad that it's showing in your dancing, Tilly." Sabrina put on the fakest sympathetic pout possible. "Guess you're not as perfect as we thought."

"I never claimed to be perfect." I met her bright green eyes. "None of us is perfect."

Sabrina raised one eyebrow as if to say, "are you sure about that," and stood up. "Well, I hope your flaws don't continue to get in the way of the show. I know how much you need that job. Your mother would be so sad if you don't achieve your goals, wouldn't she?" With a satisfied smirk, she grabbed her bag and strode out of the room. Ella looked at me nervously and scurried away after her.

I blinked in disbelief, then shook it off and went to meet Charlotte. She was backed up against the outside of the building, scrolling through her phone.

"Finally! What took you so long?"

"Sabrina."

Charlotte rolled her eyes. "What did she do this time?"

"She insulted me. Nothing new. She suggested I'm not as perfect as I pretend to be because I'm afraid of getting hurt again. Oh, and she brought up the fact that I lied to my mother again." It wasn't that Sabrina's words were that hurtful—I just wished she would mind her own business and worry about her own dancing.

"Ugh. She's such a nightmare. I mean, does she not understand that being singled out for a correction is a good thing?" We took off toward the subway.

Charlotte was right, of course. Though in the moment, being corrected is never pleasant, especially in front of your peers, I'd always been taught that it was meant to make you stronger. And, as one of my favorite former teachers told me, if one dancer got corrected, it usually meant others in the class were making the same mistake. I would need to remind myself of that if Sage asked me to step forward again.

"Exactly," I replied. I chuckled and shook my head. I needed to change the topic. This wasn't worth any more energy than I'd already spent. "So I forgot to mention this to you before, but my stepsister and her boyfriend are coming up this weekend. Do you want to hang out? We'll probably go sightseeing. We can knock a few more things off our list."

"Of course I want to go. That sounds awesome." We had reached the subway entrance and descended into the underground.

"And, uh, Paolo is probably coming too," I added, as if it was an afterthought and not really the thing I was thinking about over and over.

I was genuinely excited to see him again. And scared. There was always the distinct possibility that whatever had passed between us the other night—the hugs, the shy smiles, the electrical current of attraction—was only noticed by me.

"Little drummer boy, eh?" Charlotte winked at me as we stepped through the open train doors.

"Please, don't call him that. I will die of embarrassment."

"Fine, no death before you get to kiss him."

"Thanks for your approval." I rolled my eyes, and the train doors closed behind us.

On the trip uptown, I checked my phone to find a new picture from Abuela. She was holding up what looked like a train ticket.

> **Ginger and I are coming into the city this weekend. Mind if an old woman stops by to see you and your stepsister?**

> **We would love to see you. Glad you're getting up and around!**

> **ME TOO!**

I laughed and showed Charlotte. The weekend couldn't come fast enough.

Chapter 15

We decided to go back to the room and veg, which meant Charlotte got me hooked on watching *Friends*. I had to admit it was funny, but they all needed new haircuts. In between episodes, my mother called.

"Hi, Mama," I said. "How are you?"

"Hello, Matilda. I'm well. How is everything in New York?"

There were zero chances I was telling her about the girl who was potentially ruining my chances for a job that I wasn't supposed to be thinking about. And there was definitely no way I was going to tell my mother that I was spending my free time thinking about a boy. I stuck to safer territory. "It's good, Mama. We're close to finishing up the show and Sage is optimistic about getting it just right in time for the performance."

"I am glad to hear it. I know you'll want to be a good representative for her. I read an article that Sage is opening her own company?"

"Yes, that's right." If my mother knew about this, the news had probably appeared in a magazine or one of the dance parent blogs she subscribed to.

"Then she's counting on this show to bring in patrons."

"I believe she is." I couldn't help but feel the added pressure of dancing for me and dancing for Sage drop like bags of flour on top of me.

"Please make sure you are working as hard as you can. I know you always do. But just a reminder."

"I'm on it, Mama," I said before changing the subject. "How is the photography class?"

"Well, I doubt *National Geographic* will be hiring me any time soon, but it's certainly interesting. It has given me an appreciation for the work that artists do, if nothing else."

That was a generous comment coming from my mother. She was usually of the stereotypical "art is just a hobby" opinion. At least, she was until she realized she was living with a very talented artist—Tatum. "That's always a good thing. How is Tatum doing?"

"Her work is excellent. I have suggested to your step-father that we enlarge some of her shots and frame them. Maybe do a series in the living room." She went on to describe how she and Tatum went out to Great Falls the week before, at sunset, and Tatum caught the light shimmering over the waterfalls as the sun sank behind the trees.

"That sounds like magic, Mama. I can't wait to see them." I felt my voice catch in the back of my throat. I missed home. Just a little bit.

"Yes, well, I'm sure Tatum can show you the shots on her phone when you see her. Did you find an air mattress?"

Mama had texted me earlier in the week to make sure I had a spot for Tatum to sleep. "Yes, the dormitory had one to borrow."

"Your roommate will be there as well?"

"Charlotte will be joining us, yes. Abuela will be in the city too; she said she'd stop in to say hello when Tatum arrives, and then we'll do breakfast on Sunday. And do you remember Paolo Sansone?" Mama had met him for about five seconds when he came to the hospital, but she and I never talked about him. It felt like a million years ago, on a different planet. "Seamus is staying with him at Paolo's aunt and uncle's apartment and then all five of us are going to go sightseeing. It should be fun."

"This is the boy from last fall? The drummer from The Frisson, yes?"

"That's right. I'm impressed you remember the name of the band, Mama."

She paused before answering. "When Tatum drives, there is only one band playing in the car. It would be difficult for me to forget."

I stifled a laugh. "She's a loyal girlfriend. Plus, you have to admit they're very good."

"I like where they layer one song with another. It's quite creative."

I almost dropped the phone. Who was this woman, and what had she done with my mother? I made my words careful and light. "It's called a mash-up, Mama. I think Seamus and the lead singer, Hunter, are the ones who come up with them."

"Well, whatever you call them, yes, I don't mind when Tatum forces me to listen to them."

"I'm sure she's not forcing you."

"You're right." My mother laughed, ever so softly. I

was glad to hear she was in a good mood and that she and Tatum were getting along. A year ago, that had definitely not been the case. It was nice to think back and see how much closer we all had become.

Charlotte waved wildly from her side of the room and pointed in an overly exaggerated way to the laptop. She mouthed, "new episode" and put her hands out to the side and shrugged. I raised one finger, asking her to wait.

"Mama, I need to get going, I—"

"Yes, I'm sure you need your rest. I'll speak to you soon, Matilda."

"Send me one of your photos?"

"Right away," she said. "Good night."

"Good night, Mama."

I flopped back on the bed, my head hitting the pillow with a dull thump.

"Everything okay back home?" Charlotte took a sip from her water bottle and eyed me over the tops of her glasses.

"Yeah. They're having fun without me. My mom and Tatum. It's weird." If I was totally honest with myself, I was a tiny bit jealous, but glad for them. It was an odd place to be.

"But we're having fun here!" Charlotte said brightly and gave me a cheesy thumbs-up.

I smiled. "Super fun. And there's more coming this weekend." She was right. No need to be weirded out when I was having my own adventure.

"Do you want to finish making the list of places we want to check out when Tatum gets here?"

Charlotte answered by flinging herself across the room

and onto my bed beside me. "Yes. And when we're done, we watch another episode."

"Deal." I opened my magenta notebook and we got to work.

"I am never taking the bus again!" Tatum dropped her suitcase with a loud thud on the linoleum floor in the lobby of the Marian. The noise was so loud that the front desk lady scowled over her laptop at us. "That was the grossest, ickiest experience of my life. Besides the bathroom being not clean in any sense of the word, this dude who clearly forgot to shower this week was sitting right behind us and every time he moved, we got a wave of B.O."

"Gross," I said. "Also, hi, welcome to New York." I waved and Tatum's eyes widened as if she just now realized where she was. She leapt on me, practically knocking both of us to the floor, and wrapped me in a fierce hug. She smelled like peppermint and sugar and home.

"Hi, sister. When can we go get some pizza? I am starving."

"She's been asking that since we left the station this morning." Seamus had been hovering behind Tatum while she complained.

"Hi, Seamus. Welcome to you too." I gave him a quick hug.

"Thanks, Till. It's good to see you. The city suits you." Seamus smiled the charming grin that I knew had won Tatum over the first time they'd met.

"Thank you, I agree."

The door to the building flung open. "That cab driver was the sweetest man. He just told me all about this delicious ice cream shop down in the Village that I am putting at the top of my to-do list for this weekend. How can I come into the city and not take his recommendation?"

My abuela stood there before us in all her glory, complete with sling. She was tiny and delicate, but appeared larger than her small stature because of her big personality. I had inherited my height from my abuelo, who had been over six feet tall, but I had my abuela's bronzed skin and warm brown eyes.

"Hola, my darling," she said to me and held out her free arm. I stepped toward her and she folded me up as if I weren't six inches taller than she was.

"Hola, Abuela. I'm glad you're here." It was nice to see her away from Ginger's floral couch.

"I'm glad to be here, even though it's hotter than hades out there."

"I guess you better get your ice cream then," Tatum chimed in.

"An excellent suggestion, Tatum. I do believe the concoction the driver called the Bea Arthur is calling my name." Abuela winked at Tatum and Tatum exploded in a fit of giggles. "Of course, Rue McClanahan would've been a better choice, but no one is perfect."

"I love you, Blanche," Tatum said, barely able to speak through her laughter.

Abuela patted Tatum on the back. I looked over at Seamus to see if he knew why they were laughing and he looked back at me and just shrugged.

"Well, I won't interfere with your plans. I just wanted to say hello to my favorite granddaughters. Ginger and I have a lunch date with some friends who live right around the corner from here, then I am going to get my ice cream and head over to Ginger's daughter's apartment in Brooklyn. I hear it's trendy over there now and I'm dying to see her new place." Abuela winked at me. "Are we still having breakfast tomorrow morning?"

"Of course, Abuela. Looking forward to it." I kissed her on the cheek.

"Tatum, behave yourself."

Tatum put her hand on her hip in mock-protest. "What are you trying to say?"

Abuela made a V with two fingers and pointed it at her eyes and then at Tatum. "You know I always know." Tatum shut up. She truly believed my grandmother was psychic. I wasn't so sure, but she did have uncanny timing. Abuela turned to Seamus and squeezed his shoulders. "Don't let these girls steamroll you, young man."

"I won't, ma'am. I can hold my own."

"I have no doubt. Have a great day." My abuela blew us all kisses and disappeared out the door.

"So, where can I stash this?" Tatum pointed to her bag.

"Oh, we can take it upstairs. Shay, do you want the tour?"

He waved us off. "I'm going to wait down here for Paolo. He just texted me that he's on his way."

My stomach immediately jumped up into my throat. "Great," I squeaked. "Come on, Tatum, the stairs are over here. Fourth floor."

"Stairs? Are you kidding me?"

I gave her a "do as I say" look, patented by my mother. I thought I detected Tatum's shiver.

"Fine, fine, put the step-monster stare away, please. I get enough of that at home, thank you very much."

I snorted as we started our ascent. "From what I hear, you're getting along famously."

"Oh, yeah?" We rounded the landing on the second floor.

"Mama thinks you're quite the photographer."

"I guess so. She asked me for the files of a few shots we did for an assignment. We were supposed to shoot nature."

"I heard. She wants to print them and put them up in the house. A series, she called it."

"Get out. Really?"

I smiled at my stepsister's open mouth as we hiked past the third floor. "She's not really known for being forth-coming with her feelings, is she?"

"No, she is not."

At the fourth floor, I pushed open my door and let Tatum enter first.

"Hello?" Charlotte called from the bathroom. She stepped out, fastening a yellow beaded necklace around her neck. It matched her navy and yellow polka dotted sundress. "Are you Tatum?"

"The one and only. Are you Charlotte?" My stepsister and my roommate evaluated each other for a moment.

"The one and only," she echoed. And then, like they'd been friends for years and years, both of them laughed and hugged. It was like watching my two worlds collide. It was a little unnerving, but a smile broke out on my face as I watched them. Charlotte turned to me. "Is cute drummer here yet?"

"He wasn't when we came up, but cute pianist slash cellist is downstairs," Tatum supplied.

"Her boyfriend," I explained to Charlotte, who nodded.

"Girl," she said, putting a hand on Tatum's shoulder and taking the duffle bag from Tatum's other hand, placing it on her own bed. "Am I glad you're here. Please tell your sister that she just needs to grab cute drummer when he gets here and kiss him."

Tatum looked from me to Charlotte and back to me again. "I like her already." The two of them, two peas in a pod, linked arms. Tatum held her free arm out to me and I linked up with them.

I'd spent most of my childhood not pushing friends away exactly, but never really having time to form real, lasting connections. It was hard to care about people who felt fake or like they were only using you to get ahead. That's how it was in our competitive program. So little time to fight past the smoke and mirrors the other girls put out. This, though, was a comforting, cozy feeling. Weird and foreign, but something I could definitely get used to.

I dug my phone out of my pocket. "Can we take a picture before we leave? Without the guys?"

"My arms are the longest, I can do it," Charlotte said, snatching the phone from me. "Say cheese, ladies." The three of us squished together and grinned as Charlotte snapped the shutter. "Perfection. Three gorgeous women ready for a day in the city."

"Let's hit it," Tatum yelled.

I was about to follow them out the door when I realized I'd forgotten something. I went back in the room, put my shiny red sunglasses on top of my head, and shut the dorm door behind me.

Chapter 16

Paolo was standing in the lobby in his usual gray T-shirt, flannel, and of course, the beanie tucked into his pocket. I'd seen him in this before, and yet, my stomach started fluttering the moment I saw him. He made me feel off balance when it was literally my job to stay balanced this summer. I could feel myself blushing before he even said anything.

"Hey, Tilly," he said, with a smile that warmed my insides. "Tatum," he nodded at her. "Welcome to the city."

I opened my mouth to return his greeting when Tatum, who had a knack for not paying attention to what was going on around her, busted out with, "And boy, are we glad to be here. Let me tell you about the bus ride."

Paolo and I exchanged amused glances as Seamus held the door open for all of us. Tatum barged through in her usual brash manner, the rest of us trailing behind. Charlotte skip-walked up and wedged herself between Paolo and me.

"So, you must be the famous Paolo. I'm Charlotte, the equally-as-famous roommate. I'm sure you've heard all about me." She thrust her hand in his face, which was doubly awkward because we were walking.

Rolling with it, Paolo shook Charlotte's hand as best he could. "It's a pleasure. I don't meet many other celebrities of our stature. Do you find the fame exhausting?"

"It's the worst. I am forever dodging the paparazzi and breaking the heels off my shoes." Charlotte shook her head sadly.

"Oh, you too? I thought I was the only one with a Louboutin repair bill a mile long." Paolo turned his head and winked at me.

"He knows about Louboutin shoes," Charlotte stage-whispered to me.

"I have sisters," Paolo whispered, just as loudly.

Charlotte smiled at him, while saying to me, "Keep him. Or I will."

Tatum and Seamus both burst out laughing, stopping dead in their tracks so I almost bumped into them. My face felt as warm as the oven I preheated the other night. I knew Charlotte was kidding, but I wasn't quite ready for a conversation about "keeping" Paolo. I wasn't even sure I actually had him.

"So where are we going?" Seamus asked.

"Tilly's in charge. She has a list." Charlotte hiked her thumb at me.

"She always has a list. Is it in the pink notebook?" Tatum asked. I resisted rolling my eyes.

"Of course it's in the notebook," I said. "You gave it to me. You encourage my habits."

"I did, didn't I?" She smiled widely and patted herself on the back, literally.

"I don't care what else we do, but my aunt and uncle

said they could recommend places for dinner if we want to swing by the flower shop. It's in Little Italy," Paolo offered.

"Yes, please," Charlotte and Tatum said at the same time. They looked at each other, and both of them doubled over with laughter.

"No wonder Charlotte and I get along so well. They're the same person," I said to Paolo.

"Is that a good thing or a bad thing?" he asked.

I grinned. "I guess we'll find out."

Because my weather app was forecasting rain on and off all day, we decided to stick to indoor activities rather than end up drenched on the streets of New York.

"Let's go to a museum," I suggested. I held out my notebook to Tatum, who was standing nearest to me at the subway entrance. "Which one do you want to see?"

She took the notebook and scanned the list with her index finger. "Gosh, you're thorough. I mean, I'm not surprised. But seeing every possible museum in New York in one long list is kind of overwhelming."

I pushed her playfully and she pretended to stumble and fall over. "Pick. One. Just one."

Charlotte stepped up and read over Tatum's shoulder. "I would vote for either the Museum of Modern Art, not because I like modern art but because I just want to say we're going to the MoMa," she said, stretching out the long *o*. "Or the Metropolitan Museum of Art because I've heard there's a real pyramid in there."

"Do you think there's a mummy too? I could get down with mummies." Seamus waggled his eyebrows.

"There's also a hall of armor, including one that used to belong to Henry VIII," Paolo said.

"Of course you know that. History nerd." I smiled at him. I thought Paolo was attractive for many reason—being a drummer who wore flannel and beanies being one of them—but I really liked that he was smart. I loved how he could spout facts and stories, even if he used it as a defense mechanism sometimes.

"Card carrying and proud of it. The Met is one of my happy places. My aunt and uncle used to take me, my sisters, and my cousins there when my family came to visit. You can spend weeks in there and always find something new to look at."

If I had been encased in a block of ice, the look he gave me would have melted it to a puddle at my feet. "I can't wait to go then," I said.

Because we were only a few blocks from The Met, we walked. Tatum and Charlotte forged ahead, chattering about their favorite TV shows and books. Seamus hovered about five paces behind them—close enough to answer if they decided to include him, but far enough away that he wasn't subject to every tiny detail. Paolo and I lagged behind him, lost in our own world.

We made awkward small talk as we walked. Every so often his hand would brush against mine and I instinctively apologized. After three or four times, Paolo laughed.

"This is just silly," he said, and grabbed my hand. "That's better."

"Much," I agreed and let my fingers wrap around his. I instantly relaxed and inhaled. Even though they were all still walking ahead of us, about to march up the steep steps into the museum, our friends faded away. Being hand-in-hand magnified Paolo's presence, which was both exciting and terrifying.

We walked through the museum, completely connected. Paolo never let go of my hand, even when he grabbed a drink at the water fountain. If anyone else noticed—and I was sure they did, judging by their smirks—they didn't say a word.

Seamus insisted on checking out the pyramid first. Turns out it wasn't exactly a pyramid, but the Tomb of Perneb, a burial space from thousands of years ago. Seamus and Tatum asked a passing family to take a photo of all of us in front of it to commemorate "our first Egyptian tomb." We drifted through the rest of the museum, sometimes pausing to read the placards (me and Paolo), evaluating everything loudly (Charlotte), geeking out over the collection of musical instruments from all over the world (Seamus), and standing in front of masterpieces with our mouths wide open in awe (Tatum). Paolo was right when he said you could spend weeks in this museum. It was never-ending, with so much history and culture at every turn.

I squeezed Paolo's hand as we inspected pieces of bone that had once been used as currency. "I'm glad we ran into each other this summer."

"Me too." He gave me his lopsided smile.

We caught up with the rest of our group in the Hall of Arms and Armor. There, in all its glory, was Henry VIII's field armor from his later years. I read the information posted next to the massive pile of metal.

"This is from the few years before he died. He apparently had some kind of infection in his leg that eventually killed him. It contributed to his size; he gained a lot of weight because he was injured and ate so much." I stepped back to look at the armor. It seemed twice the size of the other suits standing at attention nearby. "What a horrible thing, to be stuck inside a full body metal cage. And with an injury." My ankle panged with sympathy pain.

"Do you seriously feel sorry for a man who killed multiple wives?" Charlotte, with a hand on her hip, looked between me and the suit of armor with disgust. "He's the ultimate misogynist. Yuck, no thanks."

I stuck my tongue out at her. "I merely expressed my disinterest at being someone his size and stuck in that suit. I do not condone bad behavior. You know that." I eyed my roommate and she nodded her agreement.

"Are you talking about the mean girl?" Tatum interjected. "What's going on with her, anyway?"

Paolo turned to me. "What's her name again?"

"Sabrina."

Charlotte and I gave Seamus the thirty-second version of the story. We added in the new part, about the stolen socks, and I said how I was worried she was plotting against me. "It adds up and then again it doesn't. She could just be a really bitter person who hates everyone, or she could be totally manipulative and planning something that could blow up in my face."

"She's a real piece of work," Charlotte said as we

drifted away from the armor and toward the Greek sculptures. "She hates Tilly. I mean, she doesn't seem to like anyone, but she really hates Tilly."

"That's because she's the best," Tatum said matter-of-factly. "She always has been. Tilly intimidates other dancers."

"I do not," I said softly, looking at my feet. I was flattered by her compliment but I didn't want to think I'd been putting others off.

"You're a brilliant dancer. And Sabrina knows enough to recognize talent when she sees it. And now she's scared. End of story. It's just unfortunate that she's acting like a spoiled child." Tatum wrapped her arm around my shoulder. "I speak the truth."

"You should talk to your director, right?" Seamus asked. "That's part of her job, isn't it? You tried to solve this yourself and now you need someone else to step in."

I shook my head. "I don't know. Sage and Sabrina's mother are friends. What if I speak up and they think I'm a terrible teammate and I get blackballed from the dance world forever? No one wants to work with someone difficult."

"I don't think standing up for yourself and the rest of your team is being difficult," Paolo pointed out.

I shrugged as if to say I'd think about it. Which was the truth. I knew I'd probably think about it too often.

We had reached the museum exit and pushed out through the doors into the fresh air. The clouds seemed to be parting, so we decided to take the subway down to lower Manhattan and walk across the Brooklyn Bridge while the weather was behaving. The train jostled us side to side as it rounded curves and we giggled at each other, trying to grip the silver poles and overhead bars. At one point, Tatum, who was making wild hand gestures while she was telling us about this guy in her and my mother's photography class who thought everything was "the greatest shot ever," lost her footing and Seamus had to catch her before she fell flat on her face, probably taking ten others down with her. As if he sensed my unease about being on shaky ground, Paolo wrapped an arm around my waist, smugly securing me to his side, while grasping the pole with his other hand.

"Wouldn't want you to fall," he said, his mouth so close to my ear that I did lose my balance ever so slightly. "Too much," he added with a little self-satisfied smirk.

We stared at each other for a long moment before my face flamed red, my knees wobbled, and I had to look across the train.

When I turned back, knees firmly locked in place, I noticed an older man, his hand holding the place in his worn copy of *The Count of Monte Cristo,* eying us. "Just kiss him already, sweetheart. He's dying for it. The whole subway car can tell."

I froze. The weight of at least thirty pairs of eyes fell on top of me, waiting to see if I'd do as this complete stranger suggested. I couldn't look at Paolo because I was sure he was either completely embarrassed or maybe even laughing. I quickly flicked my gaze at Tatum, who had a half-sympathetic and half-amused look on her face.

I wanted to kiss Paolo. How could I not—he was smart and handsome and talented and a total nerd in disguise—but I definitely did not want my first kiss with

Paolo to be on a subway before an audience. Just like when he walked me to the subway after his performance, I knew this was not the right moment.

I wasn't exactly what you would call an experienced kisser. There was a dancer in my classes in middle school who I'd had a huge crush on and he knew it. Backstage before our winter recital, he finally approached me—I was too terrified of him to do it myself—and asked me if I wanted him to kiss me. I couldn't speak, but I managed to nod my head. He came nearer to me; I closed my eyes instinctively and felt his lips on mine. Barely. It was more like his top lip tapped mine. When I opened my eyes a second later, he was gone, back on stage with the girl I found out later was his girlfriend. He'd given me a pity non-kiss, and there hadn't been any others in between.

"You don't have to," Paolo whispered from somewhere above my head.

And yet, I wanted to, so I compromised. I tipped up on my toes, leaned against him so I wouldn't crash to the ground on the still-moving subway, took Paolo's face between my hands, and kissed him gently on the cheek. I had been performing in front of hundreds of people my entire life, so for me there was no such thing as stage fright. I was just playing a part, and somehow that made performing easier.

In that moment, though, as I pressed my lips to his cheek, I'd never felt more vulnerable and exposed. Or real.

And just like when I danced on stage, the audience around me cheered wildly.

Chapter 17

*T*he moment we emerged from the Brooklyn Bridge/City Hall station, the rain started to fall. So much for blue skies.

"Did anyone bring an umbrella?" I asked, knowing the answer already.

"Of course not. Do we look like Boy Scouts?" Seamus said with a grin.

"Truth. We're musicians. We're supposed to be unprepared slackers." Paolo fist-bumped Seamus.

"I'm actually surprised you don't have an umbrella in your purse. Or maybe one of those plastic ponchos from Niagara Falls." Tatum raised one eyebrow at me. "You're the one who is so good at details, Tilly. I'm disappointed."

"I'm living on the edge these days," I told her, with an exaggerated roll of the eyes.

"Well, I for one don't mind a little water. We're washable. And we're in New York, the greatest city in the whole universe. And even if I'm going alone, I am walking across the bridge." Charlotte put both hands on her hips to let us know she meant business. "Are you guys scared of a little rain?"

"Nope." Tatum hitched her purse up on her shoulder.

"Let's go." Seamus linked arms with her and they followed Charlotte, already on the move toward the gigantic structure in front of us.

I reached for the red sunglasses on top of my head. "I guess I don't need these in this weather," I said to Paolo.

He put a hand out to push them back up. "No, leave them. I like them. They suit you somehow."

"Thank you," I said shyly. "My abuela gave them to me. She said every girl needs something red in her accessory pile and that they would give me confidence."

"Do you think she's right?"

"About the red? I love them so I suppose she was right there. And the confidence, yes, I think right on that too." I'd certainly come a long way this summer, that was for sure.

"That's good. It looks good on you. The confidence, I mean," he said. At that, I pushed my shoulders back and we both laughed.

We caught up with the others at the base of the bridge. There were lanes, like on a regular road, for people in opposing directions to walk. The wood of the bridge was already slick with water. We'd have to tread carefully.

As we walked, Paolo talked about his music program and how his director was a genius and how he was really looking forward to going to college and continuing the work he would do there. The others hung back and interjected every once in a while. We talked more about Tatum's photography and how Seamus was giving piano and cello lessons to middle school kids hoping to get into our old high school, and about Charlotte's life back home in the sunshine of California. Paolo held my hand the whole time. It felt like the gesture was not as an anchor for my safety, but as an anchor to reality.

For so long I'd been a party of one in Tilly's world of dance and school, but for once in my eighteen years, I was finally part of something bigger. This felt like a new team. A squad. A band of people I could trust. All summer we'd been working with Sage on teamwork and unity, and here I had the perfect example of what that should look like right under my nose.

At the other end of the bridge, we were completely drenched, but happy. Paolo got an Uber, and we piled into the van that took us to Little Italy. We got out at his aunt and uncle's flower shop where they plied us with towels, hairdryers, and cookies.

Once we had lost the drowned rat look, Paolo's aunt pointed us toward one of the oldest pizza restaurants in the city, where we happily lined up and waited for a table, stomachs growling. I had never tasted such delicious food, but I knew the friends I was with made it even better. We ate and laughed there for almost three hours. It felt like we were family.

The city was dark and finally dry, and the moon was out, just a tiny sliver, when we finished dinner. I would have liked to stay longer, but I knew we were exhausted from so much walking.

"Well, this is our stop, right?" Seamus said to Paolo when we arrived back at the Sansones' flower shop slash apartment.

"Yep." Paolo unlocked the door and held it open for all of us.

Seamus and Tatum took his backpack up the stairs, presumably wanting to say good-bye without all of us watching.

"I'll get us a ride," Charlotte said. "It might take a while." She looked at me and winked.

"Smooth," Paolo said laughing.

"Hey, I do what I can." She flounced out the door, her long hair flying behind her.

When the door clicked closed, it was just Paolo and me standing in the darkened flower shop, lit only by the refrigerated glass cases full of roses and gladiolas.

"Good thing the store was here so we could make a pit stop in the rain," he said with a lopsided grin.

"Agreed. Please thank your aunt and uncle for taking care of us earlier. And for the dinner suggestion. It was really lovely."

"They're good people. I think I'll keep them."

He closed the space between us and put his arms around my waist, encircling me, and I instinctively put my arms around his shoulders. It was impossible not to notice how strong and broad he was, no doubt from years of drumming. He put his face close to mine, our cheeks were almost touching, and I held my breath, just in case he was actually a figment of my imagination.

"I had a really good time today," he breathed in my ear. It tickled, and I let out a ridiculous giggle.

"I had a really good time too." I'd always thought Paolo was warm and funny, but seeing him interact with my friends—his friends—was grounding. I knew enough about the world to know that he was a little bit like a unicorn. Rare and sought after. I wouldn't let him get away again.

Paolo gently walked the two of us over to the case full of roses, opened the door, and plucked out a perfect pink one, just on the verge of bursting open. He handed it to me and kissed my cheek. "Pink roses mean grace and elegance."

I accepted it, his arms circling me once more, and held it to my nose, inhaling its delicate scent. "Thank you. I'll put it on my nightstand and dream of sweet things for days."

Paolo's arms tightened and a shiver ran through me. "I'll be dreaming about you for days," he whispered.

No one had ever said such a thing to me. It was one thing to be friends with someone, and another thing entirely to be wanted by someone. Truly wanted in all the ways that made you feel alive.

I pulled back slightly to look at him, his amber eyes bright with emotion. And then before I could talk myself out of it, I kissed him. Everything around us fell away as I leaned into him and felt the softness of his lips on mine. The electricity I had felt just holding his hand exploded between us—I was sure my skin must have been shimmering there was so much light running through me. Paolo tasted sweet and salty. He pulled away slightly and then kissed the right corner of my mouth, and then slowly, teasing, the left.

"I waited for that for months."

My stomach dropped to the floor. "Was it worth it?"

"Better than I imagined."

Me too, I thought. *Beyond my wildest dreams.*

"What would you say to hanging out next week?" Paolo asked.

"I'd say yes, please."

He planted a kissed on my cheek and took my hand, leading me to the door. "Then it's settled."

Tatum and Seamus came thundering down the stairs as we reached the door. The boys waved good-bye as we hopped into the cab Charlotte had waiting outside.

"Who got the better deal tonight? Shay sleeping above a beautiful flower shop that smells amazing or me sleeping in a dorm full of uptight interns and moody dancers?" Tatum made a fake grimace and then laughed as the cab whisked us back to the wilds of the Upper East Side.

I just sniffed my rose and smiled the entire time.

As we inflated Tatum's air mattress and dressed for bed, she said to me, "I don't know how you're going to leave this place."

"What do you mean? The dorm?"

"No, the city. I can see you here, Till," Tatum said, smoothing the blanket over the air mattress and positioning her pillow. "The energy, the people, the chaos that somehow makes sense. You fit."

My cheeks grew warm with pleasure. "That might be the nicest thing you've ever said to me."

We turned off the light, but my eyes didn't shut. Soon, Tatum and Charlotte were snoring softly, and I was still awake. I wished I was dreaming about Paolo and our kiss, but I found my mind settling on another vision—my dream of being here in New York. Which only led me to the realization that my beloved new city was far from being my permanent home.

With a sigh, I crept out of bed and down the hall to the kitchen. There was no hope of my sleeping unless I got rid of my nervous energy. I knew I had enough ingredients left to scrape something together, and then hopefully get at least a few hours of sleep afterward.

As I pulled the flour from the cupboard, I heard a soft knocking sound. When I turned, the sleepy faces of Charlotte and Tatum appeared in the doorway.

Charlotte pointed at me. "Are you anxious? You're being the carb fairy again."

I nodded slowly. There was no mistaking the giant bag of all-purpose flour in my hand.

Charlotte said to Tatum, "This one has been leaving bread out in the middle of the night. I love it. She's probably driving the other girls crazy with all the tempting calories."

Tatum sighed, understanding that my stress-baking was a bad sign, and then took the flour from my hands. She turned and opened the cupboard again and removed a packet of yeast. "Well. Let's bake then."

Charlotte came in the kitchen and hovered over the island. "What are we making?"

Tears picked the corners of my eyes. "You guys don't have to stay. This is my problem to work out."

"Um, no. It's my problem too," Charlotte said. "We're on the same team, remember? I'm just as worried about getting a job as you are. And if you're obsessing over Sabrina, I get it. She could screw everything up for me too with her ridiculous behavior. Even if she's only targeting you, we all lose."

I felt like a world-class jerk. This wasn't just about me. "You're right. I'm sorry."

"And, ahem, this is my problem too," Tatum added. "You know that if I go home totally worried about you, Belén will know and she will grill me."

Mama pressuring Tatum at this moment in time, before I had a job, was the last thing I needed. "You don't have to worry about me, Tatum. I will figure it out. Eventually." I had to. I was running out of time.

Tatum put both hands on the counter and puffed up her chest. I almost laughed because I knew she was trying to look intimidating, even though she was much shorter than me and completely harmless. "And I care about you. This isn't like when we were younger when we ignored each other. We're friends now, remember? Like it or not, you're my sister, and you're stuck with me for the rest of your life. I love you. I'm not going to abandon you in your pool of misery. I am throwing you a life raft."

Charlotte waved her hands like she was directing traffic. "Hey, yeah, me too." She pointed both thumbs to her chest. "Friend. Right here. Awesome friend. You're not alone, Till."

I grinned at them and nodded at the ingredients, an invitation to work together.

With two assistants, we made quick work of the simple French baguette recipe I had memorized. The others let me do the kneading, figuring that was the whole point of me forgoing sleep. I showed them how to press a thumb into the dough to see if it springs back. If it does, it's ready to go in the oven. As we were letting the dough rise, Charlotte's yawning became unmistakable, even though she tried to hide it behind her hands.

"Go to bed," I said, pushing her toward the door.

"I want to stay." Big yawn.

"I want you to go to bed."

"Save me some bread? I can't miss out when I was the carb fairy's helper."

"We'll save you some, don't worry."

Charlotte yawned again, one that made her whole body shudder, waved, and went back to the room.

Tatum and I worked silently to form the dough into two oblong ovals, scored the tops, and shoved them in the preheated oven. She flopped down onto the tall stool that stood at the small island in the kitchen.

"Do you feel better?"

"Yes." It never failed. Baking was my greatest stress reliever. At least temporarily.

"Do you know what you're going to do about Sabrina?"

This answer was much harder. "No. I wish I did."

Tatum sighed and rested her hand in her chin. "You know what you should do?" I shook my head. If I knew, I would be fast sleep right now, probably dreaming about Paolo. "You should talk to Blanche. I'm sure she has some pearls of wisdom for you. She's coming for breakfast, right?"

"Yeah. You're right. Abuela knows everything." If I had called her the first time I'd seen Sabrina ducking out of the dance studio, I probably would've figured all my issues out a long time ago.

Tatum stood up and gave me a hug. "You know it's going to be okay, right?"

I rested my head on top of hers. "Yes. Even if Sabrina completely ruins the show and takes all of us down with her, I have college. I have a future. I'll be fine. And maybe I'd get another chance along the way. But this one feels like *the* chance, you know? Charlotte keeps talking about the universe aligning and making things happen. If that's true, well, I'm trying to do it justice, I guess."

Tatum pulled away, her deep brown eyes boring into mine. It was the one feature we shared between us. "Then I think it sounds like you already know what you need to do."

Her words sat in the back of my throat like I swallowed a stone. "I'll talk to Abuela just to be sure."

I put the baguettes away for breakfast, and Tatum and I headed back to bed. I managed to fall asleep from sheer exhaustion, but there was no dreaming.

Chapter 18

*H*ow was your ice cream, Abuela?"

My grandmother had arrived bright and early—for her—at nine o'clock. She had her favorite leopard print flats on her tiny feet and carried a matching purse in her free hand.

Abuela grinned. "It was spectacular. Vanilla with dulce de leche and crushed vanilla wafers. Simple but packed a big punch. Just like Bea herself." Abuela smiled at me, her pink lipstick making her teeth look even whiter than usual. "I tried to convince the young man behind the counter to let me suggest a recipe for a Rue McClanahan cone, but he just laughed. He said many have offered but they're sticking with Bea."

I giggled. "Those are the actresses from your favorite show, right? *The Golden Girls?*"

"The very ones. Did you have a nice day yesterday?" Abuela smoothed my hair and kissed my cheek.

"We had an amazing day." I touched my fingers to my lips, remembering the best part. "I love New York, Abuela. I feel like I could be here forever and see something new every day."

The corners of her pink lips lifted, knowingly. "Now you understand why I don't stay in one place too long. There are so many new things to discover. Though it is nice to have such a dear family to visit, I do enjoy being on the move."

"I'm not sure I want to change locations quite so often, but I do think I'm ready for something new." It felt good to say it out loud.

"I have no doubt." Abuela clasped her hands in front of her face. "Now, I'm here for breakfast, and a little birdie told me there's fresh baguette in this dorm."

"Tatum texted you?" Abuela nodded once. Instead of joining us, Tatum and Charlotte were meeting the boys for breakfast at a diner in Times Square, one with singing waitstaff. They'd left moments before Abuela showed up. I guess they knew I needed a little alone time with her.

"I've got a basket full of fresh butter, fruit, and cheese, so let's eat. I'm starving." Abuela rubbed her stomach for emphasis. "Do you have a suggestion for a good spot for a picnic? It is a beautiful day."

"In fact, I do."

Abuela handed me the wicker basket she borrowed from Ginger's daughter, loaded with the goodies she'd picked up at a farmers' market before coming to the dorm. I packed the fresh baguettes, my stomach growling at the floury scent, and we headed out. Abuela told me how she and Ginger had tried to go see the musical *Wicked* the night before.

"She said all the young folks wait for rush tickets, cheap ones in the front row, so we tried that. I put my name in the hat and so did she, but we didn't win. So we walked around Times Square and bought kitschy souvenirs. I've got a foam Statue of Liberty crown for you back at the apartment."

"Wow. Halloween for this year is covered now. Thanks, Abuela." We looked at each other and laughed.

We entered Central Park at 72nd Street and sat down on a bench overlooking the boat pond, not far from the Hans Christian Andersen statue. I tore off chunks of the baguette while Abuela unwrapped the sliced apples and sharp cheddar cheese. I slathered the bread with home-made butter and we feasted. In comfortable silence, my abuela and I watched parents sail mechanical sailboats with their small sons and daughters, joggers circle the water, and old men shuffle in pairs with their morning coffee.

"So what is troubling you, mija?" Abuela asked as we ate. "And don't tell me nothing. You look like you're about to jump out of your skin, and there are purple bags under your eyes. Tatum may have also mentioned you didn't sleep much last night, but I would've guessed it anyway."

Abuela always noticed everything. "Well, there's this girl . . ." And I told her the whole story—leaving out the part about my intention to take a job if offered—every tiny detail, every doubt I had, while stuffing my face with buttered baguette between sentences. "Abuela, I feel so stuck."

She took a slow bite of the bread and chewed, as if she wanted to savor it. I was grateful she was enjoying what I had made, but I wanted her to answer me. I needed a little of Abuela's magical advice.

"Matilda, what bothers you most about this girl?"

"How do you mean?"

"Well, you've just described someone who is just like you, right?"

I winced. I didn't want to be placed in the same category as Sabrina. "I wouldn't say she's just like me."

Abuela put her hands up in the air as a mea culpa. "Fine. I'll rephrase. This girl is also desperate to get hired at the end of the summer, correct?"

Caught. I shouldn't have been surprised. She'd seen right through me. "Yes," I admitted, and told her about deferring Georgetown and lying to Mama.

She smiled the way adults smile at toddlers who make adorable mistakes. "I'm not oblivious, Matilda. You know, you and your stepsister don't give adults enough credit. The both of you think we don't pay any attention. But I digress. Your mother will get over your choice. It doesn't take a mind reader to know that you were upset when you injured your ankle. I know you would have been auditioning with your peers at school and trying to fulfill the plan you worked so hard on."

The plan had always been to dance for fun and go to school at the same time. Though now I was sure I would've changed my mind, even if I hadn't gotten injured. "True." As usual, Abuela knew it before I did.

"But your roommate is also trying to get a job and you aren't angry with her, no?"

An excellent point, and not one that had occurred to me before she said it. "No. I'm cheering for her."

"So what's the difference?"

I thought for a moment. "Sabrina has been horrible to me. And just me. I still don't know what I did to deserve being singled out for her sabotage." I hoped I wouldn't have anything else to add to the list before all was said and done.

"Theft. Rude comments. Potential injury. Those are

not small things." Abuela took a sip of her coffee from the leopard print travel mug she'd brought with her.

"I don't know how to deal with her," I admitted. "I keep trying to be nice—"

Abuela made a dismissive sound and waved her hand. "I hate that word. Nice. Too many people, girls in particular, think they have to be nice all the time. This Sabrina is making selfish choices that could ruin something special for you, correct?"

"Correct." I was taken slightly aback by her sudden passion.

"Who says you need to be nice to her then? You need to be civil, of course, but nice and civil are not the same things. In my opinion, you need to be assertive. She is counting on you to be silent. She's counting on your niceness. The opposite of nice isn't always mean."

"So you think I should tell Sage?"

Abuela popped a slice of apple into her mouth, chewed, and swallowed. "Maybe. If that's what you think you need to do. You could also speak with Sabrina again. You could organize the other girls and have an intervention. You have many choices."

I hadn't considered talking to the girls in the group. "Do you think the others would support me?"

"Have you been kind to them? Gotten to know them?"

My face flushed. I hadn't really spoken to them much. I'd lumped them in with Sabrina and stuck with Charlotte, who I knew would never hurt me. "Not really."

"There is an old saying that you catch more flies with honey than vinegar. You know it, yes?"

"Yes, I've heard it before."

"Kindness can be more powerful than aggression. I would wager that these dancers are hungry for it, especially if this other girl is using them to make herself feel bigger." Abuela patted my arm. "Matilda, your whole life, you have been a strategist. You make plans and you follow them. And part of being a good strategist is knowing when to change directions or when to consider new information. Choose the right tool, and you will succeed."

"I appreciate that, Abuela," I told her with a smile.

"Either way, if you need me, I'll be here. Ginger and I are going to Atlantic City for a few days. Maybe I'll come back a big winner."

I hoped that for the both of us. "Play a quarter for me."

We packed up the rest of the bread in the basket and I told her to take it home. Abuela held me at arms' length and looked me over, as she always did when we were together.

"Te amo, mija. You are so beautiful. Please get some rest and do not worry. Everything will work out the way it is supposed to. If that means you get a job, you get a job. If that means you go to college, you go to college. And if that means the whole performance falls apart, well,"—she paused and hugged me—"I do not think that is going to happen, but if it does, you haven't lost anything you have right now."

I hugged her and breathed in her floral perfume. "Why are you always right?"

"Because I am magic, as Tatum keeps suggesting. Or I just have a lot of life experience. People are more predictable than you think." She pulled back and smoothed my hair away from my face. "Even you."

I wanted to ask her if she thought I was making the right choice to dance professionally, but I didn't. I knew magicians never reveal their secrets. Abuela kissed me good-bye and we parted ways.

After Tatum and Seamus came back, we said more good-byes. I knew they would be back in no time for the show, but I missed Tatum the second she was out of sight. She had hugged me fiercely, told me to kick some dancer booty, and then ran out of the Marian so they wouldn't miss their bus back home.

Back in our room, Charlotte opened her laptop and gasped.

"Hey, did you see this?" She was pointing to the screen.

"See what?" I crowded onto her bed and read.

> Dear Team,
>
> I have a personal emergency to deal with tomorrow morning. Practice will begin at noon. Please be well rested and hydrated.
>
> See you then,
> Sage

I squinted at the screen and read it again. "Do you think everything's okay? Sage has never postponed practice." I looked at Charlotte.

"True, but it says personal emergency. I mean, what if something's happened with her hip? She's been so active with us lately—that can't be good for it."

Oh. I imagined her robot parts breaking and Sage shattering all over the ground.

"At least we get to sleep in," Charlotte said brightly. "I for one am sure that will contribute to my being well-rested. Yes, indeed."

I looked at the email on my phone. A lump formed in the back of my throat. I hoped Sage was okay. But what if she wasn't? What if her emergency, whatever it was, conflicted with the show? I was intimately acquainted with the concept of things just happening unexpectedly that ruin your plans. In all my imaginings of the way this performance could be ruined, though, not having a choreographer was never one of them.

Chapter 19

At eleven-fifty Monday morning, Charlotte and I arrived at the rehearsal space. We climbed the stairs as we did every day, but when we opened the glass door to the studio, four pairs of eyes—include Sage's stormy gray ones—swung our way.

"Nice of you ladies to join us," Sage said, her voice uncharacteristically cold. "I know I've asked you to get a good night's sleep, but noon is a little late, don't you think?"

I froze. Had I misread Sage's email? No, I was certain she'd said rehearsal started at noon. But then why was everyone else already here? My heart began beating at a marathon runner's pace and my hands went from dry to dripping. I had never been late to a rehearsal before without prior approval.

Looking around the room at Arden and Ella's bewildered faces, I could tell they were confused about why we were late too.

Ella mouthed, "Where were you guys?" Her brows were furrowed, but she didn't seem angry. Was she worried about us?

I shook my head slightly, confused. Had there been a

second email retracting the change in plans? No. At least not sent to me. I'd checked again on our way to rehearsal.

I opened my mouth to say something, but Charlotte beat me to it.

"We are so sorry, Sage. Our alarms didn't go off and we must have been really tired from last night. It won't happen again."

Sage tipped her chin up and raised one eyebrow. Her expression felt like a knife in my heart. "When I ask you to be on time, I mean that. I know this isn't the real thing," she said with air quotes, "but one day, it will be. And while one tardy won't do much damage, repeated lateness can result in a broken contract. I know none of you want that to happen."

"No, Sage," I mumbled, Charlotte nodding furiously next to me.

I flicked my gaze to Sabrina, who was smiling like it was her birthday. Unbelievable. What kind of person enjoyed her teammates' humiliation? This time, it felt like a knife in the back.

Sage crossed her arms over her chest. "Well, let's make the most of your shortened rehearsal time, shall we?"

Charlotte grabbed my arm and pulled me to the corner of the room where we quickly shed our flip-flops and slipped on our dance socks.

As we took our positions, Sabrina muttered, "Guess you need to pay closer attention to details, huh?"

I rolled my eyes. What other detail was I supposed to get out of Sage's email other than the new start time—which had obviously been some kind of mistake. But a mistake only sent to me and Charlotte?

That thought jogged a horrible memory. Back in high school, some kids got expelled for impersonating a college admissions officer. They'd tried to convince the valedictorian her acceptance had been a mistake—a misguided attempt to vanquish the competition—by setting up a fake email account that appeared to be identical to that of the admissions officer. They'd sent a note to the poor victim, saying there'd been a technical glitch in the admissions portal and she'd actually been rejected.

Had the same thing happened to us? I glared at Sabrina—who else would have made such a calculated move? She was staring straight ahead, and the slight smirk on her face was enough to confirm my suspicions.

I didn't get angry easily, and I generally tried to give people the benefit of the doubt. Sending a fake email impersonating our choreographer, with the purpose of making us late for practice and thus damaging our reputations, completely negated that privilege. Dirty looks, insults, and petty theft were one thing—actively trying to prevent me from attending rehearsal was another. If I was on the fence about talking to Sage before, there was no question that a conversation was in order. Now. Today.

Charlotte and I made it through the tail end of rehearsal without any more dings. Thankfully, I was able to channel the rage I was feeling toward Sabrina into my dancing. My angles were so sharp I might've impaled someone. My lines were straighter than arrows and my facial expressions were unmistakable. Even though our practice time had been cut in half, I fully committed myself. The fierce, intense music helped as well—it wasn't hard to use how I was feeling as fuel.

When we finished, panting and sweating, Sage motioned for us to gather around. She stood before us, shoulders back and head held high, with clasped hands. Her face was serious. Was she about to give us a lecture on punctuality?

"Team, I just wanted to let you know that I've received confirmation from a handful of companies that plan to consider dancers participating in the installation. As I warned you earlier in the summer, there are very few spots available. They may think about offering an apprentice-ship or student spot for younger dancers, but those of you looking for a permanent position need to wrap your heads around possibly not having an offer when this is over."

I did my best to keep my face stony and still. I needed one of those spots.

"That doesn't mean that you're not talented enough or that it won't happen next time, but if you are not offered a job, it is most likely that they think you're not quite ready yet." Sage lowered her voice and rattled off a handful of company names—including one that was very familiar. District Ballet of Washington, D.C.

My heart leapt. District Ballet was where I studied last summer, the place where I fell in love with contemporary dance. Would the artistic director, Jonathan Calsan, remem-ber me? Did that give me an advantage? I stole a glance at the other girls. Sabrina, sitting cross-legged, sat up straighter and smoothed her hair. She reminded me of a peacock. My stomach turned and I looked away. The worst thing I could've imagined was not getting a job, but what if I didn't get one and she did?

Sage continued. "It is unclear if they each have one spot, multiple spots, or if they're just here to enjoy the show." She shifted from one foot to the other, her keys jingled from where they hung off her black cargo shorts. "And you're the first to know that I'll be doing my own scouting. Sage Oliver Dance will hopefully, fingers crossed,"—she held up her crossed right index and middle fingers—"be up and running this winter."

Sage looked over at me and Charlotte sternly. She meant business with that look. I gulped, and I was pretty sure I heard Charlotte do the same. Even though we'd done well during rehearsal, we'd still violated a big rule by missing half of our crucial practice time, and so close to the performance. Unless we cleared up the misunderstanding with Sage, we could kiss our shot at a spot with her good-bye forever.

After Sage had dismissed us, I turned to Charlotte.

"I'm going to talk to Sage. You know Sabrina was behind that email. This has gone too far," I told her.

Charlotte's eyes widened as she put together the puzzle pieces. "You're totally right. That girl—" She trailed off and shook her head, her eyes narrowed. "Do you want backup?"

I pursed my lips in a sad smile. "No. I'm Sabrina's real target. You were just collateral damage. I can handle it. But thank you. I'm glad we're on the same team."

"I've got your back," Charlotte said, pointing at me and winking. "Good luck."

I hung back until the room was empty, knowing Sage was probably hovering in the hallway, checking her email or making a call, waiting for us to clear out so she could lock up the room. I cracked the door open slowly, just an inch, but it was wide enough to hear the voices in the hallway.

"I just want to thank you again, Sage, for taking Sabrina on. I know my request was out of the blue, what with how we haven't seen each other in so long, but I so appreciate this favor."

I peeked around the corner but couldn't see the speaker. The female voice sounded ever so slightly familiar.

"Donna, you know me well enough to know I wouldn't take on any dancer who isn't worth my time." Sage's voice was gruff. Curt even.

Donna . . . Donna *Wolfrik*. Sage was talking with Sabrina's mom.

I leaned a little farther into the hall, knowing I probably shouldn't be eavesdropping, but unable to stop myself.

"Well, either way, we are both grateful." A pause. "Aren't we, Sabrina?"

The muffled sound that followed was indistinguishable. I imagined the woman from the En Avant photos prodding a reluctant Sabrina in the back until she responded.

"And I want you to know that I have been working with Sabrina on the choreography in the afternoons. She's going to have it all down by showtime. Don't you worry."

I winced. Mrs. Wolfrik confirmed everything I had suspected—and she'd outed Sabrina for her extra practices at the same time. I guess my big revelation to Sage about Sabrina's extracurricular activities wasn't a secret after all.

"Just make sure you're not overexerting yourself,

Sabrina." There was a warning in Sage's voice. "I know you know this because I've been shoving it down your throat for the last several weeks, but you'll be no good to me if you are an exhausted mess."

"Oh, of course, we'll lighten up in the next week as we lead up to the performance." I wondered if Mrs. Wolfrik was saying that because she meant it or just for Sage's benefit. "And what about the other girls, Sage? I know Sabrina has just loved being in the dorm with them and making new friends. Much more fun than living at home." If Mrs. Wolfrik believed Sabrina was having fun in the dorm, the woman needed a reality check.

"I'm glad to hear it," Sage replied.

"One last thing before we go. Back in my dancing days, I always learned best by observation. Is there someone Sabrina should try to emulate?"

There was a long pause, as if Sage was thinking of the right answer. Or perhaps she was pondering answering at all. Finally, she said, "If you want to focus on a few things, watch Tilly closely tomorrow." My breath caught. It was probably like salt in a wound for Sabrina. "She's explosive and emotional at the same time. Try and mimic her. Your facial expressions are always excellent, especially when you need to show a fighting spirit, but you need to convey that with your entire body. Everything, from the tips of your fingers to your toes, needs to be screaming at the same time. Also, take a look at Charlotte. Her confidence makes you take notice. She doesn't second-guess herself."

Sabrina said something else quietly that I couldn't quite hear.

"Well, thanks again, Sage," Mrs. Wolfrik said. "And before we go, any news on your company? Do you know how many spots you're looking to fill yet?" Her tone was light, but to me it sounded like she was fishing.

Wow. Even my mother wouldn't be so forward. No wonder Sabrina had cold and calculating down pat—she'd learned from the master.

"Not right now, Donna. But you'll certainly hear when there is something to share."

"Excellent. Well, we'll see you soon. Come on, sweetheart." Mrs. Wolfrik's voice grew fainter. She must have begun down the hallway toward the stairs.

"See you tomorrow, Sabrina."

"Good night." It was the only part of Sabrina's contribution to the conversation I could actually make out.

I closed the glass door the inch it had been open and stood there, frozen in place. Sage knew about the extra practices, which meant I'd been worried over nothing. But she didn't know about the blackmail and the sabotage from Sabrina, which, judging by that conversation, were only likely to get worse now that Sabrina and her mom had me in their crosshairs.

And yet, I found myself feeling sorry for Sabrina again. Her dream was just as fragile as mine, and by all accounts she was working just as hard to achieve it. Besides, her mom made mine look like a doormat. I couldn't imagine living under that kind of pressure.

Was it worth telling Sage what was going on between me and Sabrina? The more I got of Sabrina's story, the more I understood why she was . . . well, the way she was.

And while that didn't excuse the awful stuff she'd done to me, I was finding it harder to hold onto my anger.

When I unstuck my feet from their spot on the floor, I slid my bag, now sitting in the crook of my elbow, back on my shoulder. As I was about to push the door back open, a loud knock sounded. I jolted my head up and there was Sage's face on the other side of the glass, her pale brows furrowed with confusion.

I opened the door for her.

"Tilly, what are you still doing here? I thought everyone had left." She slid her hand inside the door to the wall and flicked off the fluorescent lights inside the studio.

"Oh, I, um, wanted to talk to you about something." I willed my brain to think of something quick.

"What did you need?" Sage shooed me out and locked the door with the ring of silver keys that has been hanging from the belt loop on her shorts. "Are you going toward the subway? I'll walk with you."

"Yes, I am." We started for the stairs. "Well, first I wanted to apologize again for this morning—"

"It was very unlike you and Charlotte to be late," Sage observed. "Did something happen you didn't want to talk about in front of the other girls, other than a problem with your alarm?"

You mean that Sabrina sent us a fake email from you? "No," I said at last. "Technology just wasn't very reliable today, I guess. I'll make sure it doesn't happen again."

"Good." Sage still didn't sound happy with me, but at least I'd apologized.

I paused, deciding to push my luck. "I've been thinking

about what you keep telling us about teamwork." Sage and I landed on the bottom floor and pushed out into the bright afternoon sunshine.

"Good, I'm glad you've been thinking about it," she said, seeming amused. "Anything specific?"

Well, yeah, how one of your dancers has been making my life miserable. "No, just generally. I just, um, I like the policy. I wondered if there was anything that ever happened to you or your dancers that made you feel so strongly."

There, that was good. If she shared a story with me, maybe I could slip in what was going on with Sabrina.

We rounded a corner and the subway sign was in sight. "Actually, yeah, there is." Sage stopped walking at the mouth of the subway and leaned up against the railing. "I could go on for days, but here's the first reason. When I was a sophomore in high school, I was dancing in the corps in my school's production of *Coppelia*. My girlfriend, who was a junior at the time, a gorgeous, talented girl, had the role of Swanhilda. Some of the senior dancers were jealous of her—especially the more experienced ones who thought they should have gotten the part. So they called her names and excluded her from conversations and social gatherings, which was ridiculous because they'd been friendly up to that point. Every spare moment they were in the same room, they were on her like vultures. Always picking until there was nothing left. It was relentless. By the week before the performance, she was so anxious and sad that she was considering quitting the show to make it all stop."

I sighed. I could relate to that feeling. I knew I wouldn't quit—if I did, Sabrina would win—but the desire to take the path of least resistance was there just the same. "Did she quit?"

Sage shook her head. "No, thankfully. Everything went off without a hitch. But she *did* quit dance her senior year, we drifted apart, and last I heard, she was working as a flight attendant. I'll never know if that experience made her reconsider a career in dance." She crossed her arms over her chest and looked at me. "So much potential, you know? And the kicker is I could've done something. I could've told those girls to knock it off. Even though it didn't feel like it, I had power in that situation; I was just too scared they'd come after me too, to use it. I was a silent bystander and while I might not have been able to prevent it completely, the little voice in the back of my head is always wondering what I could've done to make it better."

That little voice had been following me around too. And it was getting louder. "So that's why you tell us to take care of each other."

"Bingo. I don't want any dancer in my fold to feel like she is alone. You have a team with a shared goal and we will work as one to achieve it. Period." Sage swiped her arms in front of her like a baseball umpire calling an out. "End of story. If she had felt supported, by me or anyone else, I think she might have chosen differently."

"Maybe," I said quietly. I felt for the poor girl who was bullied into quitting. I wondered if she chose to fly on planes because she thought she couldn't fly on stage anymore. "Thank you for sharing that story."

"Anything for someone looking to learn." Sage winked at me. "Going uptown or down?"

"Up, I think."

"Up, you think. Well, have a good rest of your day, Tilly. I'll see you tomorrow."

"Thank you for understanding. See you."

I waved as Sage took the stairs to the downtown platform, while I crossed the street to go back up.

As I waited for my train, I considered what Sage had said. Could I be the bigger person here—a vocal bystander—and let Sabrina know she had another choice? That she wasn't alone? The idea made my stomach turn, even before I set foot in the train that hurtled back up town.

On the ride, I opened my email app and checked the note that Charlotte and I had both gotten, that clearly hadn't come from Sage. Looking more closely, just as Sabrina had suggested with that stupid grin on her face, I realized the L in Oliver was actually the number one.

I sighed loudly. *Be the bigger person. Be a strategist.*

I spent the entire trip home composing an email of my own, sending it to the fake account so Sabrina would know I was onto her.

> Dear Sabrina,
>
> I'm sorry that you thought it was a good idea to further damage my reputation by sending a fake email from Sage so I'd be late. I'm angry that you made a really selfish choice. I also know you're under a lot of pressure from your mother, and probably more from yourself, which led you to make a desperate decision. I get it. I haven't always made good choices or been kind when I was stressed, either. It

comes with the territory of this competitive business. While I forgive you, please hear me when
I say that I can't stay silent if anything out of the
ordinary happens from this point forward. Please
also hear that it's not too late to do the right thing.
You told me you weren't here to make friends, but I
don't think it's too late for that either, if you should
change your mind.

Your Teammate,
Tilly

Take that, I thought. Before I could convince myself
not to, I pressed send. I had no idea if Sabrina would
hear what I was saying in my message, or if she would
even open the email when she saw who it was from, but
maybe, just maybe, she would. And best case scenario?
Sabrina might see the error of her ways and take a right
turn off her path of destruction.

At least I hoped so.

Chapter 20

Abuela had suggested that I not only needed to make things right with Sabrina, but also with the other girls. I knew I hadn't done anything wrong to my fellow dancers, but even I could admit Charlotte and I had been a little clique-y. With the performance getting closer, it was time to pull out the stops and try to make us all not just coworkers, but friends.

The following day, instead of planning an exciting new adventure somewhere in the city post-rehearsal, I enlisted Charlotte to be my sous chef in the dorm kitchen. We stopped at the market on our way home and picked up all the ingredients for chocolate chip cookies.

Instead of baking at midnight, we set to work in the golden light of late afternoon. Charlotte was an excellent sidekick, measuring just right and verifying the recipe as we went along. Once we popped the tray in the oven, she sat on the stool at the island while I rested on my elbows, legs stretched out behind me.

"Do you think this will work?" Charlotte had been enthusiastic about the cookies, but she now seemed skeptical. "I mean, they haven't exactly tried to befriend us, either. Maybe they've taken Sabrina's side in this war."

"I think they're just scared of her. And if I were scared, I'd probably want sweets." The fact that we were baking right after rehearsal was well-planned—after hours of hard work, I was betting that not even the most disciplined dancer would be able to turn down homemade cookies.

Charlotte grinned. "Point."

About five minutes later, the mouthwatering smell of sugar and butter mingled together into chocolate-chip perfection and began wafting through the kitchen and down the hall. And about two minutes after that, Arden's head poked in, her hair still slicked back in its short pony-tail from practice.

"I thought I smelled something wonderful. What are y'all making?" she said, sounding surprised to see the two of us in the kitchen. Maybe, like Charlotte, she'd also believed in the carb fairy.

"Chocolate chip cookies," I said, gesturing toward the oven.

Arden raised a dark eyebrow. "Did you leave the banana bread out too?"

"Guilty." I smiled at her, pleased. I was glad someone else enjoyed the fruit of my stressed-out labor.

"That was *good* banana bread." Arden nodded in approval. "My mom makes the best banana bread I've ever had, but yours is definitely a close second."

"I'm glad you liked it." My smile for her was genuine and she smiled back. I felt foolish for not speaking to her much before now. I still only knew that she was from Atlanta and she liked sushi—the same information I'd learned on day one. That was pretty shameful after spending a month together.

A moment later, a blonde head popped around the doorway.

"I smell cookies," Ella said in a small voice. She reminded me of a first grader, all wide doll eyes and childlike curiosity about treats.

Charlotte put her hand out to the side of her hip, where only I could see it. I tapped her palm with mine, a secret low five that our plan had worked.

"You're welcome to have some. They'll be ready in a few minutes." I put on my best friendly smile, hoping that making friends really was as easy as bribing people with treats.

The four of us stood around awkwardly, all staring at the floor or the counter, as the timer on my phone ticked the seconds down. Okay, maybe making friends wasn't as easy as it seemed. Those might have been the longest three minutes of my life.

When the alarm sounded, Ella began to giggle, completely out of the blue, so much she started crying. No one had said anything funny, leaving Charlotte, Arden, and me looking at each other, wondering what we'd missed.

"Um, Ella, are you going to let us in on the joke?" Charlotte asked.

Ella nodded and wiped a tear from her eye. "Sorry, I'm sorry." She smiled. "Whenever the kitchen timer goes off at home, without fail, my cat runs into the room, jumps up on the table, and sits at my place. Like she's going to be served. It makes me laugh every time." Ella sniffed and tears filled her eyes again, but she was still smiling faintly. "Sorry. It made me miss home."

My own heart constricted and I noticed Arden nodding her head. We'd all been here a long time. Home did sometimes feel far away. Without thinking about whether or not she'd accept it, I crossed the room and put an arm around Ella's wiry shoulders. She didn't resist. I made eye contact with Charlotte, willing her to lighten the mood.

Thankfully she got my message. "That's awesome. You have a psychic cat," Charlotte said brightly.

"I heard once that cats are really kings. That's why Egyptians worship them or something. Maybe they're smarter than we think." Arden drummed her fingers, nails painted yellow, on the kitchen island. "My cat is neurotic. Or at least we think he is. Maybe he's just manipulative and he knows he controls us."

"My stepsister pet sits for a cat like that. He's fat and lazy and takes full advantage of her." I grabbed the spatula and started lifting cookies off the pan, placing them carefully on a cooling rack.

"Cats for the win," Arden said, snagging a cookie right off the pan and then blowing on her fingers. She took a bite and chewed slowly, closing her eyes.

We all watched as she swallowed her bite and then licked her lips. A little shot of pride winged through me.

"Tilly, there's this bakery right outside Atlanta that advertises that they make the best cookies in the world. My brother stocks up every time we go. Fills the freezer."

"I'm sure mine aren't as good as theirs," I said, my face flushing.

"No, these are actually better." Arden removed her phone from her pocket, held the cookie up to her mouth, pretending to bite, and snapped a selfie. "I'm going to send this to my brother to make him jealous."

It shouldn't have surprised me to know that Arden had a brother, or that Ella had a funny cat, but somehow it did. For so many weeks they'd been the competition, lumped together in my mind with Sabrina, but really, they were pretty cool people. I wished I had baked cookies on the first day and then maybe I wouldn't have needed to backpedal now. But at least cookies, and apparently cats, were common ground. And when you found the common ground, I was realizing, you could expand and build real estate.

As we stood around the kitchen making small talk—Ella was talking about a new Broadway musical she wanted to see before summer ended—Sabrina walked by. She didn't even turn her head to look, but I was certain she knew we were all in there. The flounce of her orange ponytail was too deliberate to be missed.

"I'll be right back," I whispered to Charlotte. If I was going to kill 'em with kindness, that had to include Sabrina.

I stepped quickly down the hallway and saw her door was open. "Sabrina? I just made some cookies. There are a few left if you want some."

She was sitting on her bed, messing with her phone. "No, thank you." Her voice was clipped. She didn't look up at me.

I told myself to resist saying something snarky. "If you change your mind, we can leave some on the counter."

"No need."

I watched her tap at her phone, head down, not bothering to acknowledge me. As my stepfather was fond of saying, usually in reference to his diplomatic work with the State Department, you can lead a horse to water but you can't make him drink. I could offer her cookies, but she was the only one who could agree to take my peace offering. At least I'd made it.

I left Sabrina to her phone and went back to the kitchen.

"So, have you guys been to the Statue of Liberty yet?" I asked.

"A million times when I was little," said Ella. "But I haven't been in forever."

"Well, I've never been and I want to go." Arden was emphatic. I saw that all of her gestures were big and wide, and her voice carried. Her personality certainly reflected in her dancing.

"Tomorrow? Right after rehearsal?" Charlotte stuffed another cookie in her mouth.

"Sounds like a plan," I said with a smile.

Two days later, Paolo and I found time after all our practicing for our first real date since last fall.

"So what have you been up to? Working through your list of things to do in the city?" Paolo threaded his fingers through mine as we walked down the Avenue of the Americas.

I nodded. "We did the Statue of Liberty yesterday, actually."

At the beginning of rehearsal the previous day, I'd gone up to Sabrina and asked her if she'd like to join the rest of the team on a sightseeing outing. "Everyone is going—Ella, Charlotte, Arden, and me. We thought you'd like to come too." Sabrina had given me a short, "no, thank you," and I hadn't mentioned it again. Though, when we all left together, I'd caught a look at her face. She'd seemed sad, but she was making her choices, and I was making mine.

"Man, I loved that place as a kid," Paolo said. "My aunt used to take us every summer. My cousins were tiny then, and my sisters were still in high school. I was the one stuck in the middle, so while Cara and Giana were holding the boys' hands trying to coax them up the eight million steps, I would pretend I was climbing Mount Everest." Paolo's eyes shone, lost in a good memory.

"I can see you doing that." I grinned at him. We passed the red and blue neon lights of Radio City Music Hall and I glanced at the posters advertising concerts coming in the next few weeks. "My favorite part was the ferry ride, actually."

"I'm a fan of boats." Paolo grinned at me and rubbed his thumb on the top of my hand.

"Just not the *Titanic*, right?"

"Definitely not."

With the late afternoon sun still shining, a breeze whipping my hair around my face, I had watched the city pass by as the ferry carried us closer to the base of the gigantic green woman. As much as I loved immersing myself in New York, wrapping myself in it, there was also something to be said for stepping back and observing at a distance. I found myself thinking back to the cab driver who brought me from the train station to the Marian that first day. He'd said people get the city in their veins, like lightening or electricity. The longer I watched the skyscrapers grow smaller and smaller, the more I felt it crackle beneath my skin.

We'd waited in the massive security line and finally made it to the Statue of Liberty herself. Eventually, we climbed to the crown. The three hundred and sixty-five-degree view of Manhattan, plus Brooklyn and New Jersey, was breathtaking. At the top, we'd taken about a thousand photos, and even recruited a group of tourists to take one of the four of us together. We put our arms around each other and smiled so wide our faces hurt.

I'd realized then it didn't matter that we hadn't hung out before that day—our shared experience being part of Sage's performance was enough of a connection to build on. I got what she'd been preaching at us for so long. There was more to being part of a team than just dancing together. We were stronger, more in sync, if we knew who we were. If we knew each other deep down.

"And the other girls? Are things better with them?" Paolo asked. I was pleased he remembered that things had been tense.

"Definitely. Well, Sabrina didn't come, but the others are great. We're making up for lost time." Ella and Arden made it easy to be friends, not competitors. I was certain of one thing in that moment—Sabrina was wrong about making connections here. That was the whole point. Because in making friends, I made myself a better, more empathic dancer, and that was going to show when I stepped onto the stage.

Chapter 21

Putting an arm around my waist and bringing me back to the present—and our date—Paolo led us across the street to a wide-open space dotted with kiosks that I imagined were shops or food vendors, and a massive sea of people. Turned out his big surprise was the quintessential New York summer experience—a classic movie at Bryant Park. Paolo had bribed one of his fellow musicians to come early and set up a blanket and picnic—complete with a small bouquet of yellow primroses in a mason jar of water.

"You can actually eat these," Paolo supplied. "But I hope you won't."

I sniffed them and smiled. "I think I'll put them on my nightstand back at the Marian, next to my rose, and save my munching for those sandwiches."

"Your wish is my command," Paolo said with a nod, handing me a sandwich and opening one for himself.

The movie was another New York essential, *Big*, which was one of my stepfather's favorites. As the sun slipped behind the tall buildings, turning the sky the color of cotton candy and Easter eggs, the movie began. I'd seen it so many times I could've recited the lines, but watching it in New York, at the tail end of what I hoped would end being a life-changing experience, it took on new meaning. A young person was experiencing life as an adult, before he was fully ready, and doing it in a city full of possibility and opportunity. He was forced to think in new ways, rely on his friends, and figure out which of the new people he met could be trusted. It all felt awfully familiar.

When the summer air cooled off and goose bumps appeared on my bare arms, Paolo magically produced a fleece blanket and wrapped it around my shoulders.

"Thank you." I leaned over and kissed Paolo on the cheek. In the glow of the movie screen, I could just make out his subtle blush. I smiled to myself, feeling content.

At the end of the movie, as our date was nearing its close, it hit me. What happened next week when I went back home and Paolo left for college? What would happen to us? Did we only exist in the confines of New York? He knew what he was doing for the next four years. I had no idea where I'd end up. I squeezed my eyes shut. I didn't want to think about losing him just when I'd managed to repair the damage I'd inflicted.

"You okay?" Paolo asked as the credits rolled.

"Yeah, just happy, I think."

"You think?" His voice was amused.

I sighed. "I'm glad to be here with you. I keep thinking about all the time I wasted. You know. Last year."

Paolo shifted so we faced each other. Even in the darkness, he was beautiful. Maybe more so as the dim light hit the angles of his face. "I'm glad we weren't together last year."

What? "You are?"

"Hear me out." He took my hands in his. "You were obviously not in a good place when you got injured."

"Understatement of the year."

He smirked. "You needed time to process what happened and to figure out what you wanted." He paused and looked at me as if to say *you know I'm right.* "I think you needed to do what you did on your own. Get to the place of clarity and own your choices. Luckily, you figured it out and somehow someone up there saw fit to put us back in the same place at the same time."

I laughed. "Charlotte says the universe is conspiring in our favor. She says we were supposed to end up together in the park that day."

Paolo offered me a mischievous smile. "I don't think all these little things that happen are random. Even though the year sucked for you, and really for me too because no one wants to be rejected by a girl he really likes," I covered my face with a hand and he gently pulled it away. "We're in a better spot to try this now."

"You're right." *Try. This.* My heart fluttered.

I knew, without thinking about it, without having to make a pro and con list, that I was all in. Ending up in the same place for the next year wasn't possible, so we would have to be long distance, seeing each other at holidays and breaks, potentially on the weekend if I wasn't too far away. I'd try it. We were worth it. I just wasn't sure if he agreed and I didn't think I was quite ready to ask. If Paolo was going to tell me this was just a summer thing, I'd rather let the magic last a little longer.

After the movie, he rode all the way back uptown with me and walked me to my doorstep.

"So, are you coming to my show?" I asked, pressing my cheek to his shoulder.

Paolo held me at arm's length. "Are you kidding? Of course I'm coming. I thought that was understood. I'm almost offended you had to ask." Then he laughed and shook his head.

"I don't want to make any assumptions." I put my hands up in protest and then cracked a smile. "But I'm glad. You know my whole family will be there. My mother included."

"I remember what you and Tatum have said about your mother. I have a week to prepare myself."

"Yeah, she might not be a fan of your tattoo." I loved it, the way it looked and what it stood for. But Mama definitely wouldn't see it the way I did.

Paolo quirked an eyebrow up. "Maybe I'll wear a tank top. Then she and I can discuss it."

I tilted my head to the side. "I would be interested to hear that conversation."

"Maybe I'll get another one on the other arm this week. Just to really amp up the fun."

"I mean, I'd like it . . ."

He closed the space between us and bent his lips to my ear. "I knew you liked it. Admit it. You're a tattoo girl. *You* should be the one to get one this week."

A shiver ran down my spine. "Any suggestions?" I couldn't see myself getting a tattoo but I knew better than to say never. I'd tried plenty of new things lately.

"What about bailarína?" he whispered.

I might have guessed he would say that. It was *dancer* in Spanish.

"That would kind of match yours." I liked the idea of matching tattoos more than I wanted to admit to myself, even though I always laughed when Tatum showed me pictures from her celebrity magazines of couples who did it.

"You're very observant."

Paolo leaned in and kissed me with a smile on his face. I closed my eyes and let myself get lost in him. His lips were soft on mine, gentle and almost teasing. Something stirred inside me and I kissed him back. I loved being friends with him and bantering and talking about music and dance, but I could now say without a doubt that kissing him was definitely the best part. I reached up and ran my fingers through his hair. He kissed me softly on my cheek, my temple, and then the top of my head.

"I don't want to say good night but if I don't go now, I won't go at all," Paolo said at last. "We've both got busy days tomorrow, unfortunately."

I smiled at him and he smiled back. "I know." I hugged him, kissed him once more square on the lips, and ran inside. Before I even got to the stairs, I sent him a text.

Thank you for tonight. I included a heart emoji.

He sent a string of hearts back, and mine exploded.

Charlotte was asleep when I crept into the dorm room. As I was in the bathroom, washing the day off my face and thinking about how soft and silky Paolo's hair had felt running through my fingers, my phone buzzed on the counter.

"Hi, Abuela. What are you doing up?" Not that my abuela was an early-to-bed kind of woman, but it was almost midnight and she *was* my grandmother.

"Oh, just playing solitaire to tire myself out. Thinking of you. How are things?"

I knew when she said "things," she meant Sabrina. "Well, the other girls and I are on friendlier terms now. I plied them with cookies," I said, proud of myself for that tactic. "Sabrina is still a work in progress, but I'm optimistic."

"That's my girl. I knew you could do it." I could hear the smile in her voice. "Now, indulge an old woman. How is your young musician?"

I blushed in the fluorescent bathroom light. "Paolo's good. Amazing. I just got home from a date actually. He brought me flowers and everything."

A pause. "What kind of flowers?"

"Primroses."

Another pause. "He must really like you then, Matilda."

"I mean, I think so. I hope so. What makes you say that?"

Abuela chuckled softly. "Primroses are generally given to someone you can't live without."

My breath caught in my throat and I struggled to respond. "Really?" There was no way someone who knew so much history didn't know the symbolism behind such a meaningful gift. Especially when that someone was sleeping above a flower shop.

"Your abuelo gave them to me on our twentieth anniversary. I'll never forget it. Not only because of the beautiful flowers, but because that was the year I searched every used bookstore I could to find a first edition of Gabriela Mistral's completed works from 1958. I finally found it, and he cried like a baby when he unwrapped it."

I remembered the book. It was the one that I'd seen on Abuela's bookshelf growing up. Mistral's words had certainly inspired my dancing this summer, but I wondered what my abuelo had loved so much about them.

"Why Mistral, Abuela?"

She hummed to herself, as if she were trying to find the right words. "Well, as you know, they are simple but so powerful. Your abuelo was the same way. I think, though, he liked her because these poems took him back home to Chile. They made him proud of where he had come from and grounded him, while still embracing our new life. It is important to have reminders of the past to anchor us, even as we walk toward the future."

"Yes, I understand," I murmured. My heart ached for home. No matter where I ended up after this summer was over, I was grateful to have a family who loved me and a safe space to return to if I needed it. And forgave me when I messed up.

"You have to know who you are to figure out where you need to go. Your abuelo used to say that a lot." Abuela sniffed a little, and I knew she was remembering their time together.

If she'd been next to me, I would've hugged her. "I love you, Abuela. Thank you for telling me about Abuelo."

"Te amo, mija. I think I might be ready for bed now. You too?"

"Me too. Good night," I said, a yawn surfacing at the mention of sleep.

"Good night, my love. See you soon."

In the week before the dance installation was to take place, Charlotte, Ella, Arden, and I covered a lot of ground. Not only were we all feeling more confident about our performance, but we also managed to hit up several sightseeing venues I wanted to make sure were crossed off my list before I left the city. We were ambitious in our mission, but there were only a few days left. We managed to combine several stops into one trip three days out—the New York Public Library, St. Patrick's Cathedral, and a stroll down Fifth Avenue, as Charlotte and I had done earlier in the summer, though this time it was more fun because there were more friends to share it with. We even went into Tiffany's and pretended to be principal dancers, imagining all the things we might buy if we had the money.

As it stood, I only had a few items left:

- Highline—X
- The Met—X
- Empire State Building—X
- Little Italy—X
- Chinatown—
- NY Pizza—X
- Broadway show—
- Brooklyn Bridge—X

- *9/11 Memorial—X*
- *Union Square—X*
- *Central Park—X*
- *Macy's—*
- *Times Square—X*
- *Cheesecake—*
- *Bagel—X*
- *Rockefeller Center—X*
- *Bus Tour—*
- *Guggenheim—X*
- *Museum of Natural History—X*
- *Whitney Museum—*
- *Fifth Avenue—X*
- *New York Public Library—X*
- *St. Patrick's Cathedral—X*

The night before dress rehearsal, Ella surprised us. She pulled some strings with her father, who did something important with fundraising for local officials, and got us tickets to see *Oklahoma!*, which was in previews for a revival with all new staging and choreography. I'd seen the movie once years ago, but it didn't even compare to the rush of energy and emotion I felt seeing it up close and personal.

After the show, we went one block away to a diner called Junior's that Ella said had the best cheesecake. She also knew to ask the hostess to seat us near the floor to ceiling glass windows on the far side of the restaurant so we could watch the stage door across the alley, to see if any actors came out.

"One time I saw a couple of TV actresses leaving from the stage door of the play they were starring in. I was going to run to see if I could catch them for an autograph, but then I decided it would be a little on the stalker-y side," Ella said with a laugh.

We all dug into our cheesecake—we shared a huge slice between us—and chattered about how great the show had been and how nervous we were about our own show. Despite the fun outing and light conversation, the tension sitting at the table like another member of our team was more than obvious. Everyone involved in this show had something at stake—a job, an apprenticeship, exposure to directors, and for Sage, money.

The closer we got, the more apparent it became how easily those things could slip through our fingers.

Chapter 22

The morning of dress rehearsal, my phone was flooded with texts.

We are on the train to come see youuuuuuuu. Almost there!!! Tatum attached a selfie of herself, Seamus, and our parents crammed into a booth in the restaurant car. Ken looked mildly amused, my mother seemed annoyed that Tatum was making her take the shot, and Seamus was kissing Tatum's cheek—I guessed at the last minute because her eyes were squeezed shut and she seemed like she was laughing. My heart ached for them. I couldn't wait until they got here, even though I knew I was in for some tough conversations. Unless the school had emailed her, my mom still didn't know I'd deferred Georgetown.

I am looking forward to your performance. You will no doubt be magnificent.

Abuela's confidence in me made me smile.

I feel like the thing to say is break a leg, but you need them, so how about a break an arm?

I laughed out loud at Paolo's message.

I'll keep my legs, you keep your arms.

Good plan. Can't wait to see you tomorrow.

I couldn't wait for tomorrow for lots of reasons.

Sage had triple-checked that we knew all the information about the dress rehearsal and where we could pick up tickets for our family and friends who were attending. We were to be at the Whitney by five that evening, dressed and ready to warm up.

When I got there, the museum space took my breath away. All my senses felt heightened—one, because every performance was exciting and two, because my grand adventure was almost over. Sage worked out the lighting and the blocking on our new "stage" as we ran through the routine for the first time there. I felt lighter than air, carried on the wings of my adrenaline, as if I could spring to the top of the tallest skyscraper. With every lift of my arm, every flex of my feet, my heart raced in the same way I'd felt knowing Paolo was about to kiss me. The rush was otherworldly.

When we broke for water, I checked my phone.

Hope everything is going well. Paolo had sent a string of sunflower emojis.

Thinking of what Abuela had said about the primroses, I quickly looked up the meaning of sunflowers. As I expected, they meant happiness, but I was pleasantly surprised to see they also meant loyalty and adoration. I grinned at the floor. I loved the way Paolo's mind worked.

Thank you! Emboldened, I sent him back a kissy-face emoji, symbolizing what I was hoping for at the end of the performance.

He got the message and sent one back. I put the phone down before I melted to the floor, took a swig of my water, and got back into position to begin again.

The second short section of our piece was just Ella and me on stage, like magnets that attracted and repelled each other depending on our positions. Right as the singer lowered her voice to pianissimo, Ella and I froze, staring at one another, as if waiting to see what the other would do next. And just as we were to swing back into motion, a loud, metallic ringer cut through the silence, ultimately clashing with the music that swelled to a fortissimo.

I cringed inside, willing my embarrassment to not show on my face. It was my phone. I could've sworn I turned the ringer to vibrate, but maybe my thumb bumped it acciden-tally back on. I sent Charlotte, waiting for her turn on the far side of the room, a telepathic message to shut it off before it ruined the dance. Unfortunately, she didn't pick up on my signal.

As I pretend-pushed away from Ella, I saw Sabrina, the closest off-stage dancer to my phone, reach into my bag. Well, at least it would stop ringing. Relieved, I turned my back and continued circling the room, thrusting one arm out in front of me and then the other. On the next pass, to my horror, Sabrina had not only picked up my phone, but she appeared to be talking to whoever was on the line, one finger in her free ear to block out the music. I clenched my jaw, knowing I couldn't do anything about it.

I could only hope it was a wrong number.

I had to wait until the entire production was over before I was able to lunge for my phone, sitting atop my bag where Sabrina had dropped it. I clicked through to the recent calls and saw my abuela's phone number on top.

Sabrina was in the corner, a protein bar resting on her leg, nonchalantly brushing her long red hair.

"You talked to my grandmother?" I asked.

Sabrina nodded. "Yes, but she didn't sound very good. You probably want to call her back."

My heart skipped a beat. "What do you mean she didn't sound very good?"

Sabrina rolled her eyes. "Exactly what I said. It was hard to understand her. She said something about the doctor, I don't know—" She waved her hand dismissively.

I didn't wait to hear more. We only had a few more minutes break before Sage wanted to run through the whole thing again. I ran outside the museum lobby and pressed "call" next to Abuela's name. It rang. And rang. And rang.

"Hello, you've reached Blanche. I can't answer my phone, but please leave me a message. I'll get back to you when I'm done with today's adventure. While you're waiting for the beep, why don't you ask yourself why you're not having an adventure too?"

The beep sounded.

"Abuela? Are you all right? Sabrina said you didn't sound very good, so I'm calling back to see what's wrong." I glanced over my shoulder through the big glass wall to see Sage rounding everyone up, probably to give critique and corrections. "I won't be able to pick up but please call back or text and let me know you're okay. I'll call you after rehearsal. Te amo."

Cold sweat formed at the base of my neck. What if she was hurt again? Abuela's shoulder was much better now, but at her age, it was much easier to reinjure herself. She could have done something to her arm, or fallen, or— My stomach clenched. I needed to make sure she was all right. I glanced inside again. Sage was watching me and I thought I saw her toe tap.

I quickly dialed Paolo.

"Pick up, pick up, pick up," I whispered frantically, hopping from one foot to the other.

"I picked up, what's wrong?" He sounded concerned.

"Can you please call my abuela and make sure she's okay?" I gave him the ten second version of what had just happened.

"Of course." Paolo didn't hesitate. "I'll go to the apartment if she doesn't answer, okay? Just breathe, Tilly. I'll keep you posted."

I hadn't realized I was holding my breath until he reminded me. I inhaled, thanked him, texted him the number and address, and dashed back inside. Sage's foot was definitely tapping, but she said nothing. Charlotte looked at me quizzically, but I just shook my head. I couldn't even look at Sabrina.

All through the rest of dress rehearsal, which included two more full run-throughs and fifteen minutes of reminders, I told myself to breathe, just like Paolo had said. If something happened to Abuela . . . well, I didn't know what I would do. I tried to calm myself down by saying it was probably nothing. It didn't work. I missed the same cue twice and on the final set of jumps, I came down awkwardly, causing my bad ankle to roll and pain to shoot up my calf. I was so caught off guard I cried out, which caused Sage to look at me with a mix of concern and annoyance. My nerves were doing absolutely nothing to instill confidence in her that I could be a competent professional.

By the time Sage dismissed us, I felt like I needed to run laps around the building, despite having just danced to the point of muscle failure. I leapt for my phone.

The first message was from Paolo.

She's fine. I called a few times and was walking to the subway when she finally answered. She says she was on a train when she called, so the connection was probably spotty. Call her when you get done.

And the second message was from Abuela.

Mija, don't worry about me. Sorry for the misunderstanding. I was on my way to a check-up with the doctor and just wanted to tell you to enjoy the last day before the rest of your life begins. Te amo.

I sank to the floor. Abuela was fine. Everything was fine. I squeezed my eyes shut, thanked the universe for keeping her safe, and wiped the sweat from my brow.

Charlotte put a warm hand on my bare shoulder. "Hey, what's going on?"

"Nothing," I breathed. "Absolutely nothing."

"Are you sure?" Charlotte's furrowed brow told me she wasn't convinced.

"Positive." My eyes flickered to Sabrina. "But there's something I need to take care of."

Arden and Ella stopped over to see if we wanted to grab food, but I waved the other girls to go on and said I'd catch up.

Sabrina had just finished packing her bag, and when she straightened up, we were standing face to face. Her blank expression betrayed nothing. Had she been deliberately obtuse when she told me Abuela didn't sound so good? A crackling phone connection made sense, but she couldn't clarify?

"This needs to end. Now." I was quiet, but firm.

"I have no idea what you're talking about," Sabrina said, but she didn't look me in the eye. Or couldn't.

"You know exactly what I'm talking about. You hit a new low today. It was one thing to try to sabotage me, but you do not drag my grandmother into this."

"It's not my fault if you misunderstood me." She hitched her bag over her shoulder, still not looking at me.

I made my voice ice-cold, so there would be no confusion. "I'm tired of your mind games and your petty threats. You have as much riding on this performance as I do. So instead of trying to bring me down, why don't you worry about yourself?"

Sabrina blinked a few times, but said nothing.

I stepped back. "See you tomorrow. Have a nice night."

I turned and strode away after the others. I had no idea if she'd leave me alone, but I'd said what I needed to say. I could only hope she'd find her conscience and let go of whatever bitterness she was still holding where I was concerned. Either way, I wasn't going to waste my last few precious moments of the summer worrying.

The four of us took the train out to Brooklyn and had an early dinner with Abuela and Ginger. When the food came, Charlotte banged her knife on her glass. "Hey, how about a toast?" She raised her water. Everyone else followed suit. "To the dragon slayers. May our feet be light and our faces fierce."

"To us. I hope we all get what we want tomorrow." Ella grinned and sipped her iced tea.

I glanced at Charlotte and she reached for my hand under the table and squeezed. I squeezed hers back.

"To Sage," I said. "May we make her proud."

"Cheers," everyone said and clinked.

The relaxed meal was the perfect way to end what had turned out to be a more stressful day than originally anticipated. For a cherry on top, I called Paolo before bed.

"Thank you for being my hero today."

"It was nothing. You would've done the same for me." And he was right.

"Well, you saved me, so I owe you one."

I knew he was grinning into the phone without seeing him. "I can be paid in kisses."

"You drive a hard bargain."

We both laughed, he said he'd see me tomorrow, wished me luck, and we said good night. I fell asleep that night knowing that whatever happened the next day, I had done everything I could to make my dream come true and that I'd made the most of the opportunities I'd been given—both with Sage and with Paolo.

Chapter 23

The next day, ninety minutes before show time, I stood outside the Whitney Museum, staring up. The late morning sun was pouring down between the tall buildings, and the scent of the river wafted through the warm air. My stepfather had just called to tell me Abuela had arrived at their hotel and that the whole family plus Seamus would be making their way to the museum shortly. Dry mouthed, I told him I'd see them soon. Charlotte's family had flown out for the show, so she was meeting them ahead of time. The other girls had scattered, perhaps perfecting their hair or makeup or meeting their friends and family.

I walked toward the museum, the place it all would end, by myself. I stared at the modern structure, which was not as tall as the skyscrapers I'd been so intimidated by when I first arrived, but just as imposing. I hoped that today would also be the beginning of something.

I passed through the glass door, noted the empty chairs set up in the lobby where we'd be performing, and felt my heart skip a beat. I made a beeline for the make-shift green room, which was really just a meeting room used by the museum staff, and dropped my bag. I stripped off my plain T-shirt then slid my loose skirt down my hips and let it puddle at my feet. Underneath I had on a simple black tank and dance shorts.

Sage had wanted us to be blank canvases, so our costumes didn't detract from the movement and our expressions. "Be the emotion," she'd said. So basic black it was, for all five of us.

I pulled my hair back into two braids and wound the braids into a pretzel shape at the nape of my neck, secured with a few bobby pins. Then I set to warming up against the conference room table, stretching my legs and rolling my ankle until it felt loose. I wasn't cutting any corners. The last thing I needed was for my ankle to give out like it had yesterday.

Arden came in next, the sleek black clothing making her warm brown skin luminescent. She gave me a bright smile. "Ready for this?"

"Ready as I'll ever be," I said, smiling back. I knew it didn't reach my eyes, but I was doing my best. The nerves were beginning to filter into my veins. The electricity I had been assuming was helpful, making me buoyant and spiriting me through the city, was beginning to feel dangerous, almost like a shock. I took a few deep breaths and reminded myself that everything would be fine, no matter the outcome.

Ella shuffled in with a friendly wave, her stage makeup applied to perfection. Charlotte stomped in behind her with slapping flip-flops. "Do I have lip prints on my cheeks?"

I inspected one cheek and then turned her face to see the other. "There is a very faint pink outline here, yes."

"My mother and her smothering," she grumbled, but she was smiling at the same time. "I love her, but sheesh. I need to carry a wet washcloth or some makeup remover wipes when she's around."

I pressed my lips into a thin smile. "She missed you."

I continued to stretch and bounce in the conference room, wondering where Sabrina was. I knew this performance was important to her—maybe more than the rest of us because she seemed to have the most at stake—so it felt odd that she wouldn't be here with everyone else. I poked my head out and looked left toward the lobby. I could just see the edge of the bank of chairs where the audience would sit. With an hour to go, there were a few bodies in seats. I hoped, for Sage's sake, that we would have a full house. I looked right. Past the restroom and a set of doors I figured had to be offices, stood Sabrina.

She was practically hunched in the corner, like a cat that had been backed against a wall, fur standing up, ready to pounce. Her mother towered over her and appeared to be talking a mile a minute. Sabrina was silent. Her arms were crossed at her chest, like a shield, and she had turned her face away from her mother. She seemed resigned, but there was no anger. It was almost as if she was just letting her mother's words bounce off her and fall to the floor.

I watched until Mrs. Wolfrik appeared to give up. She threw her hands up in the air and strode down the hall-way, hips swishing as she hurried past me without turning her head my way. I felt like a well-dressed tornado had just blown by.

When I turned back to the other end of the hall, Sabrina

had sunk to the floor in a heap. I approached her cautiously, my anger from the day before not quite gone. But I couldn't let her sit there miserable and dejected either.

"Are you okay?"

Sabrina lifted her green eyes, watery with the beginnings of tears, to mine. "Define okay."

I knelt down so we were eye level. "Well, I just saw your mother make a dramatic exit, so I thought the question was appropriate."

"How did you—" she stopped herself. "That's right. You were internet spying on me."

I shrugged. "You did it to me first." Sabrina shrugged back, like we were even. "Is everything okay with your mother?"

She sighed so heavily I could see her chest move under her black tank. "Well, considering I haven't spoken to her in over a week, probably not. I believe the term 'massive disappointment' was used more than once."

My heart lurched. My mother might have had high expectations, ridiculous ones sometimes, but I know without hesitation that she would never call me a disappointment. "Why would she say that? I mean"—I stumbled over my questions—"why would you stop talking to her? Did something happen?"

Sabrina paused and sighed again, louder this time, as if she'd decided she had nothing left to lose by holding back. "As you so astutely figured out, my mother and I were spending our afternoons in her dance studio practicing. And the other week, she showed up after our rehearsal to talk to Sage. To thank her," Sabrina said, practically spitting the word "thank" out. She shook her head and closed her eyes. "Thank her for allowing me to be in the group. Thank her for taking on a pathetic loser who has zero talent. Thank her for taking pity on me." Tears welled in her eyes.

"But she said she wouldn't have chosen you if she didn't think you were a fit. Sage isn't like that. She would never have given you a pity spot. She's too into hard work. Obviously she saw something in you."

Sabrina's eyes flew open. "What did you just say?"

"I said you were talented . . ."

"No, you said *exactly* what Sage said. How would you know that?" She narrowed her eyes and clamped her jaw tight. "You were listening."

My cheeks grew hot and I knew they were probably bright pink. "Yes, I was there," I said softly. "But I didn't mean to be. I was leaving the studio, pushed the door open, and caught an earful."

My explanation did nothing to soften Sabrina's hurt expression. "Yeah, I'm sure it was just a coincidence," she muttered.

"Look, I know it was wrong. I wouldn't like knowing someone I hate overheard such a personal conversation. But in my defense, I thought it would be more embarrassing if I busted through the door."

"Maybe," she conceded. "And I don't hate you."

"No?" I sat down on the floor next to her, our backs up against the wall.

"Shocking, I know." She laughed bitterly.

"For what it's worth, I don't hate you either," I offered.

She inhaled slowly. "My mom wanted me to stop you

today." Sabrina's voice had shrunk. She sounded almost scared.

"Stop me?"

She nodded. "That's what she said. I knew who you were before we started this summer. I saw everyone's social media accounts and websites. She told me to collect information. Data. Why do you think I was living in the dorm and not at home?"

Sabrina raised an eyebrow and I understood. Her mother wanted her to spy.

"On the first day of rehearsal, she asked me who my biggest competition was. And I said you. It was obvious. Plus, Sage had made it pretty clear you were the one to watch from the get-go." Sabrina frowned at the memory. "So my mom said I should do what I needed to do to make sure nothing prevented me from getting what I deserved." Sabrina's voice was hollow and robotic. Gone was the angry passion she spoke to me with earlier in the summer.

"So that's why you were so awful to me. Tripping me. The socks. The email. Lying about my abuela."

"Yes. I'm sorry about those things. All of them." She sounded like she meant it. Her voice wavered a little as she spoke. "I felt like scum yesterday. All the days, really, but especially yesterday. I knew exactly what I was doing, hurting you, making you anxious about your grandmother, and I did it anyway. And then your ankle—"

I didn't hesitate to respond. "I forgive you. And my ankle is fine."

Sabrina sucked in a shaky breath. "My mom wanted me to lock you in the green room. Or drop laxative pills in your water bottle." She turned to me, her eyes rimmed with red. "She tried to put them in my hand, did you see that?" She broke our gaze and looked at her feet. "I just ignored her. I couldn't do it. Not to you. Or to Sage." At barely a whisper, she said, "Not to me either."

I realized how horrible Sabrina must have felt. This wasn't just about being talented enough to get a job. This was about whether or not her mother believed she was talented enough to get a job. And Mrs. Wolfrik's actions had proven that she didn't believe Sabrina could do it on her own.

Without thinking about it or worrying that she might shove me away, I put an arm around Sabrina's shoulders. "I'm so sorry." She sniffed and I just let her cry. I thought about sharing how hard my mother had been on me over the years, but stopped myself. This wasn't about me. I wondered what Abuela would do. She told me there is power in being assertive and kind. "What do you want? For you?" I asked. I bet no one had ever actually asked her that.

A loud sniff. "I don't know."

"Do you want to dance well today?" The problems with her mother wouldn't be resolved in the next hour, or any time soon, but maybe the performance could give Sabrina some confidence. And if she did get a job offer in the end? Well. That would certainly show her mom a thing or two.

"Yes." She sat up straighter and pushed her shoulders back against the wall. "Yes, I do."

"Do you want to do it for your mother?"

Sabrina frowned. "No. I want to do it for me. And for all of you. Sage too. I know you want a job. I know this is your last chance too. And Charlotte's. And I know Ella and Arden want the exposure." She sniffed again. "I'm really not this kind of person. At least, I don't want to be."

"I believe you." I stuck my hand out. "Truce?"

Sabrina shook it with a surprisingly firm grip. "Truce. I really am sorry, Tilly."

"I'm sorry I stuck my nose in your business."

"No, I'm glad you did. Not only did I stop talking to my mom, but I've been resting this week. I feel a thousand percent better without all those extra practices. I spent weeks being on edge and exhausted, and now I feel pretty good, actually."

"See, Sage was right! We'll have to go tell her and then she'll hold it over our heads for the rest of our careers."

"Can't have that, can we?"

We both laughed and a summer's worth of trading barbs, lies, and intimidation started to fade.

Sabrina stood up first, wiped the mascara smears from her cheeks, and dusted herself off. Then she extended a hand to me. I took it and allowed her to help pull me up.

It was show time.

Chapter 24

Right before we took the stage, Sage gave us her version of a pep talk, which was less football coach and more birthing coach. She reminded us to breathe and focus and assured us that everything would come out just fine. Charlotte giggled through the whole speech.

We filed out of the green room one by one on silent cat feet. I kept my eyes down until I took my spot, on the left, legs in an inverted V, bent at the middle, flat back, arms outstretched, as if I were asking the audience to give me something. Perhaps I was.

The advantage—and disadvantage—of having the performance in a glass-lined room in the middle of a summer afternoon was the light. The room was blindingly bright with sunshine. Normally on a stage, you can't see a thing, but here I could see every single detail. Every person's face. Hundreds of pairs of eyes all on me.

As Sage introduced us and I waited for the music to begin, I swept my eyes around the room. I recognized Jonathan Calsan immediately, from District Ballet Company, and there to his left was his principal ballerina, Alyona Miller. She was grace personified. Last summer I'd worshiped her.

My heartbeat picked up slightly just seeing her. A few rows over, I spotted my family. Tatum was flashing me a less-than-subtle thumbs up from her lap while Seamus closed his hands over hers, rolling his eyes in embarrassment. My stepfather grinned at me and waggled his gray eyebrows. My abuela was there, with her friend Ginger, and they both winked in my direction. And then, there was my mother. Her dark hair was cut shorter than it had been in years; it made her look younger. She had on a new shade of lipstick and a summer pink dress. If she hadn't been sitting next to my stepfather, I might have passed right over her. I wondered how much Tatum had to do with the new, fresher look. Perhaps, if she was feeling as light as she appeared, telling her my plans after the show wouldn't start World War III.

There on my mother's other side was Paolo. His favorite gray beanie was nowhere to be seen and he had on a blue collared shirt, rolled up sleeves, and a braided twine necklace peeking out at the neckline. His hair, still wet, curled at the ends. He looked like he'd just come from the beach. I wondered what my mother thought—it must have been positive enough for her to allow him to take the seat next to her.

All the people who loved and supported me, in a row. It was enough to put the pieces of me that seemed to be floating in midair back together into one, solid Tilly. And just in time.

When the first few strains of music began, we flew. With every step, I leapt into orbit, around the moon, and then back down. I was grounded as the ball of my foot hit the floor and I thrust my arm above me. I circled around Charlotte and Sabrina, warriors, and turned my body inside out. I kicked next to Arden and rolled past Ella. We became the dragon slayers Sage wished us to be. When the music slowed to a sad defeat, we crawled and tiptoed. When it picked back up to a forte triumph, we flew again. I could feel the trickle of sweat making its way down the small of my back. I ignored it. I felt strong and solid and confident and completely myself.

I knew, chest heaving and clothes soaked, that I'd already won. Even if there was no grand prize for me in the end, I'd done what I came here to do. I'd proven to myself that I could do it. I could belong to a city that scared me at first but had accepted me, welcomed me with open arms and shared her secrets, at least a few of them. I could survive dancer drama in a way that didn't compromise the direction my moral compass was pointing. And I could make connections with friends without feeling like they were distractions on my walk through the snarling forest of doubt to happiness and success. Best of all, I could hold their hands and know we would get through the woods stronger and more confident together.

It didn't matter if I was offered a job or not. The dream I didn't know I wanted had already come true.

When the music finally stopped and we were frozen like the marble Greek statues in the Met, the audience rewarded us with wild applause. I glanced at Charlotte out of the corner of my eye and she was grinning from ear to ear. The edges of my own mouth lifted. There was nothing in the world that felt better than an audience recognizing the blood, joy, tears, and sweat you laid out for them on a stage. No one would ever be able to convince me otherwise.

I searched out my mother in the sea of awed faces. Her eyes were shining, wet with happy tears. I felt them spring to my eyes as well. She'd never cried at any of my performances before. That felt like one more victory, perhaps the best one of all.

Sage appeared and motioned for us to stand at ease. She pulled a wireless microphone from the back pocket of her black tuxedo pants and fiddled with the matching black bow tie until everyone quieted down.

"Friends, thank you for joining us today. It is with supreme admiration and gratitude that I recognize the Collective Arts Foundation"—she waved to three people in suits in the front row—"who conceived of this wonderful project and allowed me to be a small part of it. Dance has changed my life many times over the last few decades, in surprising ways, and I am so grateful to have the opportunity to share it with all of you." A polite smattering of applause. "I hope you will go see as many of the other performances this weekend as you can fit into your schedule. So many hardworking young people have exciting things to share with you. We are thankful for your support of the arts."

Sage took a deep breath and continued, "This was a personal show for me. All of them are in some ways, but this was my homecoming. I want to quickly share my story—apologies if you've heard it before." She side-eyed us on stage and we smiled. No one minded. "Twenty years ago I was poised to become a principal ballerina here in New York. Unfortunately, my partner, a brilliant young man who went on to have a short but bright career, accidentally dropped me, and I ended up changing my direction. It was hard, I won't lie, but I fought back. I found strength in working with young dancers and teaching them to push through the pain to find the shiny bits."

She turned back to us and smiled like a proud parent. My heart swelled. "These strong, tireless women here are the finest examples of that I could ever ask for. They rose to the challenge of working with me, and let me say that I am not always a peach," she said raising one eyebrow at us. We laughed. "But they stuck with me and what you saw was the result of purity of heart and fortitude of mind and all out warfare of the body. I asked them to find inspiration in people who fought their demons. Maybe they didn't always win, but they kicked some booty along the way. Team, can I put you on the spot for a second?" She handed the microphone to Ella, who was standing closest to her. "Tell our esteemed audience who you chose to think about today while you were dancing."

Ella blinked a few times, her long dark lashes fluttering and then finally she said, "Cleopatra and Malala Yousafzai." Sage nodded and Ella passed the microphone to her left.

Arden was next. "Michelle Obama. And Daenerys Targaryen."

Sage, and the audience, laughed. "The mother of dragons. I approve."

Charlotte said Esmerelda Santiago and Gerda Weissman Klein, and I noticed a number of nodding heads in the audience. Then it was my turn.

"Little Red Riding Hood," I started.

"A literal wolf slayer. I like it," Sage said approvingly.

"And Gabriela Mistral." I glanced at Abuela and her hand flew to her mouth, eyes shining.

Sabrina was last. I turned my head to watch her. I had no idea what she would say. Her face was paler than normal and her chest rose and fell as if we had just that moment stopped dancing.

"Myself," she said quietly.

I reached down and squeezed her free hand.

"Thank you, Sabrina." Sage nodded once at her, stepped back, and spread her arm out to the audience, gesturing back to us.

The audience clapped once more and we took small bows.

"Thank you all for coming. Enjoy the rest of your weekend!" Sage waved and led us back into the green room.

She shut the door behind us softly and put her hands to her chin, as if she were about to recite a prayer. "Thank you. All of you. That was far beyond magnificent. You made my vision a reality and I will forever be grateful. I'm going to leave you to get changed, but I hope you'll introduce me to your fans when you come out, okay?"

She smiled widely and disappeared.

When we emerged, I rushed to my family. Ken got me first, giving me a bear hug and telling me he was proud of me. Abuela held my hands in hers and told me she wished Abuelo had been here to see it just before Tatum and Seamus tackle-hugged me.

"He would have recognized the Mistral in you, no question," she whispered in my ear.

My mother stood there next to Abuela, her hands holding her matching pink purse at her hips. I walked slowly toward her and she broke into a teary smile.

"That was the most beautiful thing I have ever seen, Matilda. You were transformed." She kissed the top of my head. "I didn't know you could dance like that." Her voice was reverent.

"Thank you, Mama. I didn't know either. Sage is an exceptional teacher."

"It certainly seems that way. You'll have to introduce me so I can thank her." My mother hugged me to her side. She bent to whisper in my ear. "And how about Paolo? Did he contribute in any way?"

I blushed against her shoulder. "I like him."

"I like him too." In a very un-Mama-like fashion, she nudged me forward, toward Paolo, who was standing with Tatum and Seamus, watching me with his golden eyes. With her blessing, I went.

Paolo's grin spread across his face the closer I got to him. I went in for a hug but he planted a kiss square on my lips first and then picked me up and spun me around. "That was some show," he said.

"Some show, eh?"

"Some amazing, jaw-dropping, terrifying show."

"Terrifying?" I raised an eyebrow at him.

"Only in the best way. But, remind me not to get on your bad side. You might try to slay me."

"Good. Stay in line and you'll be safe."

"Yes, ma'am." The gravelly voice hit me right in the stomach and everything grew warm inside. "Seriously, though. Bravo. I'd hire you."

"Thanks. For saying that. And for being here."

"There's nowhere else I want to be."

I smiled into his cheek. "This is *everywhere* I want to be."

Chapter 25

We stood around chatting, the whole giant group of us, with jaws aching from grinning. I startled when an arm slid around my shoulders. Sage.

"You did good, kid."

I grinned. "Thank you, Sage. It's all because of you."

"Shucks," she said with goofy false modesty. "Who are these fine people?"

I introduced my small herd, saving my mother for last. Sage held my mother's hand a few seconds longer than everyone else's and nodded as they locked eyes.

"Ma'am, it has been my extreme pleasure to work with your daughter. Thank you for sharing her with me. She truly has a gift."

My mother blushed as if she'd been in the sun too long. She rarely blushed, so I knew she was taking the compliment to heart. "Thank you for giving her this opportunity. It was not an easy year for Matilda. I am grateful to you." Her voice caught in her throat. I noticed Sage put another hand on top of my mother's, patting it to comfort her. Though Sage didn't have any children of her own, it was as if there were two proud mothers before us.

Sage turned to me. "Tilly, could I borrow you for one quick second?" I nodded and followed her down the hall, past the green room, and into one of the small offices. Jonathan Calsan and Alyona Miller were seated behind an oval-shaped table. All the air rushed out of my lungs. Sage ushered me in, winked at me, and left, closing the door behind her with a soft snick.

"Hello, Matilda," Jonathan said. "That was quite a performance. Alyona and I were impressed with the tremendous growth you've made in the last year, especially given your injury."

"Thank you, sir," I somehow managed to say. "That's very generous of you."

He cleared his throat. "I won't drag this out. We happen to have one spot open for a permanent company member at District Ballet, and we're offering it to you."

On the outside, I forced my face to stay neutral and professional. Inside, though, I started turning my joyful cartwheels and screaming in disbelief. I'd done it. I'd danced well enough to catch the eye not only of someone who had a job to offer, but also someone I knew and respected. Relief flooded through me as I realized that if I accepted this job with DBC, I had a place. I had a path to follow toward a future. My future.

For a second, though, I paused the celebration. What if it was the wrong choice? What if I was meant to hold out for Sage or another New York company? I shook my head a little, brushing the doubt away. New York was the biggest of big dreams for me, but that didn't mean that I couldn't come back after taking full advantage of the amazing opportunity Jonathan was handing me with DBC. I hadn't come this far to second-guess myself.

I looked at Jonathan and then at Alyona, whose eyes were practically sparkling. DBC was known for being innovative and fresh. They took chances. Plus, being close to home wasn't necessarily a bad thing. The tiny voice in the back of my head reminded me that Paolo would come back to Virginia during breaks and it would be easier to see him, if he was interested in doing the long-distance thing. I knew Washington, D.C.—it was home. If New York was a pair of red patent leather boots, D.C. was pointed, black snake-skin flats. One definitely more exciting, but the other comfortable and still able to make a point.

Jonathan cleared his throat. "I'm sure you're aware that new company positions come with a probationary period."

I nodded. I wasn't afraid of that part. I wasn't going to shy away from hard work and I'd proven to myself that I could handle high-pressure situations without falling apart . . . completely.

He continued. "And, I also expect you to continue to work with a physical therapist. We want to make sure that ankle is in top condition."

I nodded again. That part made sense too. I had no delusions that my ankle wouldn't roll again at some point.

Jonathan leaned back in the chair and clasped his hands at his stomach. "So, what do you think?"

I smiled at Jonathan and Alyona, my decision clear. "I accept," I said as evenly as I could. The second the words flew out of my mouth, Alyona leapt from her chair, not unlike the way I'd jumped around the stage only moments before, and hugged me.

"I'm so glad," she said.

Jonathan stood and offered me his hand to shake. "I'll have the contract drawn up. You won't regret this. We're going to do great things this season."

"Thank you, sir. I look forward to it."

I walked out of the office, dazed. I had a job. I'd done it. Years of classes and performances, of cracked and bleeding toes, of ripping up toe shoes and sweating through socks, of shiny tights and too much makeup, of aches and pains, watching my lines and falling into bed dead tired from rehearsal, lying to my mother once or twice about what I wanted, of surviving my injury and baking myself out of a stressed-out frenzy, and thinking my dream was dead, all led me here. To this moment. I had done it myself.

I could barely breathe as I made my way down the hallway to my family. To my mother. She had her back to me when I approached. I forced my breath in and out, one foot in front of the other.

Like a heat-seeking missile, Charlotte launched herself at me before I could get to my destination. "Tilly! Sage offered me a position in her new company! I'm staying in New York! I'm dying, *dying* I tell you."

A tiny pang of jealousy hit me, and then I brushed it off. Charlotte was my friend. I was going to be nothing but thrilled for her. And, I thought with a small smile, I could come visit her in New York any time I wanted.

I took Charlotte's hands in mine and squeezed them. "That is amazing news. I'm so, so happy for you."

She grinned and started jumping up and down. Her enthusiasm was infectious. I laughed and started jumping with her, hands still connected, in the middle of the Whitney Museum. We slowed down, breathless.

I let go of Charlotte's hands gently and pulled her into a hug, whispering my own good news in her ear. "I just accepted with District Ballet Company."

She gasped and hugged me harder. "We slayed the dragons, Till."

"We sure did."

When we pulled away, we both had tears in our eyes. For a couple of girls who were looking for second chances, we certainly could've done worse.

I looked away from Charlotte, sensing someone was watching us. My mother. No longer turned away, I could see that she had witnessed the exchange with Charlotte. And she knew. It was written all over her face. Had someone told her? Abuela? No. I knew she wouldn't have done that. Maybe I'd been fooling myself for months that I'd been keeping my true desire a secret, but from a single glance I knew she'd known all along.

I walked the fifteen feet that separated us while and noticed a tear forming in the corner of her eye. There was no need to spell it out for her. I stared into my mother's brown eyes, the same dark shade as mine, as she looked back at me, seemingly so sad. My palms began to sweat, waiting for her to say something, but she didn't. Normally, when my mother was upset, her face went pale and blotchy, and sometimes her lip trembled. But she was so still and her cheeks were flushed.

She was going to tell me I couldn't go. She was going to tell me I'd broken her heart by lying. She was going to say I'd have to go to college or move out. I opened my mouth, ready to list all the reasons why dancing was the right choice, why it would make me happy and I could go to college later, when my mother cleared her throat and finally spoke.

"Where?" she asked. Her voice wavered a bit.

"D.C. The District Ballet Company."

She sniffed and nodded. "You'll be nearby. That will be nice."

My heart stopped. She had said *nice.* "I thought so too. Just as close as Georgetown."

"And this is what you want?"

"Yes, Mama." With all my heart, I didn't add. I didn't need to. I knew she knew that part.

My mother blinked, her long lashes still wet with tears. "It won't be easy. Are you prepared for this life? You'll need to develop a thicker skin than you already have."

I tried to look confident, as if everything would roll right off my back. "I believe I'm ready for that." I hadn't been training for so many years only to not be able to take criticism.

Mama's lip finally began to tremble, betraying her real fear. "And . . . what if it doesn't work out? What if you take this leap and . . ."

"And I crash and burn?" I smiled to let her know I could handle it if that happened.

My mother shook her head. "I worry about you. College is so much safer. Dancing as a hobby is safer."

"Mama, if I don't do this, I will regret it for the rest of my life." The passion in my voice surprised me. I meant it. And I was one thousand percent certain I couldn't live a real life with regret. Which meant I needed to tell her the whole truth. "Besides," I took a deep breath, "I actually already deferred Georgetown. I know I should've told you, but I was afraid." I looked at her cautiously, bracing for the worst. "I didn't want you to be disappointed, but I had to do this. For me. This is the only thing I want in the whole world."

Mama's pink cheeks paled and the familiar blotches appeared. "You cancelled college and you didn't tell me." It wasn't a question.

I felt my face fall. "Yes. I'm sorry." We stood there for the longest time as I waited for the other shoe to drop. I'd asked my mother to forgive me in the past, but this was the most serious lie I'd ever told. When she stayed silent, I took her hand. If she couldn't see how much I believed I was doing the right thing, maybe she could feel it.

"I wish," she started and then stopped, her voice wavering slightly. "I wish you didn't feel you had to lie to me."

"I'm sorry. I didn't mean to hurt you, Mama." My voice caught in my throat. "No more secrets. I promise."

Mama's jaw tightened, but she didn't let go of my hand. "And what about the scholarship money that was so generously given to you? And the deposit we sent to Georgetown?"

"I'll return the scholarships. In person if I have to. I'll apologize and beg them to give it to someone who deserves it." I would grovel at their feet and beg their forgiveness

if it would make any difference. "And I'll pay you back
the deposit. With my tiny paycheck until you have every
cent back."

Mama sniffed again and wiped a finger under her eye.
"Well. Then it's a good thing the comforter and desk fan I
bought last week can go back to the store."

She looked at me and I looked at her, still for a moment,
and then we both burst out laughing. She hugged me to
her chest, her woodsy perfume tickling my nose. "We will
continue this conversation at home. But for now, you know
I am very proud of you, yes?"

"Yes, Mama."

"And that will never change. You are a good girl. And I
know this is your dream. You work hard. You deserve it."

"Thank you, Mama."

She kissed the top of my head and just held me, and all
the residual anxiety I'd had, from performing, from Sabrina,
from the job, and from telling her, all drifted away. After
what felt like a lifetime, my mother gently stepped back,
wiped her eyes again, and straightened up.

"Your stepfather has made a reservation. You must be
starving. We should go celebrate." Mama smoothed her
dress and looked at her watch.

I nodded and then noticed someone hanging back in
the corner of the room. "Give me five minutes, Mama."

Sabrina looked lost. Her mother was nowhere to
be seen, and I hurried over to her. "You were great out
there," I said to her.

"Thanks. I heard you got a job."

"Wow. News travels fast around here."

Sabrina pursed her lips together. "Well, in case the bad news gets around, I wanted to tell you myself. I wasn't offered a job. And before you ask, I'm fine."

Her face told a different story, and I put a hand on her shoulder. "Are you really okay? I mean, I know you wanted this."

Sabrina sighed. "Maybe. I don't know. Maybe I didn't really want it as badly as I thought."

"No?"

She shrugged. "I like winning. Losing sucks. But you know what I feel more than anything right now?" I shook my head. "Relief."

I smiled slowly. "Maybe it's a sign."

"Maybe it is."

"You can do anything, you know? Go travel the world. Go to community college. Get a job as a barista until you figure it out."

Sabrina paused, like she was considering her options. "Maybe this sounds weird, but I think I might like to teach. Dance, that is."

I smiled at her. "I don't think that's weird at all. You have years of experience to share." I glanced back toward my family. They all looked ready to go. "Let me know what happens, okay?"

"I will."

We smiled at each other. "And if you're ever in D.C., give me a call."

"Okay." Sabrina's eyes scrunched up at the sides. I didn't know if she'd actually call, but I was glad we'd gotten to a place where I was happy to make the offer.

I rejoined my family just in time to hear Tatum shout, "I am so hungry I could eat a horse. Let's blow this popsicle stand."

She linked her arm through mine. "Can I just tell you that I'm glad you're coming home? New York is awesome and all, and I would've been perfectly cool coming up on the bus like every other weekend to crash with you and your seventeen dancing friends in a studio apartment, but I'm glad you'll be nearby. It'll be nice having my sister around for my senior year. I might need your help." She looked at me pointedly. "I hear you're really good at writing college essays."

We both laughed. "I'm glad I'll be around too," I told her, and I meant it.

Chapter 26

After the show, I took a cab back to the dorm with Charlotte and Arden. Our families were taking us out to dinner, respectively, and though we knew they would love us no matter what, we all thought showers would make the dinners more pleasant. I also didn't want to sit next to Paolo smelling like, well, like I'd just danced the performance of my life. Charlotte let me shower first, because, as she said, "You'll probably take extra-long picking out your outfit since you have someone to impress."

"I'm not dressing for anyone but myself, thank you very much," I told her, sticking my tongue out childishly. When I swapped places with Charlotte, I chose the last new outfit I'd brought with me—a silky black tank and white shorts with a scalloped edge. I pulled out a pair of wedges I hadn't had the courage to wear yet—an impulse buy—combed out my hair so it would dry in long waves down my back, and secured my red sunglasses on top of my head. Even though the sun would set soon, I didn't want to leave them behind. Abuela had given them to me for confidence, and they'd certainly done their job.

"So what did you think about Arden's offer?" Charlotte called from the shower.

Arden had been offered an apprenticeship with a company in Colorado. She would finish high school out there, study dance with the company, and hopefully become a full company member when she graduated.

I cracked the door open so she could hear my voice over the running water. "I think it sounds good. There were some kids from my high school who took similar offers. I don't think she's excited about being so far away from her parents though."

"Yeah. That's what I was thinking too. She sounded nervous in the cab. It's one thing to be gone for a summer and another one entirely to be gone for years."

"Definitely. Either way, I'm sure she's flattered to have been noticed. And Ella seemed upbeat. She told me her dad was taping the whole thing and planned to send it as part of her portfolio to casting directors." Ella hadn't been offered a job, but she was definitely on her way to her dream of dancing in the theatre.

"She may end up in musicals one day and then we can say we knew her when and go backstage," Charlotte said with a wicked giggle. I heard the water turn off from behind the cracked door. "But really, more than half of us ended up with job offers. That's pretty good, I think, considering how few spaces were available. That says a lot about Sage." She came out of the bathroom wrapped in her bathrobe with a comb in her hand.

"I think that says a lot about you, my friend. Of all the dancers she could have chosen, she picked you. And speaking of being far away from home, how do you feel?" I grinned at her. I knew Charlotte was more excited than nervous.

"My mother said she'll keep a studio apartment in New Jersey for when she wants to come visit. She's willing to get rid of cable to afford the plane tickets back and forth." Charlotte shrugged as though her mother was being ridiculous, but I could tell she was happy, thinking of family visiting. My mother would probably do the same if I were moving to New York full time.

"She loves you." I smiled and put on a pair of silver hoop earrings.

"So does your mother, apparently." Charlotte looked at me over the rims of her orange glasses. "I knew she wasn't going to be mad about Georgetown."

"I'm glad you knew, because I sure didn't. And she was a *little* mad that I deferred and didn't tell her."

"Still. She was supportive about dancing, which shouldn't have come as a surprise. But then again, it's always easier to see the truth when you're looking from the outside."

"You might be right about that."

When she was dressed, and we were both ready to leave, Charlotte stepped forward and hugged me tightly. "I'm going to miss you."

"I'll miss you too. You were the brightest spot for me this summer."

"Yeah?"

"For sure. Thanks for showing me that I needed more people in my pictures."

She laughed. "Any time."

And as if to prove her point, she pulled out her phone and we took one last photo together, two wide smiles of two girls who had an amazing summer.

Tatum used a very scientific method for choosing the restaurant for my celebratory dinner.

"It was between one of Mario Batali's restaurants—he has a million—or Scott Conant's Scarpetta. I went with Scott because I strongly dislike the fact that Mario wears clogs with shorts on his show." She said this as if it were a perfectly valid reason.

"Did you look at the menu?" I asked.

"Yes, I did, smarty pants. Both looked good, so the clogs were the tie breaker."

We were able to walk to the restaurant as a family from their hotel. When the front door of the restaurant was in sight, so was Paolo. My stomach began to flutter at half a block away. As soon as I was within reach, he took my hand and kissed my cheek.

"Have I told you how much I love those sunglasses?" he said softly in my ear.

"Once or twice."

Once we were seated, Ken ordered a bottle of champagne for the adults and a round of mocktails recommended by the waiter for the rest of us.

When we all had our drinks, he lifted his glass. "To our girl, Tilly. She makes us so proud."

"Thank you, Ken." In the world of stepfathers, my mother had certainly picked me a good one.

"Salud," said Abuela cheerfully.

"Salud, Abuela." I clinked my glass with hers.

"My turn," Tatum insisted. "To the most talented sister I could ever ask for." She grinned at me over her Shirley Temple.

"Here, here," chimed in Seamus.

Everyone looked at Paolo. He cleared his throat and lifted his glass. I was grateful he was a good sport about being put on the spot. "My Italian family says cin cin, which means *all good things to you*. So, cin cin." He raised his glass higher as everyone else echoed his words.

My mother looked at me across the candlelight of the table, and nodded. "Congratulations, Matilda. Please don't forget about us on your rise to fame." I knew it was meant tongue in cheek, but I reassured her nonetheless.

"I could never forget you, Mama. You'll have front row seats to all my shows. Even the ones where I'm only on stage for a minute, and I'm way in the back." I knew I wouldn't be front and center until after I'd paid my dues, and that could be years.

"Comp tickets all around," Tatum shouted, probably a little too loudly, but we all laughed.

Dinner came and was completely delicious. I was so ravenous after the performance, and all the anxiety, that I cleaned my plate and had room for dessert. As we were finishing up our salted caramel tarts, my mother pointed her fork at Paolo, who had held my hand under the table for most of dinner when we weren't cutting things on our plates.

"And what are your plans, young man? College? Conservatory?"

Paolo sat up a little straighter, shoulders back and proud. "I'm going to Oberlin to study percussion and history. My two loves."

Mama eyed me, as if she were asking me the question I wanted to ask Paolo. "Well, at least Ohio isn't terribly far away. I'm sure your parents are glad about that."

"Just far enough away that they won't be able to come visit if they just feel like it," he said with a good-natured laugh. "Though I think I'm going to have to invest in a bigger data plan for my phone, with all the video chatting I plan on doing with this one." He tapped heads with me gently.

I smiled, the corners of my lips feeling like they were stretching to my ears. Tatum covered her mouth with a hand and looked down at her plate, giggling covertly.

"Maybe I'll convince her to get a tattoo during one of our chats," Paolo said wickedly.

I wished it was socially acceptable to crawl under the table. My mother's eyebrows practically flew up toward the sky, while Tatum's jaw unhinged. I gave Paolo a hard side eye.

"I'm not getting a tattoo, Mama. Nothing to worry about." My cheeks glowed red.

Paolo chuckled next to me and mouthed "yet" to me. I smacked his leg under the table. He snatched my hand and held it tight.

"I was thinking of getting a tattoo, actually," Abuela said with a sly look on her face. "Maybe you can help me pick one out, Paolo."

"I would be honored, ma'am."

Abuela smiled at him and then winked at me. In that moment, I would bet it was my *mother* who wanted to crawl under the table, and I laughed.

The next morning, after she'd pressed the snooze button on the hotel alarm three times, Tatum rolled over and asked, "Do you wish you were staying here in the city?" Her pillow half-muffled her voice.

I slumped down further under the covers and stretched my legs as far as they would go. "No. Not really. I mean, yes, it would've been great to live here and get to experience this every day, but maybe the novelty would wear off?"

Tatum lifted her head and gave me the Belén look. "Are you kidding?"

We stared at each other for a second and then collapsed into giggles on our beds. "Okay, so maybe not. I'm probably just trying to convince myself that I want to go home. Which really doesn't take much convincing because I won't be at home. I'll have my own place in the city and it will be fun to rediscover D.C."

"That's the spirit," Tatum said, stretching her arms above her head.

"And besides, we have an awesome day planned. I'm not going to be sad about my last day here. I want to enjoy it."

We got ready and met the rest of our family, plus Paolo, outside the hotel, ready for one last adventure.

"Did you know I had a dream about riding a big red bus once? Last summer. So bizarre that we're doing it now," Tatum exclaimed, staring up at the tour bus before us.

The bus tour had been Paolo's suggestion. He'd told Ken and my mother at dinner that it was an easy way to see the city and decide what you wanted to go back and visit more closely.

Paolo grinned. "We did this every few years when I was a kid. To see if anything had changed."

"Well, that sounds like a great idea, son," Ken had sounded excited. "Let's do it."

Seamus had given Paolo a quick, covert fist bump, as if they had shared some "win over the dad" tips before we all met up.

Fifteen minutes later, we were sitting on the upper deck of the bus, flying down Broadway as the driver told us about the history of New York. I settled into my seat, fixed my red sunglasses firmly in place on my face, and smiled to myself. With Paolo's hand in mine and my future just about to begin, the electric city crackled softly in my veins. I wasn't a New Yorker just yet, but I knew, with every fiber of my being, that I'd be back one day.

Acknowledgments

While working on this book, one of my dearest friends from high school passed away suddenly and quite tragically. A few weeks later, the unimaginable happened, and we lost another friend. In the days following, though, despite the shock and sadness, something beautiful happened. The other members of our circle came together and shared photographs and stories and reconnected, despite physical distance, in ways we hadn't in a long time. Though I've always known I was lucky to have had such a positive experience in my teen years, it was comforting to reflect on how wonderful and influential these people were, and still are, in my life. WSHS friends—you are the reason I had such a great time in high school. You're the reason I write about kids with strong friendships and allies and passions. Thank you for being my friends—then and now—and for being awesome.

All the gratitude to my editor, Jillian Manning, for wanting this book and working so hard on it. I'm so glad that you found Tilly "fascinating" and that you understood that sometimes the quieter characters have hidden depths. I'm lucky to have you on my team.

Thank you to my agent, Kevan Lyon, for challenging this story to be the best it could be, and for not tossing my stream of conscious emails out the window.

Thanks to the whole Blink team—Mary Hassinger, Sara Merritt, Liane Worthington, Marcus Drenth, Ron

Huizinga, Denise Froehlich, Londa Alderink, Annette Bourland—I am so grateful to have such an enthusiastic group of people working with me. To Amy Sisoyev, thanks for all your help and support. And all the champagne to Darren Welch, for creating such beautiful covers for me.

Writing is not done in isolation. I couldn't create anything without Katherine Locke, Rebecca Paula, Leigh Smith, Rebekah Campbell, and Sarah Emery. You make my books, and me, better. A huge thank you to Lauren Karcz, Catlihn Nguyen, Melissa Roske, Chloe Roske, Nadine Jolie Courtney, Sunhi Keller, Katy Upperman, Angele McQuaid, Olivia Hinebaugh, Kristin Lippert-Martin, Heather Maclean, Stephanie Morrill, Alison Gervais, McCall Hoyle, Sonia Belasco, Leah Henderson, and Heather Van Fleet for your candor, your comradery, and your thoughtfulness.

I am grateful for the love and friendship of Suzette Henry, Melissa Donoghue, Kat Pacenka, Amanda Summers, and Amy Burns. Thanks for sticking with me all these years.

Thank you to all the librarians, teachers, readers, and bloggers who have championed my books—you are my people.

Thank you always to my family for their unending love and support. I have the best cheerleaders ever.

And to the ones who have to put up with me every day, my buddies, I love you forever. Thanks for everything.

About the Author

Christina June writes young adult contemporary fiction when she's not writing college recommendation letters during her day job as a school counselor. She loves the little moments in life that help someone discover who they're meant to become—whether it's her students or her characters. Christina is a voracious reader, loves to travel, eats too many cupcakes, and hopes to one day be bicoastal—the east coast of the US and the east coast of Scotland. She lives just outside Washington, D.C., with her husband and daughter.

It Started with Goodbye

Christina June

> "An unfailingly entertaining and thoroughly engaging read from cover to cover ... highly recommended." —*Midwest Book Review*

Tatum Elsea's summer has gotten off to a rough start, but neither strict stepmothers nor community service will keep Tatum from chasing her dreams, especially when those dreams involve starting a graphic design business and getting a first date with a smart and funny musician who may just be her Prince Charming.

Check out this excerpt from
Christina June's novel

It Started with
GOODBYE

Chapter 1

*T*atum, they have your license plate on camera. This is as good as it's going to get." Mr. Alves stood at the head of the table in the plush conference room.

I stared blankly at him, still trying to process what he was saying. My head was spinning, and it sounded like he was speaking Greek while his cheeks were stuffed full of mashed potatoes.

My stepmother, Belén, poked my shin with the toe of her pointy pump. "Tatum Elsea, Mr. Alves is trying to help you."

I yelped, even though it didn't hurt. "You didn't need to kick me," I said loudly, making sure my dad, Mr. Alves, and the people in the next office over heard me.

"Tatum," my dad warned, putting a hand on my shoulder. "Tom, could you please run through the deal again? Tatum, you need to listen. This is your future."

"Yes, sir," I said, eyes down, guilted. The temperature in the room seemed to increase with each second that ticked by on the wall clock. I wiped my palms on my skirt.

Mr. Alves cleared his throat. "Right. Here we go again." He looked at me over his glasses. "You're expected to confirm the figures seen on the security camera at four thirty-seven p.m. on June ninth, exiting Mason's Department Store." He pushed his glasses back up on his nose and glanced down at the paper in his hand. "Ashlyn Zanotti and Chase Massey. Is that correct?"

"Correct," I said, and checked out my reflection in the table's polished surface. This was torture.

"The official charge for both is grand larceny, because the total amount stolen exceeds two hundred dollars. Normally in Virginia, you would be charged with the same felony, since you were the driver. However, as you have no record, you're issuing this statement, and there was no merchandise found on your person or in your car, the commonwealth attorney has agreed to reduce it to a misdemeanor instead."

"Thank goodness for small favors," Belén said. "This is still going to affect your college applications, you know. I was reading on the Focused Parent blog about the impact of criminal charges. You'll have to disclose it, Tatum."

It was so typical of her to bring up that ridiculous blog. Just because the author was an "expert" and was on TV all the time did not make him the authority on life. If I'd had the power to take away her voice temporarily, like in *The Little Mermaid*, I might have used it. I bit the inside of my cheek instead.

"The silver lining is that we can petition to have your record expunged." Mr. Alves offered me a sad smile, while Belén exhaled the biggest sigh of relief the world has ever heard.

"That's good," I said quietly, to the table. At least this snafu wouldn't follow me forever.

Mr. Alves continued. "Mr. Massey, age nineteen, will obviously be charged as an adult."

Had I heard that right? I picked my head up. "Um, Mr. Alves, did you say nineteen?"

"Yes," he said, his glasses sliding lower on his nose. "Why?"

My eyes grew wide. "He told her he was seventeen."

Belén's hair rustled against her blouse as she shook her head, no doubt with disappointment over the ineptitude of teenagers, especially that of my best friend, Ashlyn.

"It seems that Mr. Massey did more than falsify his age. He also chose not to disclose his long list of previous offenses." Mr. Alves flipped through the pages in his hand. "Vandalism, assault, petty theft—it goes on and on."

"Huh." I'd always known Chase wasn't good boyfriend material, for sure not good enough for Ashlyn, and his finer points were sadly the reason I found myself in what the commonwealth attorney wanted to call "the getaway car" that fun-filled afternoon. But a repeat offender? For Ashlyn's sake, I'd tried my best to look past the scruff on his face, the ink peeking from beneath his sleeves, and the way he leered at me when Ashlyn's back was turned. And for my trouble, for trying to watch out for her, it landed me here, in this uncomfortable wooden seat, between my dad and the stepmonster, facing completely ridiculous, unnecessary charges.

"These are the people she's keeping company with?" Belén sat up straighter and eyed my dad from over my head. Not only was she pretty, if you liked robotic, she was tall and often used that to her advantage when she wanted to remind all of us that she was in charge.

"I didn't know, all right?" I protested. "I hope you realize I wouldn't have been spending time with a criminal if I'd been aware of that piece of information."

My dad and Belén exchanged another look I interpreted as skepticism. I was sure that any trust I had earned over sixteen years of being Dad's daughter and eight years as Belén's stepdaughter went right out the window the second the security guard came charging out of Mason's after Chase and Ashlyn, but still, I thought they knew me better. Clearly, I thought wrong.

Dad patted me on the shoulder to remind me that this wasn't the time to argue. I sighed as Mr. Alves called for his secretary to come in and take down my statement. A young redhead sat down next to Mr. Alves with a laptop, and started typing as soon as I began speaking.

"Well, after school that day, Ashlyn had told me she wanted to go to Mason's to get a new pair of flip-flops and some nail polish." The weather was finally warm enough to wear sandals and short skirts, and Ashlyn wouldn't be caught dead with bare toes. "She let me know on our way to the parking lot that Chase was coming, which ticked me off."

"Be polite, Tatum." Belén narrowed her eyes in disapproval.

I sighed and rested my chin in my hand. "I drove because I knew that if I was the one with the wheels, I could make sure we weren't there all day. The less time I spent with Chase, the better." When Ashlyn and I got to my car—the sensible navy hybrid I shared with my stepsister, Tilly, on weekends—Chase's hulking frame was leaning against my trunk. A cigarette dangled between two fingers, smoke curling upward. I wrinkled my nose, not just at the nasty smell but at Chase himself.

"So is it accurate that you questioned Mr. Massey's character right from the beginning of his relationship with Miss Zanotti?" Mr. Alves gestured to the redhead to make sure she got that.

"Of course I did. I know appearances aren't everything, but I never thought he was a good guy." Chase and Ashlyn had been "dating" for a couple of months. They'd met at the gas station where he worked. She spilled fuel on her hands while pumping—possibly on purpose, knowing Ashlyn—and was "forced" to go inside the convenience store and ask for the restroom key. He flirted, she batted her eyelashes, and suddenly my closest friend was involved with someone she knew almost nothing about.

Chase had been Ash's first real boyfriend, but the guys she'd crushed on in the past were good students, wore clothes that were hole-free, and used hair product generously. Chase, on the other hand, told her he'd dropped out of high school due to "family issues" but was planning to "get a GED real soon, baby." She fell for it hook, line, and sinker. I'd hoped he was just something she needed to get out of her system. There was no doubt that her father,

Arthur Zanotti, millionaire real-estate developer, would freak out as soon as he learned his precious princess was spending time with someone like Chase. Luckily for her, he hadn't picked up on that tiny detail of Ash's life. Until now, at least.

"Chase wasn't exactly the kind of guy you'd bring home to meet the parents," I told them. I started doodling on the pad of paper in front of me, until Belén closed her hand over mine, halting the pen from moving. I scowled, but stopped drawing and continued.

"Anyway, I drove to Mason's while Ashlyn and Chase sat in the backseat." Him whispering and her giggling, me feeling like a chauffeur. "After we parked, I went to the art supplies and they went to the makeup." I remembered wandering through the racks of crayons and markers, grabbing a set of charcoal pencils and a small sketchpad that would fit perfectly in my favorite hobo-style shoulder bag.

"And then what?" Mr. Alves nodded for me to keep going.

"I went upstairs to check out the tablet computers." I was saving to buy one, but babysitting money only went so far. I almost passed out when I saw the price for the one I'd been admiring, which had led to a disappointed sigh. I still hoped that by the end of the summer, maybe, I would score enough cash to get it.

"Lynn, make sure you make a note about our client having been in the electronics department," Mr. Alves said to his secretary. "Tatum, did you notice anything odd while you were there?"

"On my way back downstairs to pay for my stuff, I saw Ashlyn and Chase making out in the cell phone aisle. That made me want to throw up, so I turned around immediately and went to pay." Ashlyn had been up on tiptoe, her mouth suctioned to Chase's, while his hands roamed over her back. Blech. I liked kissing as much as the next girl, but in the middle of a store, where anyone could walk by? No thanks. I'd sent Ash a quick text telling her I'd be in the car and not to take all day.

"You didn't happen to notice any Mason's employees near them?"

"Nope." I paid for my pencils and pad, went to the car, and pulled it up in the loading zone, hoping they'd see me when they came out.

"Okay, and what happened when they exited?"

"When they finally came out, Chase went to open the backseat door, but it had automatically locked." When he couldn't get in, his face had turned stormy. I had fumbled with the buttons to let them in, which in hindsight was probably lucky. Those extra few seconds were enough time for the Mason's security guard to come marching out, black walkie-talkie in hand, shouting.

"Once the guard showed up, things started getting bad, fast."

The doors had finally unlocked, and Chase clambered into the car, knocking his elbow into the metal doorframe in the process. He swore loudly. I looked behind me at Ashlyn, who was cowering next to him like she wanted to slide down under the seat in front of her. The security guy pounded on Chase's window so loudly, I screamed.

"Shut up, Tatum." Chase had glared at me in the rearview mirror with his teeth bared, like he was ready to bite me. I looked away and found myself eye to eye with the livid security guard, gesturing for me to roll down the window. I did.

"Is something wrong, sir?" I'd clasped my hands in my lap to keep them from shaking.

"You and your friends need to exit the vehicle, miss."

Mr. Alves glanced over his secretary's shoulder to make sure she was getting all of this. "Go on."

"I got out of the car right away. Ashlyn did too." With what can only be described as a guilty look on her face, eyes downward, refusing to look at me or the guard. "Chase foolishly remained seated and cursed at the guard, until three more came and physically removed him from my car." The men had patted us down; legs spread, arms wide like wings. I'd never been so utterly embarrassed in my life. Even though the evening air was warm and humid, I'd shivered on the sidewalk, waiting to find out what was going on.

"They got nothing from me and Ash, obviously, but I guess you know what they found on Chase." The men pulled four brand-new iPhones from Chase's ragged jeans, and a stack of gift cards from the waistband of his boxers.

Mr. Alves checked his papers. "The monetary amount Mr. Massey stole totaled over three thousand dollars, and it seems he had a little help from a Mason's employee, who left the locked cases open for him and activated the cards."

"What a jerk," I said under my breath.

We had taken a little ride in the cop cars that showed

up minutes later, and Ashlyn and I ended up together. I remembered looking at her pointedly as we sped to the station.

"Did you know he was going to take that stuff, Ash?" She didn't answer me. I stared harder, hoping the weight of my glare might force her to turn her head, but no dice. "Ash? Did you know? Did you help him? Because if you did, you not only put yourself in danger, but me too. I thought you were smarter than this." It was a cheap shot, and I knew it.

At *smarter*, she'd turned her head, her blue eyes neon with emotion. "Everything is going to be fine. This isn't a big deal. Why are you being such a brat?"

My cheeks flamed. "Excuse me? Not a big deal? You and your loser boyfriend shoplift and try to use me as your getaway driver, and I'm getting scolded for being mad? No way. This could ruin our lives. You do not get to call me a brat. I have every right to be upset. You do not. Right now, you don't get to be anything." I glanced forward and realized the policeman driving the car was watching us in his mirror.

Ashlyn waved her hand, dismissing me. "Whatever. We didn't do anything wrong. Chase's friend gave him the phones. He said he put them on layaway and they could be paid for in installments. It'll all get sorted out."

I'd gaped at her. Who was this person, and what had she done with my intelligent, fun, loyal best friend? "If you believe that, there's a beach in Antarctica I'd like to sell you."

My cheeks warmed with anger again, just recalling

that awful scene. Next to me, my dad squeezed my hand under the table.

"So just to wrap this up, you talked to someone at the police station, and you were then released to your father, correct?" Mr. Alves leaned back in his chair, appearing satisfied with my answers.

"Yep." When we pulled in, Mr. Zanotti was already there, wearing his ever-present dark suit, perfectly coordinated pressed shirt, and shiny tie, with cell phone in hand, shouting almost as loud as the security guard had. As soon as I stepped out of the cruiser, my dad's sedan parked next to us.

Once we'd answered their questions, the police finally let Ashlyn and me leave. When I slid into the front seat of Dad's car, I spied Ashlyn in her father's black SUV, the car he carted his clients around in, clearly getting an earful from Daddy. Her eyes were pointed at the floor, as they had been for most of the evening, and I thought I saw a tear falling down her pale cheek. For half a second, I felt bad for her . . . and then I remembered how we'd gotten here.

The ride home was just as uncomfortable for me as I'm sure it was for Ash. I gave up trying to defend myself when my dad started using words like "disappointed," "unsafe," and "poor judgment." Hearing how I wasn't living up to my potential stung. When he said it made him sad that I hadn't come to him when I first realized my friend was dating someone I didn't trust, my heart broke a little. I couldn't find the voice to say I thought I could handle the situation by myself.

In the past when I screwed up, my dad had given me

the proverbial eyebrow raise and let Belén deal with my consequences. She had very specific thoughts on right and wrong. And if I felt she'd been too harsh, he'd always found a way to smooth it over quietly—when she wasn't looking, of course. Which meant his speech hurt that much more, because I knew he felt I'd let him down. It felt like we'd crossed some kind of barrier I didn't even know existed.

At the house, Belén stood in the kitchen, hands on her hips, mouth turned down in an angry frown. Tilly was at the kitchen table, AP Calculus book open, punching the buttons on her graphing calculator. She didn't even bother to lift her head when we came through the door.

"Well?" Belén's tone was sharper than her favorite steak knives. Tilly finally looked up at me with feigned interest. Actually, she was probably very interested, but she'd never let on.

"Well nothing," I replied, immediately going into evasive mode, my best defense against the stepmonster. I poked my head into the refrigerator and pulled out a ginger ale.

Dad cleared his throat. "We have a meeting with Tom Alves scheduled. It seems the girls may be charged with grand larceny."

Tilly's eyes got so big, I thought they might fall out of her head.

Belén's finger tapped her hips like she was itching to wave it at me, and her face was a blotchy patchwork of pink and red. I'd never seen her this mad. "*May* be?"

"Well, Tom's going to dig around and see if he can

find anything to use as leverage. We'll discuss it with him after he speaks with the commonwealth attorney."

I opened the soda can with a loud popping noise, and tiny droplets of ginger ale splattered my nose. I wiped them away and backed myself up against the counter, cold marble pressing into my back.

Belén let out an annoyed sigh. "How can you be so casual about this, Tatum? Do you know what you've done? The danger you put yourself in?" She could be a little dramatic sometimes. It was probably all her time spent in litigation. And on the parenting blog.

I took a slow sip of my soda, swallowed, and eyeballed her. "Yes, I know exactly what I've done. And that would be a big fat nothing wrong. The only thing I'm guilty of is trying to protect my friend from her sketchy boyfriend, and failing. No, I didn't know he was going to steal that stuff. No, I didn't help him. My plan was to go to Mason's, buy some pencils, maybe help Ashlyn pick out some nail polish, and come home. Contrary to popular belief, a field trip to visit our city's finest was not on my agenda today. So can everyone please calm down?"

Belén's jaw clenched shut and her eye started twitching. I wondered if steam might start coming out her ears next. Tilly had turned her face back to the math book, but I knew she was listening and probably filing this conversation away for later. My dad remained quiet, a sign of danger. My father is a pretty thoughtful man. He ponders his words before he speaks, and the majority of time he's able to come up with a solution, if needed, and to say it calmly. But when he stayed in his head too long, I knew it was because he didn't know what to say, or was afraid to say what he was thinking. That conveniently made it easier for him to defer to Belén, who was always happy, thrilled even, to speak up.

He finally shook his head and, barely above a whisper, said to me, "Tatum, please go to your room for the rest of the night." I opened my mouth, like a bass about to bite, and then shut it. There was no use arguing against that point. I'd wait until everyone had calmed down and then plead my case again. I climbed the stairs and didn't look back.

"And here you are with me. Thank you for being candid, Tatum." Mr. Alves continued reading me the terms of our agreement with the CA. "You're being asked to pay a fine of five hundred dollars by September first."

"Which you will be paying out of your pocket," Dad said. I groaned. Goodbye tablet.

"The CA is also requiring one hundred hours of community service. You can choose the location as long as there's a supervisor who can sign off on the paperwork. Same completion date as the fine."

Somehow, I knew that was coming. "And Chase and Ashlyn? Am I allowed to know about them?"

"Mr. Massey's fate will be decided at his trial. I feel confident saying he's likely going to jail."

I sucked in a breath. "Ash?" I whispered.

He looked at his papers. "It appears all charges against Miss Zanotti are being dropped. Perhaps she provided some additional information about Mr. Massey."

I was glad Ash wasn't facing jail time like Chase. I was

decidedly not glad that she was getting off scot-free. I kept that precious thought to myself.

My lawyer stood, marking the end of our meeting. "Ken, Belén, always a pleasure. I'm sorry this meeting wasn't under better circumstances, but I think for the most part, this issue ends here."

I was so glad he thought so.